According to
Sofia

ALSO BY ØYSTEIN LØNN

The Necessary Rituals of Marien Gripe

Tom Reber's Last Retreat

According to Sofia
ØYSTEIN LØNN

Translated from the Norwegian by
Barbara J. Haveland

Published in 2009 by
The Maia Press Limited
82 Forest Road
London E8 3BH
www.maiapress.com

First published in Norwegian as *Ifølge Sofia* by Gyldendal
in 2001
Copyright © 2001 Gyldendal Norsk Forlag AS
English-language translation by Barbara J. Haveland

Øystein Lønn asserts his moral right to be identified as the
author of this work
Barbara J. Haveland asserts her moral right to be identified
as the translator of this work

All rights reserved. No part of this publication may be
reproduced, stored in a retrieval system, or transmitted in any
form or by any means, electronic, mechanical, photocopying,
recording or otherwise, without the prior written permission
of the publisher, nor be otherwise circulated in any form of
binding or cover other than that in which it is published and
without a similar condition including this condition being
imposed on the subsequent publisher

ISBN 978 1 904559 34 4

A CIP catalogue record for this book is available from the
British Library

Printed and bound in Great Britain by Thanet Press
on paper from sustainable managed forests

Translation supported by Norwegian Literature Abroad
and Arts Council England

*Only when the dust has settled
do we know whether what we have
is a donkey or a camel*

BEDOUIN PROVERB

1

Bird was fumbling with the key to the door of his office when it was opened by his editor-in-chief.

'You're late,' he said.

Bird, whose head was spinning, was no longer surprised to find his friend the editor-in-chief sitting in the blue office chair, but on this particular evening, after dinner at The Stables, he had been annoyed when Simen called. Bird had been in the middle of a conversation about Carl Lewis, about calf muscles and sprinters' reflexes, when Hansen the old waiter bent down to his ear and whispered that the editor-in-chief needed him back at the office. 'He said you should take a taxi.'

Seasoned waiter that he was, Hansen could make himself almost invisible. Sometimes, when no one was looking and because they lived in the same building, he had been known to lay his hand on Bird's shoulder. On this evening he both whispered in Bird's ear and brushed his arm.

Bird found this very disturbing.

'Dear, flighty Sofia,' Simen said as he trailed back and forth across the office, moving piles of papers over to the desk by the window. He glanced dubiously at the dripping branches of the ancient lime trees rearing up out of the tarmac in the car park. 'It's drizzling,' he added appeasingly before continuing: 'I received another rotten report from the doctor regarding my inner organs. It was worse than usual today. They found a haemorrhage. Precious drops of blood leaking out and mingling with the coffee and all those bananas. I'll trouble you with that later. Right now you ought to read the fax that's stuck up on your computer screen.'

Bird put on his half-moon glasses and peered at the message.

'Fucking bitch,' said Simen.

This outburst moved Bird, who had known Simen for over thirty years and had hardly, if ever, heard him swear, to hunch his shoulders. It wasn't the import of the two words which caused this reaction, it was the virulence of his tone. Simen did not have enough of a voice to be surly. He tended always to wait for things to blow over.

Bird turned to face the wall and eyed the reproduction of Monet's water lilies. He liked Monet's soft light, the water with the white flowers floating on it, the grassy bank, the red of poppies, and the shimmering blue of the sky. He had read that it had been Monet's best summer, that one.

Then Bird shut his eyes.

When he opened them he saw Simen's face; he looked not only shaken, but painfully grey, and suddenly Bird understood that Simen was the kind of man whom women left.

That was what Sofia had done. Not just four weeks ago, but whenever the mood took her. This last was an expression used only between Sofia and Simen, but Bird divined it. Simen was alone again in the expensive flat with the sea view and the marbled balcony.

'She's your sister,' Simen said, lowering his voice. Bird detected a note of accusation in his voice. That, too, was a first. He polished his glasses. He felt awkward, unwell, he read the message. 'The slightest thing can break her,' he whispered in a way that made Bird look up. He turned to Simen. 'Is she hurting, do you think?' Simen went on. 'Do you think it's serious this time? I mean, it's happened before, but it has always passed.' And

According to Sofia

as usual Simen cut short all answers by reaching for his mobile. He clicked down the list of selected names and called Inger. She was Simen's secretary, as close at times to the editor-in-chief as an elderly aunt, and Bird had not forgotten that she trimmed his ear hair.

'Your sister has left the flat. It has happened before,' he informed himself.

He turned to Bird, who stood quite still.

'Leon has set off for Colomb Bechar,' Simen continued. 'It seems more serious this time. It's certainly more unusual. Why does everything resembling chaos always have to come my way? Leon obviously felt he had to fax this message to me. He couldn't take the local bus out into the desert like a normal person. Not Leon. That wouldn't be his style at all. He's bought an ancient Renault. A Renault with an air-cooled engine that'll suck dust and desert sand into pistons and valves. He means to drive across the desert in a car with an air-cooled engine,' he added, well aware that Bird did not know the first thing about cars. 'That's today's headlines, if you like,' he muttered under his breath. 'Your sister ran off ten days ago and has at long last sent word of herself from Vitoria in the Basque country. Leon is headed for the desert and Colomb Bechar.'

Bird leaned both hands on the desk.

'Leon doesn't buy French cars,' Bird ventured. 'I bet you anything he bought a Toyota.'

Simen ignored Bird, who didn't know the difference between a distributor and a carburettor. 'I'll bet you the salesman has foisted the biggest heap of junk in Algeria on to him. In a car dealer's in Beni-Saf. In Africa. In a backstreet in Beni-Saf. Think about it. Do you see what this means? He's going to drive out into the sandstorms. Out to the camels. The Bedouins. Are there any Bedouins living in North Africa, by the way?' Simen put a hand to his brow. 'He took the boat across to Africa from Almeria in Spain. Can you imagine Leon in a fishing boat on the Mediterranean? A run-down Renault with an engine that has air vents in the rear wings. That old banger will break down after three hundred miles. He's going to drive out on to the burning plains. Into the sea of sand. Deep into it. In among the sand fleas, lice, snakes and cars with shattered sumps. Isn't that pathetic?' he said. 'Leon all alone amid the dun-coloured sands with a flashing oil indicator? With an engine that's red-hot. All the filters are clogged and he gazes despondently at his toolbox. He's over a hundred miles from the nearest garage. Can you imagine Leon lying under an old Renault, repairing a sump with plaster of Paris? Without a jack?' he added.

Simen paused and considered his mobile. It was so quiet in the office that Bird could hear Simen breathing. 'Leon has just left your dear sister,' he announced. 'Now *that* I had not expected. You can expect just about anything from Sofia, but *that* . . .' he proceeded. 'Leon and her. Somehow it doesn't quite fit. It's too much, somehow. She's a wreck, of course, worn out, with a headache and another gumboil in the offing. She bites her lips and presses her fingers to her brow. They make bombs in that part of the country. She *would* be stranded in a part of Europe where the people buy new automatic weapons and conscientiously buff their collective neuroses. A Basque minority showing the way for nationalists great and small. I bet you anything that right now she's sitting on a plastic chair in a café wondering just what she's doing there.' Simen looked at the clock, eyed its hands askance and breathed deeply through his nose, aware that the deadline for tomorrow's leader was approaching. 'Oh, yes, she's in Vitoria, in a Basque country which is doing its best to resemble a Greek tragedy.'

Bird was not sure whether he was addressing him or Inger. But the fax from Leon was indeed stuck to the screen of his computer. 'This is Sofia's doing, I'm sure of it,' Simen continued. 'This madness has her name written all over it. Do you think Leon is numbered among the men she sleeps with, or those she doesn't sleep with? My money is on the latter. She's been playing Gustav Mahler lately. Nothing but Mahler. The flat has been filled with

According to Sofia

the grumblings of Teutonic melancholy. Teutonic infidelity. Teutonic madness. The mournful Mahler of the period when every note he produced sounded like a protest. Maybe that's why she went to see Leon. She has been down there for four weeks. She needs an explanation. She has tapped from him everything he knows about music. Can you imagine? It's too much, even for a sensitive piano player. Poor Leon. Do you think she makes him feel even smaller than he is? She's more than strong enough. She could carry him in her arms. Leon must have lost his mind. Really lost it,' he added. 'Oh, it's complicated all right. I already called Bird,' he said. 'He's sitting in the chair next to me.'

So he was in fact talking to Inger, and again Bird noticed how he relaxed when he spoke to his secretary.

Bird was not sitting in the chair. He was on his feet. He was standing perfectly still in the middle of his own office, looking out of the window as if seeing those lime trees for the first time. He was genuinely sick and tired of thinking about his lovely sister with the gorgeous brown hair. Sick of all the fuss. Sofia was always surrounded by so much noise. Including the click-clack of shoes, and the scent of creams and telephone conversations with people who, in a previous century, would have been described as lovers. 'You have a beautiful sister' – since the age of fifteen he had been hearing those words. He still heard them. 'How does she look in the morning just after she has showered? How does she look when she's padding around the house in a towel?' Sometimes, especially when he was only fifteen, he understood why they asked, because it was impossible not to like Sofia. She had a laugh which made Bird realise that not everything was in vain. She gave him heart. He always felt more heartened when Sofia laughed. She stood up for him. When necessary she fought for him. She knew what he wanted long before he knew it himself. 'You must sign every piece you write 'Bird',' she commanded him on his very first day in the huge newspaper building.

Since then, not a single person had ever called him anything but

Bird. He was Bird. In his dreams he was Bird. 'Pull yourself together, Bird.' When he talked to himself, he said Bird. It was as if he had crawled inside the name. He was suspicious of anyone who called him anything but Bird. He liked that name so much that he actually tried to adopt it instead of his Christian name.

But it was complicated. Everything had become so complicated. Simen always tried to stick close to Sofia. He had been doing this ever since she turned fifteen.

In the morning, before they cycled to school, he would be there on his bike at the garden gate, waiting for her. He had a newspaper round and was quite happy to hang about for half an hour, eating apples while he waited.

She would arrange herself on the carrier with her schoolbag on her lap and off they would ride to school. He bought her custard pastries. He was in love with her. He always had been. Bird removed his glasses in surprise. It was as simple as that.

Simen never complained. He did not pester her. He did not follow her around. He hardly ever called her. But when he was not working, he thought of her. He talked about her to everybody he knew, in the bathroom mirror, in the car, the newspaper office and the sauna, and occasionally when he was dining at The Stables.

'I like her almost no matter what she does,' was one remark oft quoted by his fellow journalists.

Then they would look at one another and shake their heads. 'Sofia's beautiful, but even so?' they muttered.

Is it really possible to feel like that about a woman today, Bird wondered. Never mind let it be known. Telling your workmates while they wiped the beer froth from their beards. Bird regarded the lime trees, which dripped and dripped. Winter seemed to lurk in those slender branches. He turned and looked at Simen, who was pacing up and down the moss-green felt of the office carpet, mobile in hand. Bird was sure that Simen had not given the next day's leader a single thought. Two hours from now it needed to be lying written and ready on his desk. Even though Simen could

According to Sofia

write a leader incredibly quickly, it always had to be done at the last minute and should preferably ruin the sleep of as many people as possible. Or, at the very least, act as a kick in the pants to bishops, vicars and ordinary men of power. 'I'm running a newspaper. A perfectly normal madhouse,' he was wont to declare when he got worked-up. 'I am an editor and hence friendless,' he would grin. But that did not have much to do with Simen either.

He was observant. He was receptive. Patient. He picked up the slightest vibrations of impending unpleasantness. Not many people knew this, but Bird could read the signs. Simen started sneezing and contracted a fresh bout of sinusitis whenever livewire reporters stayed at the office until late at night, staring at empty screens. His heart sank when hopeful recruits wrote useless articles. He used Inger as his spy in the newsroom when he had to shut himself in his office to write. 'I really have tried. You know that. For years I've tried, but I've never understood what it is that troubles Sofia,' he said, with a look which made Bird turn away.

He had worn the same ironic look when they were out on the marbled balcony, watching the rockets blazing into the new millennium. Simen had been standing alone, with his arms crossed as if defending himself. Bird recalled how Simen had looked up, studied Sofia, noticing how her eye was caught by a young Indian over beside the cold buffet: mathematician, numerical wizard, shipowner, millionaire, with an open line to the Asian stock exchanges. She had flushed with delight, her eyes riveted on the Indian genius. He was festooned with gold that jangled around his wrists. He munched salad from a bowl while rockets filled the sky and coloured the wavelets in the harbour with their gaudy light, and Simen who was footing the bill for the festivities, tugged at his lower lip, cleared his throat, walked over to Sofia and rested his chin on the top of her head.

Bird remembered Sofia's laugh.

She bit Simen's ear. She promptly forgot the filthy-rich Indian with the Rover, diamonds and peach-bloom skin. He had a handsome, haughty face. The sort of face that comes only from having a wealthy father who sends his offspring to the celebrated universities of that despised country, England. He believed in both a spiritual and a capitalist God and was, therefore, as self-assured as he was invulnerable. But he cut a fine figure in an Italian suit and hand-sewn shoes. Bird had to admit it. Sofia curled her hands round Simen's neck in a way that eased Bird's mind. They were so good together. God, how good they were together. In truth, they were inseparable. May they be spared from all Indians with Rovers and bank accounts, Bird thought to himself. Seeing them standing there with their arms round one another, laughing at the new millennium, he did not only feel easier in his mind, he felt almost happy. He looked up at the rockets and heard the church bells in the distance.

2

So they saw the new millennium in in style. With not a single word of abuse. No rows. No one got particularly drunk. Bird did not feel like going home, so he slept on a sofa. The last thing he saw before he dropped off was Sofia laying her head on Simen's shoulder.

Simen's peaceful expression stood clear in his mind.

They were both sober: they had drunk iced water with lemon slices and cocktail cherries on the quiet all night, and looked out of the window at the promenade and the folk weaving up and down it.

Simen worked too hard, of course. His office at the newspaper, with its enormous desk, two chairs and discreet divan decked with cushions and throws was where he felt most at home. He didn't drink. In fact he was something of a teetotaller. He had realised long ago that one beer before dinner was one of many ploys designed to enable one to carry on drinking. It seemed so simple. 'How's about a little gin and tonic?' 'Fancy a quick one at The Stables before bedtime?' Simen had long since cracked the code, he was wise to all the excuses. He did not have time to get drunk. But he slept very badly. Had done so for twenty years. In fact he didn't fall asleep before two in the morning. If he was not asleep by then he opened the drawer of the bedside table and took out his notes. Was it really worth writing that article? Was it merely a rumour? Who was currently having sex romps in the cabinet minister's bed? Sometimes – it was not such a big world – he would call the newsdesk, mention a particular piece of gossip and suggest that a little discretion would not be a bad idea. He did not miss the evenings at The Stables. His fellow journalists were, as always, perched on their bar stools, vociferously discussing the year's newest football hope. 'Twenty million,' Simen might cry, on one of his rare visits. He did not know a thing about football. 'Two hundred thousand's a reasonable price for a good forward.' A remark which was roundly applauded. His colleagues occasionally talked about him. About Sofia. About the sorties she made when the mood took her. She could be away for a week or a month. 'Have you noticed, the first streaks of grey have appeared in her hair,' Simen heard someone say when he walked into The Stables one evening. He had examined her hair when he got home, but in the lamplight he could not detect so much as a hint of grey.

'What are you trying to say?' were the words which caused Bird to turn away from the lime trees and sit down on the chair at the computer. As usual, he laid his glasses in the middle of the pile of papers.

'You know what this means,' he said to Simen, who was trying to slip his mobile phone into his breast pocket.

'I have to go to the toilet,' Simen said, sinking his head down between his shoulders. Bird smiled. Again, it was like being back in the playground. One thing had not changed. Simen on his way to the toilet and suddenly the office smelled of girls with freshly washed hair, apples, goat's cheese, new-baked rye bread and milk in cartons. Simen, Leon and Leif.

Bird frowned.

As a boy, his name was Leif. He had been tall and skinny, lazy, no: languid, sleepy, always sleepy, but good at running. He saw it in

According to Sofia

the trainer's eyes. He read it in the sports pages of the newspaper. He was sent to running camp. Often it was the only thing he could be bothered doing. He was a sprinter. When he left the starting blocks he could tell when his hips were at the right angle to the track. At that moment he was utterly content. The only thing he collected was pictures of sprinters. He never forgot Carl Lewis's coolness. He never forgot Ben Johnson's eyes. Now and again, just before he fell asleep, he saw Mike Tyson's look of rage.

He was a boxer, but forever on the run.

Bird had always been poised to take to his heels. He was always on the starting line, so to speak. He made furtive visits to the library and read biographies of sprinters. When absolutely necessary he would fight with anybody at all over anything whatsoever. He covered his face with his arms and whispered to himself: 'Don't get mad. You win when you don't get mad.' More often than not he did win, and his mother, who changed the plasters and bandages, laughed as she went to fetch scissors and ointment. 'Don't you give in, Bird. Not for a moment. It does no good. Understand?' She snipped the bandage with the scissors she had taken from their place in the sewing machine drawer among all the reels of thread. She mended Bird's shirts and trousers. He asked her to.

She had raised him alone. She was a shop assistant and a member of the local Labour club who spent all her free time with her friends in the Party. She was happy to speak from any platform. She had a message to impart, she was one of the devout. It was the only thing Bird did not like about her. She gave him all the freedom he could wish for, but if he was gone for more than two days he had to call her at the shop. She never told him not to get into trouble, only that he should use his common sense. 'You've been blessed with more than enough to get by on.' To Sofia she said: 'Leave Leif alone.'

Sofia grew more and more beautiful, while Leif got more and more gangly. 'Another five years and you'll look like an Indian cow,' Sofia told him, as she outlined her lips with lipstick.

He did not forgive her. He did not look like an Indian cow. He did not forgive her until she objected to him being called Leif.

She dubbed him Bird.

She insisted on naming him thus, not after Charlie 'Bird' Parker, but because he had a dovecote to which he retreated whenever he came a cropper. He did so because his bony knees showed through his trousers and because Sofia, who never tattled, always knew which blonde girl he was gawping at when he wasn't being jumped on in the playground. He remembered the tarmac in the playground, which shimmered with heat in the summer, and Simen shuttling endlessly back and forth between the stairs and the toilets.

'I keep having to pee,' he said and put his mobile down on Bird's desk. He had eventually given up trying to slip the phone into his breast pocket.

'Bird, we have to do something. Your sister is maundering about down there in the Basque country and Leon is on his way to Colomb Bechar. It's hilarious. Too easy. Not very realistic. Romantic. Necessary even, perhaps. I understand it, but I'm worried.'

Bird bowed his head.

'A lot more worried than I was before,' Simen went on. 'Leon hasn't been his old self over the past few months. I can tell from his e-mails. There's something not quite right about Leon sitting in an hotel room, sending text messages on his mobile phone. On the bed. In a dressing-gown and boxer shorts. He's making money. Lots of money. He's playing in the most exclusive jazz clubs. He turned down the chance to play in Paris. He's been invited to *the* in places in New York. He's doing well. That can be a dicey business.'

Simen paced up and down the room. He looked at the clock and Bird was sure that for the first time that day his thoughts went to the next day's leader. 'You're going to have to fly down to Spain for a few days. To Bilbao. Or San Sebastian. I'll call the

Hotel Internacional on the promenade. Is it still there?' he asked Bird. 'Do you think?'

'I doubt it,' said Bird.

'Just a few days,' Simen ventured. 'A week maybe. The paper will pay, just remember to let me have all the receipts. Every single one. Could you try to bring back all the receipts? Don't tell Inger. She'll give me a bawling out. I can't bear to think of the look she would give me.'

3

Simen, the wealthy editor-in-chief with shares in the newspaper, was regularly quoted at party offices on the strength of his political leaders. He knew this, but never mentioned it. He trod carefully and did not relent until the reporters had dug up the whole story.

'I want every detail. The lot. Facts. I'm not asking what you think, I'm asking what you know. What is the story here!' he had been heard to roar at the morning meeting while opening the window.

'There is to be absolutely no smoking in this room until I have left it,' he would add, knowing he was wasting his breath.

Occasionally he would cough unrestrainedly, point to his sinuses and turn helplessly to Bird, who grinned and looked at the papers in front of him.

It was all part of the morning ritual accompanying his fifth cup of dark-brown coffee.

The reporters regarded Simen as he stood by the open window, saw how he took great gulps of fresh air and was subjected to the dirty looks of those who defied the doctors' warnings. They went on smoking as before and greeted all protests with the air of the bereaved.

Simen liked to be presented with all the facts in an orderly fashion, preferably point for point, preferably typewritten and

According to Sofia

with a straight right-hand margin. 'Could you explain this whole mix-up with Leon and Colomb Bechar to me one more time?' he said to Bird, who had turned round because he felt silly about staring for so long at the dripping lime trees.

'It's started snowing,' Bird said. 'Snowflakes in the rain. In October,' he added. He raised a hand as if to shield himself.

'It can't be,' said Simen.

The newspaper building was quiet at night. That was why Bird liked it there. The new computer hummed reassuringly. The corridor was hushed and there was not a sound from the photocopier. There was no one to bother them. No phones ringing. No smokers' coughs. Not so much as a giggle from the newsdesk.

'Your trusty secretary is going to have another sleepless night,' Bird essayed. 'Do you think she talks to her husband about you absolutely all the time? Do you think she refers to you as poor Simen? Poor Simen who is married to Sofia. Do you think her husband is fed up hearing about you when he's writing, eating, reading, brushing his teeth? When they go to bed and she plumps up the pillows?'

Simen did not laugh as he gazed out of the window. 'It's snowing,' he said. 'Enormous snowflakes. I can't bear it, it's snowing in October. I've no idea what Inger's husband knows or what they talk about. I'm glad to say,' he added.

They sat at the desk and Simen squirmed about in one of the newspaper's blue chairs, with both hands now covering his face. He had grown thinner, he had a harried look about him, Bird observed, but right now he was in one of the newspaper's snug offices. 'Your office here is like a fortress. A sanctuary. You have your things here. I don't know how you manage it?' he declared. 'There is this stillness about you. I wish I knew how you do it. How many years did it take for you to feel reasonably at ease?'

Despite the fact that Simen remembered every crucial statistic from the last three elections, he found it impossible to remember arrangements made with people he liked. He could recall politicians and ministers both living and dead, the weirdest details: the names of their mistresses and lovers, their breakdowns, perversions, true loves, embezzling, alcoholism, curious facts and bits of gossip. He rarely consulted the paper's database.

'Would you mind switching off your mobile?' Bird said. 'It's beeping,' he added and pointed to the phone amid the pile of papers.

'Would you like coffee?' Simen asked.

'Inger's gone home, remember,' Bird replied. 'She has the key to the cupboard. She keeps a close watch on the coffee tin and the cream.'

Simen eyed Bird glumly. 'Tell me again – what is all this really about? Does Leon mean to kill himself?'

'I assume so,' Bird said.

Simen removed his glasses. He looked at them in surprise. 'Assume?' he repeated. 'This isn't the sort of thing you go around assuming. I'm asking what you know.'

'I think he is slowly going to kill himself. Little by little. One day at a time.'

'Slowly?' Simen said.

He did not look too bright, sitting there with his glasses now perched on the tip of his nose, a bit forlorn, his fingers trembling as he ran a hand over the back of his neck. 'Slowly,' he repeated.

'He has finally given up,' Bird said.

'Given up?' Simen said.

'He's so vulnerable.'

Simen stretched his back.

'Would you mind not?' he began.

'What?' said Bird.

'It's so embarrassing.'

'What's embarrassing?'

'That he's so vulnerable. Who isn't?'

Bird pursed his lips.

'Don't give me that.'

'He's in a bad way,' Bird hazarded.

According to Sofia

'How come?'

Bird looked at the lime trees. Wet leaves stuck to the tarmac and the freshly polished car roofs. The evening was wet, clammy; chilled crows hopped about among the cars. Bird stood quite still. Why should those four lime trees have caught my eye on this of all evenings, he wondered. They've always been there. I've been working here for over twenty years. I've been using this office for just as long, but I have never noticed those lime trees till now.

Leon was not a dwarf. He could only just manage to work the pedals on the piano with the stool at its lowest setting and his legs were the longest part of him. And yet years before, when they were walking home from school with Leon hobbling along between Bird and Simen, it had not seemed the least bit laughable. Bird and Simen were both well over six foot, they stepped out smartly, Leon keeping up with the aid of his crutches. They were always, always deep in discussion, and Leon was always angry. He roared with anger. There was far too much aggression packed into a very small body. He was the one people looked at when they went to the cinema. Leon fumed, but he enjoyed it. His fingers and arms were almost normal, but even in the darkened cinema he shielded them from draughts. He protected his fingers from frost, cold water, axes and saws, hammers and nails and garden tools. He ordered specialist journals and electric drills. When he was bored he tucked his hands into his armpits. He blew on the tips of his fingers, lowered his arms to let the blood flow down into his wrists. He stretched his fingers. Pressed the tips together. Polished his nails. Massaged the joints. He talked non-stop and nineteen to the dozen, mostly about music, but also about boxing and boxers. He had not forgotten Muhammed Ali's words: it's the punch you don't see coming that knocks you out. He stopped short on the pavement. 'Or was it Joe Walcott who said that?' When he lost. Joe Walcott knew how to draw back that essential hair's-breadth to let the decisive blow go whooshing past. He was lazy. He practised the finer points of boxing and never moved more than was absolutely necessary. Leon talked about Mike Tyson's eyes.

Leon was the most arrogant individual Bird had ever met, and when he was not at the piano he was to be found in halls where he learned the most lethal moves in the martial arts. 'I'm constantly on the hunt for illegal moves,' he declared. 'Nothing is more revealing than an illegal move. They pay off. I need every one of them.' He spoke Japanese. He was the son of two missionaries and had lived for five years in Hiroshima. 'The Japanese have simple, but ruthless rules which I am trying to learn.' When his parents were called to bring Christianity to a Berber mountain tribe in North Africa he yearned to return to Japan. The very absence of the smells of Japan made him feel sick.

'I couldn't read one word of Japanese, but I learned to speak the language. That was the best thing about those years in Japan. I couldn't read. I lived in a world without newspapers or books. I have never felt so good. I understood only what people said to me. Not only that, but hardly anyone was more than a head taller than me.' He was quick, sharp and garrulous. Leon never got drunk, but when his dander was up he would yell at his friends out of a downturned mouth.

Bird did not like him.

Sometimes, when the three of them had spent a whole day together, Simen would suddenly reveal to Sofia:

'Bird likes Leon when he's playing the piano. Only then.'

And when Sofia told him this, Bird removed his glasses and polished them, a sure sign that he was endeavouring to buy time.

'Maybe so,' he said to his sister.

At any rate, and this never failed, he could tell right away when it was Leon who was improvising. He sat perfectly still on the piano stool with his eyes open, head tilted to the right, towards the audience in the auditorium, and after a few simple bars Bird knew for sure. That was Leon playing.

According to Sofia

He might be having a good night or a bad one. But it was Leon playing, and those very first bars were enough to make Bird look round, almost as if divining that Leon was once again about to play a tune the name of which he could not remember. He improvised constantly. A couple of tentative notes, a little silence, then a little more silence, occasionally a fresh attempt, and then he was off and running, and Bird, who never drank when he was listening to music, had his first glass of iced water with lemon slices and cocktail cherries.

Leon could mute the piano to the point where the keys seemed to have sunk into the casing, leaving only the bass, drums and guitar chords drifting over the stage. He appeared smaller at the piano, in the slanting spotlight beam only his arms and fingers were clearly visible, and it sounded as though he was simplifying existence not only for the drums and the bass, but for anyone who felt like listening. A hush fell over the place, the clientele refrained from picking up their glasses and the waiters stood motionless by the door.

He played for an hour. Never more. No amount of applause could elicit an encore. He tipped himself off the stool, smiled, but did not bow, and left the stage.

There was no fathoming him. Leon was in all ways obscure. Except when he was playing. Then he slowly bent his head over the keys and became distinct, precise, pregnant, and so technically superior that Bird sometimes felt the piano was about to crumble away. He conjured up stillness in a way which led Bird to notice details he had not known were there. He deconstructed a melody, took it apart, improvised on the piece he had altered, built it up, slowly, but unwaveringly, to reveal possibilities that no one else had heard. Bird had never seen him look surprised by this when it happened. It was natural, inevitable and always unexpected. Afterwards, Leon disappeared into the dressing room to wash. He rubbed olive oil into his fingers. He took as much care with his hair as a woman. He got deodorants and scent out of the cupboard. It took time. Bird sat with his iced water. Laughter rose from the tables again. He came in suddenly through the back door. He hobbled along: when it snowed he used crutches, they banged off the floor. Everybody knew he was there. And he hoisted himself adroitly up on to the bar stool.

'Polish vodka and beer,' he breathed. They were already there in front of him. 'I held back,' he said. 'I don't know what's got into me, but I've started holding back. I didn't want to let it show. Not tonight. Nor last night. It's been months since I let anything at all show. You heard?' He drank the vodka first, in one gulp.

Bird fished the slice of lemon out of his iced water. 'Yes,' he said, nibbling the lemon slice. 'I heard.'

'It's so simple,' said Leon. 'The only way to survive is to create your own niches. I have to construct them. At the piano I can make my own laws, which no one else can change. When I play, I know how it should sound. Do you know what I mean? It's embarrassing when it doesn't work out.' Without any sign of concern he then affirmed this: 'When I'm not at my best, I know it will come back. I know it will. Do you understand?'

Bird did not answer.

'I can't be bothered changing anything at all,' Leon went on, murmuring into the froth on his beer. 'There's too much of everything and it's all too massive. I want to produce works of art and fill in certain gaps with which I was presented when I was born. Fortunately, what I do is levelled only at myself. Sometimes I'm really quite boring.'

Bird swallowed the lemon slice.

'You're not answering.'

'No,' said Bird.

'I don't want to let it show any more,' Leon had reiterated. 'But I can't make out why I can't play what I actually hear. I don't though. Not any more. It serves no purpose. Not today. I mean: not now. Right now everything is a consumer good. There's always a market for the second-rate, it's the only commodity the barrow-boys are interested in. In order to produce the very best I have to find my own niche. I have to be alone. For weeks on end.

Totally alone. Do you know what I mean?'

'Not really,' was Bird's answer.

He was still standing by the window in the newspaper office, watching the crows hopping around the cars and noticing that the mangiest looking bird had sought refuge under the warm engine of the delivery van. Simen inserted the nozzle of the spray bottle into his nostril, inhaled, coughed and dabbed his nose with a tissue. He put his hands to his brow and massaged his sinuses. This made Bird feel at home. He liked Simen. He liked being in the same room as Simen. 'Do you think he's dead?'

'No,' said Bird.

'Are you sure?'

'Yes,' said Bird.

'How can you be sure?'

'Such things take time,' said Bird. 'He would have called. I'm sure he would have phoned at least three times to tell us not to do anything.'

'Do you really think so?'

'Yes.'

'You sound as if you're absolutely certain,' Simen said.

'I am absolutely certain.'

'I don't get it,' said Simen.

When Bird felt helpless he hunted for his cigarettes. He stuck his hand into the right-hand pocket of his jacket, then his trouser pocket and his shirt pocket. He did not give up until he had patted every single pocket with his right hand. He scanned the top of the desk. He did not swear, but he felt helpless.

'You quit,' Simen said. 'Eight years ago. There's not a trace of nicotine in your system.'

'Do you really not remember how Leon feels about Colomb Bechar?' ventured Bird. 'What it stands for? He's been telling us for as long as I can remember. All those speeches. All the speeches about how he's going to lose himself out there in the desert when he can't take it any more. He intends to lose himself out there in the desert at the end. When it really is the end.'

'Do you believe that?' Simen asked.

'I think it's possible,' Bird said. 'If Sofia could take herself off to the October rain in the Basque country, then it's possible.'

Simen put a hand to his mouth.

'What about you?' Bird continued. 'You're the one who knows him best.'

'I don't believe anything at all,' said Simen.

'It's not possible.'

'What's not possible?' said Simen.

'That you've forgotten.'

Simen smiled. 'You've no idea what it's possible to forget when you have Sofia in the house. When you're married to her,' he added. 'She won't be able to cope with this. I bet you that at this very moment she's wondering what she's doing down there in that neurotic Basque country. She lives dangerously because she's always trying to make someone happy. What was she doing in Northern Ireland a year ago, what is she doing among Basque bombers right now? Does she go looking for disasters? Is she waiting for trouble to break out? Does she feel it coming? I bet you that as we speak she's drawing her shoulders up around her ears and smiling hesitantly at the waiter. As usual she thinks it's all her fault. Hers alone. She won't cry. She loves to be plucky, you see,' he said and smiled at Bird. 'She'll call me.'

Again Bird was surprised. He looked at Simen. So far he had said only two negative words about Sofia. He missed Sofia. Sofia's hair. Her lips. Missed the smell of her. He missed the sounds she made. She sang in the shower. She even sang when she got out of bed. And she laughed when she ate. She drove Simen to the newspaper office in the morning and picked him up in the evening. She nuzzled into Simen's neck when he eventually got away from the office and climbed into the car. She kissed him. They were still liable to hold hands in a darkened cinema. They were that strangest of phenomena: good friends. Still, Bird thought.

According to Sofia

'You really don't remember what we agreed?'

'Not really, no,' Simen said.

Bird smiled. 'You're footing the bill?'

'No,' said Simen. 'The paper will pay. I'm doing my best to forget it.'

'So you do remember.'

'Yes,' said Simen.

4

I am forsaken, Sofia smiled. He forsook me. This is the first time that anyone has ever left me. It was quietly done. She thought for a moment. No, silently, she concluded.

It's lucky I can see the funny side of it. Here I am, sitting all alone under the awning in a Basque café, drinking coffee that tastes of chicory and deceit. Today I have the feeling that all is deceit.

It is October and chilly, and the other customers have retreated indoors. They sit at tables inside the warm café, wondering why I stay out here in the chill wind off the mountains. Those much vaunted mountains. I'm feeling sorry for myself and it always shows and it's always comical.

Here I am in the Basque city of Vitoria, stirring my coffee. I know only one person here. I arrived yesterday. I arrived yesterday on the local bus from San Sebastian. I ought to have been so upset today that I wouldn't remember the slightest thing about that bus journey.

Not so.

I remember the driver telling us that we were driving over the famous pilgrim way. The driver stopped the bus. Then: crossings and faint cries from devout passengers, accompanied by the drone of the diesel engine. We called in at the grey village where the

According to Sofia

Virgin Mary showed herself to a little girl. Four silent men nipped into the crypt to confess their sins to her. I had coffee in the bar and ate a sweet lemon cake. I remember almost everything of the trip. I sat quietly in the air-conditioned bus, looking out at the countryside. The grey mountains of Northern Spain are always a disappointment, the villages are a disappointment, the lemon cake was a disappointment and I loathe those green hillsides. I loathe Basque cows, which are in fact horned cattle from the plains of the East, and I hate the sheep. I have no time for Basque berets, Basque wine, Basque peasants or the Basque brotherhood.

Although it was a while ago, I was barely twenty at the time, I can still recall the sounds from the back rooms of the bars and how the voices altered once wine, food, cigars and battle cries had been consumed. When grown men congregate in lodges with food, wine, cigars and battle cries then everything is in vain. There is no point. We might as well give up. What perverse hormone is it that runs riot in men when revolutions are being planned and false names chosen? It cannot be boredom. Or at least: not boredom alone. Maybe it has something to do with the grey villages strung out across the mountains? They are as changeless as the moon. Remote genetic codes? Dirty-grey, age-old poverty and green algae. It poured with rain. We popped into cool bars at crossroads and I drank even more coffee. I stood firm and drank only coffee. I have not been really drunk in ten years. I don't dare. I have witnessed too many embarrassing incidents. When one of the company drinks a bottle of wine or two, a weariness steals over me. I can't take it. All the words. All the usual words, repeated in every land, in every age. After two bottles of wine all men say the same. Things always become more complicated when I'm a little bit drunk. I no longer have the heart for it.

She could feel the corners of her mouth twitching. The waiter sweeping ash and crumbs off the table with a cloth was sure she was smiling at him. He was still young enough to be happy at his work and he looked at both Sofia and the glass he had been polishing. I deserve it, she thought. It had to come. This pain in my right shoulder has to be more than a standard warning sign. It's sharp. When I raise my right arm there's a sharp pain. Could it be the apex of my right lung? A cancer is really only a bunch of rogue genes. It's not fair. I can't have smoked more than ten cigarettes in the last two years. But I've been living in a city where the air is thick with asphalt dust and industrial fumes. In Norway, if you want to get on you have to live in the city. I know the right people, I'm on first-name terms with waiters, *maître d*'s, politicians, brokers, bank managers, artists and hucksters. I live in a flat by the sea. We bought that flat with our own money. I bought the flat. Simen took care of all the other bills. No fathers with fat bank accounts for us.

Five years ago I found that I couldn't lift my hands. All of a sudden I couldn't lift my hands. One perfectly ordinary day in May five years ago I sat at the breakfast table and couldn't pick up my coffee cup. From one moment to the next lifting a fork became an impossibility. I couldn't switch off the hotplate on the cooker. I had to be fed. I sat at the table and looked at the food. Simen always lays the table. He has to have everything in a set place. I could see that the cucumber was in its usual bowl. The bowl I bought from a ceramicist in Risør. And I could see that the marmalade was in its jar. The blue jar. I couldn't cut a slice of bread. Whatever I had to eat, breakfast or dinner, might as well have been sitting on a table in another country. It was just as unattainable. It could have been sitting on a table on another continent. Sometimes it strikes me that it wasn't all that unpleasant. I had sort of got used to it. For the first four weeks Simen had to feed me. I drank milk through a straw. I hardly ate anything. Some bread, soup and chocolate. And yet I put on almost nine pounds. I wasn't getting much exercise. I went from the living room to the kitchen. From the kitchen to the bedroom. I showered. For some reason I didn't need any help to take a shower. I showered three times a day. For eight months I dropped everything I laid hands on. I dropped keys, the bread knife, cups, my scarf, gloves. I can still hear the sound of my keys hitting the floor. That exasperating sound. I knew it was no use bending down to pick up the keys. I spent the first eight weeks on the sofa. I dozed for eight weeks. I hardly slept at all, just dozed.

After two years one of my fellow doctors came up with a diagnosis. I knew that just about every bit of that diagnosis was a fabrication. A load of waffle. A sop. Empty talk. Everybody knew it. 'You'll come through this, Sofia. You've been working too hard. You're suffering from exhaustion, but it's only temporary. You haven't taken a holiday in three years. It won't last. It's often the most brilliant minds that are hit like this. It's an understandable reaction. You've been working your arse off. For years.' I knew that. Of course I knew that. And in any case I had discovered that after four Valium I was fine. My hands were as right as rain after two Valium and two glasses of wine. For weeks I sat staring at those traitorous hands. At the wrists. Those supple wrists which I had been so proud of during tricky operations. How many weeks did I spend staring at my hands, I wonder? For how many weeks did they fail me? It took a while to admit it. It led to incidents that I'd rather not think about it. I lost something. I've no idea what. I don't want to know what I have lost. It's just too stupid. Too much. But I've been with too many men. I've lain on my back a little too often. I don't regret it. Somehow regret is impossible. 'I got a hole in my heart the size of a truck,' an American voice roared out of the loudspeakers in that jazz club in San Sebastian. I used to be able to roar like that. A long time ago. That clever-clever, goody-goody Sofia Linde. The one who became a doctor, surgeon, famous. It all happened so fast. 'It won't be filled by a one-night fuck.' Must be Lou Reed. While Leon was washing his fingers after that evening's gig I heard Lou Reed's voice.

Through the smoke and the din around the bar in the Mr Duke jazz club I heard a voice that suddenly prompted me to glance down at my wrists. They had been x-rayed from all angles. They had been examined, discussed, analysed and dismissed by all those professors who also happen to be my friends. But I came through it. I got well. Does that sound stupid? It's not stupid. Believe me. It's a comfort. It's a dangerous comfort, but I came through it. It has led to incidents I would rather not think about. I have strong hands. I can lift a bag of cement. When I'm building steps at the cottage I can lift a hundredweight easy. Luckily there are all sorts of things wrong with me. I still have catarrh and stomach cancer, enteritis, atrophying muscles and aching joints. It becomes a habit.

She smiled.

The waiter misunderstood. He fussed about her, the crucifix round his neck swinging against the hair on his chest. He's hairy, horny and stupid as a mule, thought Sofia. She shut her eyes, opened them slowly, looked at the waiter, unspeaking, long, a little too long. He wavered, cleared his throat, lifted his face to the rain drumming down on the awning. He spoke serviceable English, Sofia answered in Spanish. He thought he was an expert on women from the north and was sure he knew what that smile meant.

Sofia waved him over.

'Pay,' she said.

'You mean now?'

He looked at her in surprise.

'Yes,' she said.

'Already?'

'Yes,' she said.

'Will you be back this evening?' the waiter asked. 'It's nice here in the evenings. We play music. Basque music. The band is famed throughout the country. The Basque country,' he added. 'We have a really good time. Not to mention what we get up to once all the customers have left,' he said, flashing his teeth.

'What's your name?' she asked.

Sofia smiled. She smiled because she found it amusing to have yet another waiter standing dutifully behind her chair. She lifted her hair slowly with her fingers because she knew that this made men restless. She let her hair fall down her back. The waiter stood there stock-still. He looked like a gun dog the moment before it begins to whine. 'They call me Alfredo,' said the waiter.

She made no reply.

'Will you be back this evening?' the waiter said again.

That's all I needed, she thought. Alfredo. His name's Alfredo and he's a waiter in a café in Vitoria.

'No,' she said.

'You won't be here?' he said in astonishment.

'No,' she said.

'Why not?'

'You're too skinny,' said Sofia.

'Skinny?' repeated the waiter.

'Skinny men have no staying power,' said Sofia. 'They just lie there. Fumble about a bit. Sweet-talk. It's always over almost before it's begun. I can't take that, you see. I need time. Long fingers are a good sign. Not always. But often,' she added. She had noticed that he had short, stubby fingers that he hid behind his back.

'Fingers?' he said.

'Yes,' she said. 'They're important.'

She was sitting next to the wall under the canopy of the roof. They could just hear the rain on the plastic of the awning and Sofia shifted her chair, presenting her profile to the waiter. She looked her loveliest in profile. She had been drinking coffee, she placed her hands on the table.

'What did I do?' said the waiter.

'Do?' said Sofia.

The waiter looked at her.

'Nothing. That's the sad part.'

'Will you be back?' the waiter asked.

'I won't be back. Not today, not tomorrow, nor any other day. I simply will not be here,' she smiled.

She looked at him. 'You little slime-ball,' she said in Norwegian. She reached for her handbag and took out her nail file.

'You'd better clear off, Alfredo,' she said, studying the nail file. 'You'd better clear off to somewhere where it's hot.' Sofia fixed her eyes on him. 'Hot and steamy,' she added. 'You know what I mean by steamy. You know what it smells like when you take off those black underpants of yours.' Calmly she proceeded to file her nails, eyeing him mildly. 'You're actually quite good-looking and you think you're always going to be good-looking. But you're such an insufferable pain in the neck. You can't come up with a single lusty fantasy that hasn't been so done to death that even the primmest old maids in the Basque country wouldn't yawn with boredom.'

The waiter was still standing by the table.

'You are disgusting, Alfredo,' she said. He heard her mention his name and edged closer to the table. 'If you bend down to me, I'll stick the point of this nail file right between your eyes,' she said, in a voice so soft that Alfredo smiled. 'All the way in to the part of the brain that controls what little sense you have. It so happens that I am a doctor. A surgeon. I was a promising surgeon. I was ambitious. For ten years I worked under the electric lamps, slicing my way in to liver and kidneys. I can tell right away when the liver is swollen because a person has been drinking too much, or when the prostate has passed the point of no return. It's true that it is some years since I last cut into a human body with a scalpel, but I am a surgeon. I know exactly where to slip this nail file in behind your ear. I have more than half a mind to twist the nail file round about in there a couple of times, and I would take some pleasure in it,' she added, feeling quite calm. She inspected her nails. 'That would make me happy,' she went on. 'Today I ought to be drunk. Drunk as a skunk. Leon packed his bag and took himself off to Africa. I sat on the bed in my dressing-gown eating a sandwich while he threw CDs into his bag. He wasn't angry, just worn out. He'd been working too hard, these deep hollows had appeared at the corners of his mouth. 'To Africa,' she repeated. 'Why can't I get drunk the way men do? It scares the life out of them. I'm a sort of a virgin who's contemplating

According to Sofia

sleeping with everybody I fancy. And that's something your average man finds hard to understand.' She turned and looked at the waiter standing behind her chair. 'You are a perverted little pipsqueak from the Spanish sticks who goes to mass every Sunday. You weep and you wail. You weep and wail in the confessional every Monday. You confess your sins. And you're actually sorry. You bemoan your lot. You tell some country priest about all the women you've slept with the week before. He feels old and weary after Sunday, his sinuses are blocked from the dank air in the cathedral and he would much rather be back in his office. The parish registers are on his desk, and there's a glass and some red wine in the cupboard. He metes out your punishment, five Hail Marys, a little repentance, a bit of a chat and you can start all over again. Nice little set-up you've got there, Alfredo.' The waiter listened intently to the torrent of Norwegian in which his name occasionally cropped up. 'You don't know anything about real perversion, you bloody little runt. Not the slightest thing.' Sofia was aware that she had raised her voice. She grabbed her handbag.

'Why that stupid bag? Can you imagine anything more womanish than using a handbag as a weapon? I felt such a fool,' she wailed down the phone at Simen four hours later.

'I should have used my nail file. Don't you agree? Say you agree, Simen,' she whispered into the phone.

Sofia grabbed her handbag, got up, slammed the bag into Alfredo's jutting Adam's apple then ground the catch into his eyes. She knew this was dangerous. The Adam's apple does not stand up well to pressure. Not a lot of pressure, at any rate. Besides which, Sofia knew exactly where to hit and how to angle the blow. All of this she worked out even as the thought crossed her mind: I'm going to ruin my bag. It had been a gift, outrageously expensive, soft calfskin, bought in one of Rome's chic-est shops on the Via Condotti.

'Why didn't I laugh?' she asked a silent Simen on the phone. 'Is Bird there?' She knew that everyone in the café was under the impression that Alfredo had just broken up with her and that she had gone crazy. Love had driven her mad. She had had a taste of Basque passion and could not imagine living without it. They thought she had lashed out with her bag because she could not live without the young waiter. She screamed insinuations in Spanish regarding Alfredo's endowments and his mother's gold-plated dentures – the latter having been a reward for certain services rendered to the bishop. She shrieked unmentionable things about certain tricks that can be employed when all else fails. All of this was received by the people in the café in profound silence and with a certain respect. It is quite permissible to go off your head for a few minutes in the Basque country. To the best of her knowledge concerning mitigating circumstances she ought also to laugh hysterically and tear at her brown locks. She ought to laugh out loud. Whinny, if she liked. It would have been quite all right for her to whinny like a mare. Eventually Alfredo made a mistake. He touched her. He laid his hands on her. Soothingly. Sofia gave a Wagnerian screech, hands to her brow, then she pointed to her wallet, passport and money. He had touched her breasts, she cried. He had pawed her sacred breasts. She let fly with her right fist and hit him behind the ear. He tottered and fell back between two blue plastic tables. Good, she thought and threw herself on top of him. Fucking brilliant. She whacked him on the brow with an ashtray. Bull's-eye. This blow momentarily stopped the flow of blood to the brain. 'He put his hands on my breasts,' she shrieked like a fat and frantic shepherdess at the opera. The head waiter stepped out on to the street. He saw the blood oozing from Alfredo's forehead and roared to someone inside the café to call the police. 'Bloody great oaf,' Sofia hollered, and struck Alfredo with the ashtray. She remembered the way the Cinzano logo on the ashtray glinted in the light.

'Know what,' she said to Simen on the phone. 'At that moment I had the upper hand. Not for long. But I had the upper hand.' To

According to Sofia

the people in the café she was a crazed mistress who had been deceived by a Basque peasant lad. She sat astride him, hammering away at him. Laying into his thigh now. 'Who is that waiter?' asked a well-fed man sipping Tio Pepe. He was sitting at a table by the window, he stroked his beard and raised his glass. 'He's not hitting back,' the well-fed gentleman said, pointing at Alfredo. 'That is so Basque. We have our honour. We have our dignity. What was his name again?' he asked. In the distance he heard the faint wail of the police car. 'Is he alive?' Simen asked, glancing at Bird's notes. 'You could have killed him. You can't go on like this, Sofia. No good can come of it.' Slowly, Simen put a hand to the mouse for the computer and moved the arrow to 'Shut down'. He pressed the left-hand button on the mouse and listened to the little carillon by which Bill Gates has decreed the world will be steered. 'Yes,' he said. 'You're in a bad way. I know and there's nothing I can do about it. Not right now. Not from here. No, Bird's not here. He went off to make some coffee. Yes, he's here at the newspaper office. No, I don't know where exactly. Yes, he did get a fax from Leon. I don't know how you can manage to kick up such a shindy in such a short time. What's that? I shouldn't call you?'

Sofia went on hammering away at Alfredo until she was arrested by two policemen with pencil moustaches. 'A common Nordic whore who does not understand the meaning of Basque dignity,' said one of the policeman, digging his fingers into Sofia's hair. He hauled Sofia off the bleeding waiter, who covered his face with his arms. The policeman had gentle eyes and was sure she did not understand a word of what he said.

'That's right,' Sofia shouted. 'A common Norwegian whore who learned Spanish at that flaming university in Salamanca. Nowhere else in the world will you find so many perverted professors gathered inside the one mausoleum. A thousand years of isolation. No Middle Ages. Nothing but wine and mutton. Nothing but convents and nuns. Nothing but secret drinking and jerking off. Eight hundred years of Moorish and Berber muck. Five hundred years of dignified debasement. Don't you lot ever have enough?'

'Did you really say that?' Simen murmured into the phone. 'That wasn't very smart, was it?'

'No,' said Sofia. 'It wasn't.'

'Then what happened?'

'They drove me to the police station. The policeman sat on me. He smoked a cigarette. I was greeted by a police chief who knew what he was doing. He was one big smile. He grabbed me round the waist, just far enough below the right breast for decency. He was a real pro. Then he called a lawyer.'

The lawyer poured a wineglassful of brandy down her throat. 'Take it easy,' he said. 'Everything's going to be all right.'

5

Lawyer Antonio Nerida had streaks of grey in his thick black hair, long pliant fingers which slowly unscrewed the top of his fountain pen, and when he smiled his teeth glinted with gold. When he looked at Sofia he did not smile, but his eyes softened.

'Don't you remember me?' he said. 'My name is Nerida. Antonio Nerida. I remember you from the university in Salamanca. You learned Spanish in five months and two of the professors wanted to marry you? You were eighteen, but seemed older. Do you remember Miguel? The guy who walled himself up in his office and smoked forty Celtas a day. He had a chronically sweaty upper lip. Other than that, he didn't do anything but love you, Real Madrid, volcanoes, Rome, earthquakes, Pompeii and disasters. He had a house on Santorini. He was given to quoting Robert Burns, was the Dean of the university and pursued you all the way to Hamburg when you left for home. Word was that you had lived with him for five months. I envied him.'

Nerida paused.

He eyed her over his half-moon glasses and edged his chair closer. She is so fragile, he thought to himself. Everyone is so fragile. The slightest thing can break us. The weak fall sick due to the demands on them. The strong become sick with disappointment. 'I gather you visited a café yesterday.' He spoke like a doctor. Sofia was surprised to find that he knew what she was thinking. 'Yes,' he said. 'I know you are a surgeon.' She turned away and Nerida saw her in profile.

'I called the proprietor from the police station when your name came up. It was the first time you had been there, the proprietor said. You arrived yesterday evening on the bus from San Sebastian and were staying at the hotel across the street.' He waited, but Sofia made no reply. 'What were you up to with that waiter? Nothing? I bet you had never laid eyes on him until this morning. You met him for the first time today, isn't that so? There was a spot of bother. Are things always this lively when you're around?'

Sofia nodded.

'What number shall I call? Whom shall I call?' he asked. 'I'm betting that you're the sort of person who calls someone.'

'Simen.'

'Is that your husband?'

Sofia nodded.

'Where is he living?'

'In Norway.'

'Would you like some more brandy?'

'Yes, please,' said Sofia.

She produced her notebook from what was left of the expensive handbag and pointed to the mobile numbers. 'There,' she said, pointing. 'He's a newspaper editor who keeps trying to stick his mobile into his breast pocket. He always has it on him. You'll have to speak English to him.'

'English?'

'Yes, English.'

Nerida sighed and keyed in the number. He raised his chin, put his hand to his mouth to conceal his smile, cleared his throat, waited. He had eyes which said that he could hang on the telephone for hours. He glanced at it accusingly. It's so boring, he thought, boring and unpleasant when absolutely everything happens at once. So far, the worst thing with the new technology is that everything happens at once, and that nothing can be kept secret. I am benumbed. My senses are deadened by information for which I never asked. A group of hackers has invented the future on the quiet. They nail us to the future before we've had a chance to give it any thought. I am constantly plagued by facts and knowledge the scope of which I cannot comprehend. A hacker with a laptop can paralyse air traffic over Paris. Some little pedant in Pakistan can cut off the electricity supply in Oslo and Malaga. Everything is so fragile and it is so unpleasant. A stone-cold sober woman wallops a waiter in the Basque capital with a handbag. She is arrested and three hours later her husband in Norway knows all about it. Useless messages are being transmitted by millions of chirruping mobile phones. What am I supposed to do with all this information? Is it any good to anybody? He raised his chin even higher and noticed that the fan on the ceiling had gone into hibernation. It's horrendous, he thought to himself, pressing the keys again with his long fingers. There is nothing we cannot discover at the push of a button or two. All the world's foolishness is digitally transmitted, soon the only ones taking it seriously will be the people in the Tokyo and New York stock exchanges. If I were living in the desert I could sit back, chew khat and observe the whole masquerade from afar. 'What was your brother's name again? I remember him. Wasn't it something to do with animals?'

'Bird,' said Sofia.

'Bird,' sighed Nerida. 'I'd forgotten. I remember he used to jog. He was a typical sprinter. He wasn't interested in studying. I've often wondered what he was doing at university? Did he run all the time? I remember he used to stop at crossroads and check his pulse. He trailed chaos in his wake. Way too many feigned sick days. He received at least ten letters a day. What *was* it he bought at the chemist shop? At the chemist shops,' he added. 'When people were at work he would run for miles and miles on ordinary, dusty Spanish roads. Of his own free will. He wasn't interested in doing anything. He ran. Occasionally he would put on a brief spurt. It was my first experience of interval training. He wore spikes. He smelled of dust. Dust and sweat.'

Sofia drained her glass.

'Didn't he . . .?'

'Yes,' Sofia cut in.

*

She cut me off, Antonio Nerida thought. So there is a limit. A definite, unspoken limit. Good. Then I won't have to reveal everything I know about Therese Somoza. I won't have to think about what I know about the Somozas, that well-to-do family from the ramshackle town on the banks of the river Ebro: their wealth, their heaps of money, the vineyards lining the stream which, for generations, supplied them with riches, power, a somewhat threadbare honour. Talent, even. It's a downright disgrace. The wine. That superb wine, not to mention the price of it, has endowed them with talent. Traditions, genes. Don't forget the genes. I married into all the mess with Therese's aunt. That is, without a doubt, the stupidest and the smartest thing I have ever done. I have no intention of trying to work out the difference. I do not need to dwell on the fact that Sofia Linde is the mother of the famous Therese Somoza, that Bird is her uncle and that hardly any scandal will still have the power to shock twenty years on. Most people will have forgotten all about it. Most people will smile at the idea of a run-of-the-mill scandal resulting in a child. It so often does, Antonio Nerida smiled. Therese Somoza is still young. I can leave it at that for now. I can concentrate on the fact that Sofia belted a waiter with an ashtray, was arrested by a policeman who had to sit on her, and that she was not the least bit frightened. Not for one second. The desk sergeant was brusque. So she outlined her lips with lipstick and her hand did not shake. She did not try to conceal the fact that her trousers were grey with the dust from a Basque pavement. She washed her hands in cold water and asked for a towel.

According to Sofia

Nerida rested his feet on the desk while he waited to get through to the newspaper office in Norway. He glanced across at Sofia who had got the colour back in her cheeks, and tried to forget Therese Somoza, her family, the greedy, grasping Somozas with their money, talent and connections in Madrid. He tried to forget the family estate east of Ronda, with its bulls, then he suppressed the thought of the mind-numbing speeches made when Therese won a national award. Therese at the piano. The television. The papers. Reporters with notepads and the din of the telephones when the news was announced. In the parish register and income tax records she is given as the daughter of Remi Somoza. He was rich, thrifty, ate fried potatoes for breakfast and drove out to the fields every morning in his jeep, paid his workers a fair wage, spent most of the morning in the back room of a country tavern drinking water, eating nuts and playing cards.

Antonio yawned.

It was all so long ago. He yawned again. He drank the family Rioja. Seldom, but nothing except that. Therese Somoza was genuinely fond of her name. Because it was in the Somoza family that one found talent, heritage and misfortunes aplenty. The Somozas died early or not at all, he had often thought. He was happy when they moved to the top of the hill on the other side of the city. She is like Sofia, he thought. Therese is more beautiful, but Sofia is the type to whom every eye is drawn when she walks into a restaurant.

'Engaged,' he said, pointing to the telephone.

'Terrie,' Sofia said. 'I know you all call Therese Somoza Terrie. Isn't that right?'

She's a mind-reader, a resigned Nerida noted with a little puff that rounded and softened his cheeks. He put the phone to his ear, remembering as he did so that half an hour ago he had been in his nice, snug den in the basement at home, trying out his new music system by playing Bill Evans's version of 'Alice in Wonderland'. So clever, he had thought. With brilliant backing from Scott LaFaro on bass. He had smuggled the system in from the Canary

Islands two days earlier, it had been so expensive that when he got home he hid the loudspeakers under a rug in his study. When his wife discovered them she would scream blue murder. He could already hear her, but Bill Evans's peace when he touched the keys would loosen the knots in the back of Nerida's neck for years to come. He thought of LaFaro's cool insouciance and his closed eyes. That was enough to stifle any regrets he might have had, and he looked at Sofia. She is magnificent, he told himself, and felt his throat tighten. I had forgotten that brown hair. How could I? Her face. Her skin. It's strange, but I had forgotten. And he remembered how the Dean, who had been seized by a poetic frenzy when Sofia went back to Norway, had ensconced himself in a ridiculous garret and written verse, and how all of his poems had been unreadable. He had received rejections from every single publisher in Spain and whiled away his last two years there in dimly-lit bars where he played snooker, ate eggs and bocadillos and drank muscatel. He played against fading English champions who had retreated to the dim saloons of the Basque country, there to fleece a failed poet. He remembered the face bent over the green baize, the crisp click of the cue, the silence when he lost and the bank notes on the table under the lamp. Eventually he pulled himself together and moved with his family to a treatment centre in the country outside of Oviedo. He had gone back to being teetotal, and meek and mild as any ordinary dean.

Sofia considered him.

'Yes,' he said. 'But I don't like it.'

'What don't you like?'

'Them calling her Terrie. It's a silly American name with not a single soft sound to it. It's the sort of name young American women can scream at the top of their voices.'

She looked round in surprise.

'Why so aggressive?' said Sofia.

'Was I?'

'Is she married?'

'Not as far as I know,' said Nerida.

According to Sofia

'Does she live . . .?'

'Alone,' he broke in. 'She's the only member of the Somoza family whom I like. Really like.'

Sofia nodded in the direction of the telephone.

'Still engaged,' he said. 'Rather than wait,' he went on, 'couldn't you just tell me what all this is about. And once you've done that, we'll go out for dinner. I'll call my wife and ask her to join us.'

6

So Sofia told him about the agreement that Simen, Bird and Leon had made when they graduated from high school.

She hesitated when she saw Nerida's long fingers splayed across the brown top of the desk, then proceeded, nonetheless, to tell him how they had agreed to protect one another.

'Protect?' Nerida hooted. 'Really?'

He eyed her sceptically. Then he regarded her as though she had been taken unwell and was only just recovering. He examined her features, her eyes, and shook his head: 'Who would credit it? In this day and age?' he whispered. 'In the new millennium?' he continued. 'It sounds like something out of an American epic in which three friends vow to protect each other from their fathers. Ambitious fathers. Fathers who want you to become a lawyer or a priest. Preferably the latter. I don't give a damn about fathers. Fortunately,' he added.

He stared at Sofia. He looked as if he needed to think about something else. 'Do you remember the night you crept into my bed? I'll never forget it. We drank tea and played poker.' He gazed disconsolately at his short legs. He rested his feet on the desk and Sofia peered into her empty wineglass. 'There is no way to protect ourselves from dead fathers. They're just there. They're

According to Sofia

always there. Do you mind me swearing? I try not to. It's a habit. I picked it up from my father,' he smiled. 'He was a sheep farmer and the slightest sound bothered him. He played the tuba. There is a picture of him taken at the crack of dawn one spring morning, he's all on his own, playing the tuba. Outside a bar in some village.' Antonio Nerida glanced at her to make sure that she was listening. 'He's standing on the deserted plain, lovingly embracing his tuba,' he said. 'When I was a boy, he spent most of his time up in the hills with a leather bag full of wine. He said he had a woman in every village, but that was just hot air. Nobody liked him, but he had a better life than me. Most people like me, even policemen, but that's just a nuisance.'

He studied Sofia, at length.

'I saw a picture of you in the paper last week. You were with a pianist who played to packed houses in San Sebastian. Leon was his name. I remember now. Won't you tell me about it? I won't interrupt. Not once. I promise.'

Sofia found that the brandy relaxed her shoulders. It had taken time, almost an hour.

'If you promise,' she said, and told him how Leon, Simen and Bird had made an agreement that no matter what happened, in an emergency whoever was at home would pay for the ticket back to Norway. Twice Simen had taken out a loan in order to bring Bird home from Buenos Aires. On one occasion he had got the newspaper to pay, but only after Bird had written four articles for it. Leon had never availed himself of this possibility. He had frittered away his time at home. Going from town to town. From bar to bar. 'I've learned an incredible amount that way,' he said on his return. 'Perfectly ordinary drunk men wax sentimental, the landlords become amenable and women get it into their heads that I am sensitive. This last because I sneak a bit of Bachian refinement into Gershwin's chords. It never fails, and numbers among my most exclusive memories.'

'Tell me about one of those memories,' Simen had said.

'World championship in billiards in Breda, when I played cocktail music during the intervals,' Leon grinned. He held up his hands to Simen when the latter wished to hear more.

'I don't believe it,' Nerida said. 'Friends don't stick together like that. Not these days.'

'It's true,' Sofia said.

'Since they were boys? Are you telling me that they have stuck together since high school?'

'Yes,' said Sofia.

'And never argued?'

'Oh, they argue almost all the time.'

'I don't like Leon. At least, not from what I read in the interview. No,' he said again.

'Hardly anyone does.'

'That's a comfort,' said Nerida.

'It's so stupid,' Sofia said, examining her nails. 'I've broken two nails. It'll take them a month to grow. I get a fungal infection in my nails when they're short.'

'It's ringing,' Nerida said. 'At last. Do I really have to speak English? I hate that.'

7

'The problem is – ' said Simen. He waited. The satellites up above could not decide to whom they should communicate Simen's problem. There was a crackling sound on the phone. 'The problem, as I see it . . .' Simen knew it sounded ridiculous.

'Leon is threatening to kill himself.'

Simen waited until he had a clear signal. 'When he gets back to Colomb Bechar,' he said in a voice that could only have been coming from cyberspace. 'He is to be buried beside the old city wall. There's an old white-washed cemetery where they put you into a hole in the wall. He would really have liked a sea view, but instead it will be the desert. The silence,' Simen ventured.

'It sounds terrible. I admit it,' he said to Bird, to whom the conversation was reported two hours later.

Nerida did not reply.

'Leon has been going on about this ever since he converted to Catholicism: "Free at last. At last I shall be free. At last I shall be me." But it's been getting worse.'

At the other end Simen heard Nerida snort. 'A load of crap, if you ask me,' he managed to stammer in English. 'Maudlin. Awful,' he intoned, sounding like a digital signal.

Simen did not try to gloss over it.

'Leon lived out there in the desert for almost three years as a boy. He got beaten up every day by drunken Berbers. There are still some people who think Muslims don't get drunk. Leon got fat, developed an allergy to dates and after his time in Colomb Bechar he never walked a metre too far in the sun. It's silly, it's embarrassing, and so Norwegian. I know. Don't ask me what it all means. I'm only passing on what he said. If you understand what I'm saying then you don't need to speak,' Simen went on when he heard Nerida's nasal English.

'The thing is, you see, that I believe him,' Simen continued. 'I've heard it all a little too often. Leon doesn't talk bullshit. He never has done.' Sofia stood in the centre of Nerida's office, looking somewhat bedraggled; her trousers were ripped and she had lost a shoe, but she was not in too much of a state to whip round and face the lawyer. Deep rumblings emanated from him. He sounded as if he was pumping himself up.

She was never quite sure what actually happened, but she did remember Antonio Nerida's roar of laughter. Over the weeks that followed she would wake up in the middle of the night, and when she got up she went to the kitchen, drank milk and ate biscuits while she tried to forget that roar. 'He laughed in English,' she explained to Bird on the phone six hours later. 'He gave this great guffaw, from the very pit of his stomach; it sounded as if he'd been eating gravel, too much gravel, and was attempting to cough it up along with the truth about Leon, the sensitive pianist. Antonio Nerida roared. He's a crook. I knew it. I can spot a crook a mile off. I could hear it.' Gently, Sofia endeavoured to explain to Bird that Nerida's guffaw might have been amusing had she not been so scared. 'Were you scared?' asked Bird. 'Really scared?' Sofia could tell from Bird's voice that he was having trouble taking this in. Bird sniggered. He was feeling confused. He went on sniggering just a little too long. Because Nerida had explained with some difficulty that Simen was talking to a lawyer in the Basque country. This man was in daily contact not only with the people at police headquarters, but also with the men on the beat. Sometimes he drove in an armoured car. Not just in the towns, but in the villages too. Weapons were used almost every single night. He served a city in a part of Europe which was contemplating collective suicide. With tender, loving care they nursed their age-old European traumas. Consequently, they know everything there is to know about self-torment. 'Do you think I'd let myself be scared by a crook? A dwarf. A genius. What the hell do you think? And he's a pianist to boot.'

Then Antonio Nerida yelled that he wasn't some common country lawyer living up some Norwegian fjord. He didn't go around arresting peaceable fishermen and Norwegian peasants. Two years previously he had gone on one of those fjord cruises, sailing through the idyllic Norwegian scenery; farmers stood as if transfixed in the patchwork fields, the snow lay yellowish-white on the hilltops; that majestic tranquillity, the sunshine, the romance, the mountain heartland and the new wealth – all figured on the price tag of every souvenir. The Japs snapped everything in sight, the Americans were demanding and the female interpreter had lovely long legs. He admitted it. Nerida proceeded to hold forth on the Scandinavian welfare states, on all those male Norwegian shareholders whose women sought relief from them with the men of the South. Sofia did her best not to listen.

'Bird,' she said in a little voice. 'It was embarrassing. Really embarrassing. I mean, I was arrested for belting a Basque waiter with an ash tray. I went to the big oak cabinet, took out the bottle of Sobrano and filled the wineglass without asking permission. He laughed even harder at that. It was kind of creepy. You know what I mean, Bird.' In the warm office Bird's head was spinning. He steadied himself against the wall next to the desk, swore silently, several times, his head spun even more, he bit his lips. 'Bird?' Sofia said. 'Bird. Are you there?' she repeated.

Bird cleared his throat and took a deep breath. 'Why don't you just tell me what happened?'

8

Antonio Nerida, frustrated now after having had to wait for the phone to make a decent connection with another satellite, roared at Simen that this was not how things are done. You do not fax the announcement of your own death to close friends. By the time such electronic mails are sent the person concerned is dead as a doornail with all his creditors as helpless onlookers. Leon's lies are too basic for a veteran lawyer from the Basque country. 'To tell the truth, it's too banal. It happens every day. It's too stupid,' he said, speaking slowly, as if to an overprotected adult. 'Leon is going through a bit of a bad patch. If that. It's just a standard cry for help. A bit of weeping and wailing. A little plea for sympathy from his comrades, from all his friends. This is not about money. Leon is not broke. He does not need a wad of cash. Not right now. And anyway, what he earns is neither here nor there. For some people no amount of money would be enough. Don't you know that?' Nerida glanced at the fan on the ceiling and laughed at Sofia. 'What's going on in that Norwegian sea of oil? What are you all doing up there? Are you lying rotting in your new wealth? Are you sick? You think like stockbrokers. Couldn't you all take a little break, take a moment to think? Have you forgotten how good life can be?' was only some of what Sofia recounted to Bird.

According to Sofia

And Bird, to whom this was related by Sofia later that night: at that particular moment he was at the newsdesk, making filter coffee.

'There's no taste to filter coffee,' he told a young, female reporter who had not yet got over the fact that she was on one of her first night shifts. She wandered around all the computer screens, pretending that the computers were her dear friends.

'Filter coffee is downright bad for sprinters,' he declared. 'Carl Lewis doesn't drink coffee. I'll bet he doesn't.' The reporter was young, attractive and chic in tight jeans and trainers; she told Bird that she had come straight from handball practice and had a problem with a ligament. Bird who had always been against indoor training, perked up. He liked this girl, liked her short, tousled hair-do and was so paternal in his remarks regarding aching ligaments that she put her hand on his arm, inclined her head towards his shoulder and she smelled as if she had just stepped out of the shower, bringing with her a faint whiff of deodorant, pine forests, fir cones and long runs. Bird seized the chance to talk about sprinters. They drank coffee, munched biscuits and chatted about sprinters and doping, she grew animated and spoke of Ben Johnson.

'His skin was like silk. I would have given a month's pay just to run my fingers down his arm.' She put her coffee cup down in front of the screen. 'The thing I remember most is his shoulders. When he left the starting blocks he was inches lower than all the others. He was closer to the ground. It was as if the earth's magnetism was helping him,' she said, with a fond glance at Bird. It was almost uncanny the way he burned up those first twenty metres. A little unreal. It's just too bad they found out he was cheating.'

And it was that word cheating, although he was not sure why, which reminded Bird of Simen back in the office. He had forgotten both Simen and Sofia, not to mention Nerida, while the girl was rambling on about Ben Johnson leaving the starting blocks. It was snowing in earnest now. October snow. The car roofs were white and the snow was drifting around the feet of the lamp posts. Bird shuddered. 'Some other day I must tell you about Carl Lewis's diet. I tried it for a month. It's a sort of protein bomb.'

※

But by the time Bird returned to the office, Simen had gone home. Bird cleared up, removed all traces of the evening's turmoil, looked yet again at the way the snow was drifting around the feet of the lampposts and called for a taxi. When he got home he fell asleep on the sofa. He slept soundly until the phone rang and Sofia lost no time in telling him that she had had dinner with the Neridas, and that Señora Nerida, who had sat on the edge of her chair, was so tense that she stuck her little finger in the ice cream. The waiter in the elegant restaurant, who had heard of the incident the day before with the ash tray, sneaked a peek over his shoulder at Sofia's breasts. Then he shut his eyes and spooned steak and vegetables on to her plate. He acted like a man who had been temporarily blinded, and spoke so softly and solicitously to Señora Nerida that anyone would have thought she was an invalid. He did not say a word to Sofia or Antonio Nerida, but the corners of his mouth twitched every time Sofia laughed. And she laughed because Nerida was playing the part of the omniscient lawyer.

'Anxiety,' he explained. Then he dabbed the corners of his mouth with a blue handkerchief. 'Not terror or dread, but a creeping anxiety,' he went on. 'There lies the reason for the state Leon is in. There alone. He should have brought his hands down on the piano keys and gone for it. It's intuitive. At that moment the brain is in neutral. The guy sat at the piano and analysed it. He was too busy wondering whether it was beautiful. I heard it right away.'

He looked at Sofia. 'What was the name of that bar, wasn't it Mr Duke or Lady Day or something equally original. It was so quiet in the dimly-lit restaurant that I scarcely dared to set my glass down on the bar. The acolytes of jazz in the Basque country sat with their hands wrapped round their beer glasses. They listened. Verily, they listened.' Nerida snickered. 'But on the night when I heard Leon play, everything he did was crap. Rip-offs from every American pianist from Bud Powell onwards. It was a kind of musical hodge-podge. Not even very original. He seemed calm, but was not. On that particular evening most of the material was filched from McCoy Turner, not one note could he call his own. He denied his instincts from the first chord to the last. It was beautiful, grand, intelligent, but hollow. And sitting there hunched over the piano: small, weak, forlorn and tame, he simply confirmed that he could have been great, but that he no longer had the courage for it.'

Antonio Nerida kept his eyes fixed on Sofia as he spoke. 'Poor Leon. It's a shame about him. On his way to Colomb Bechar, protected by good friends who take his foolishness seriously. What is it with you lot? What is the problem? He is under no threat now. None whatsoever. No mad impulses stirring in his brain. He is as normal as any other publican or sinner. He has discovered something sound and solid. For an artist that can be fatal. Disastrous. Worse than political convictions. Worse than believing in Stalin or Pol Pot. He has had his problems. But nothing so bad that he couldn't live with it. Not only that but he has learned to protect himself. He has learned this so well that now no one can get through to him. I mean: get to the heart of him. He has forgotten how that feels. And until he learns to let people in, he will never be as good as he used to be, and so he thinks he is going to die,' Nerida said, and proceeded to stuff steak, broccoli and artichoke into his mouth.

Then he sighed.

'Now he wants to return to the scene of his childhood debacles. Where he will be reminded that he never got things straightened out. Not even at the piano. This is a temporary setback, nothing more. Just at the moment he doesn't think that he can handle it. Eat your steak, Sofia. It's very good. No thank-you,' he said to the waiter. 'We won't have brandy with the coffee. Just coffee. I don't think it would be such a good idea to have anything to drink now,' he remarked to his wife who was discreetly wiping ice-cream off her little finger. Nerida looked at that finger, followed it with his eyes and noticed that she blushed when discreetly wiping away the ice-cream. He had a sudden urge to protect her, to put his arms around her, to pray for her, because he knew that some madman sitting in an hotel room in Madrid could detonate splinter bombs in this restaurant in Vitoria. Sometimes, especially when she was overcome by shyness, Nerida's gorge rose at the thought that he was a lawyer practising in the Basque country. He knew that nationalism is a form of insanity. It could strike anywhere at any time. In their modern guise, today's warriors could sit in front of computers and paralyse the air traffic over Bilbao. 'Everyone knows it. No one talks about it, and meanwhile here I am, sweet-talking a woman from Norway who beat up a waiter. This is too silly for words,' he thought to himself and looked at his wife, who arched her neck and put her fingers to her lips.

'He was nice,' Sofia told Bird on the phone. 'He was nice and very Basque. You have no idea how nice he was. Not to mention discreet. He acted as if nothing had happened. His wife ate pink ice-cream, looked at Antonio, was overcome with shyness, blushed and didn't seem to be quite up to the mark when she licked her little finger.'

Bird sat quite still on the sofa.

He listened to Sofia, gazed at the pictures on the wall: select little pictures, not many, but valuable. He sat silently, hunched over, almost as if he were on the starting line, listening to the torrent of words, finally managed to get a word in edgewise and asked when all this had happened.

'An hour ago,' Sofia said. 'I was given a new room in a different hotel. A fabulous room. A suite. I'm in bed. I'm

According to Sofia

drinking water because I've got the hiccups. I'm looking at the trees outside the window. Antonio fixed it. I would have been lucky to get a room if Nerida hadn't vouched for me.'

She hiccuped again and took a sip from her glass. 'He talked about respect,' she continued. 'About the respect Leon needs to win in order to move on. He is so easily broken,' she said, screwing the top on to her bottle of nail varnish. 'I know you find this tiresome, but Nerida was talking about pianists. When he wasn't eating artichokes, I mean. There's nothing difficult about playing the piano. Sometimes living can be a bit difficult,' she said in that voice which never convinced Bird. But she succeeded in convincing him that Antonio Nerida had done his best to impress his wife. 'Bloody difficult, sometimes,' he remarked. 'Sorry,' he said in response to Pilar Nerida's look, 'but I could tell from his touch that Leon could have been one of the greats. Do you know what I mean? Anyway, I've had enough,' he added.

There was silence on the phone.

'Was that all?' Bird asked.

'Just about,' said Sofia.

Bird considered a print of Monet's garden. He had four pictures of Monet's garden and sometimes he found himself wondering what sort of effect it had on him to look upon Monet's garden each and every day.

'Okay,' he said. 'Let me have the rest. I take it that what you have told me was really only the beginning.'

Sofia's breathing reached his ears from the man-made star up there in the chronic darkness.

'What does that mean?' she asked.

'Come on, out with it.'

'Do I have to?' Sofia asked.

'No,' said Bird.

'Do I have to tell you today?'

'No,' said Bird.

'To be honest I'm happiest not having to say anything at all. Or have I told you that before?'

Bird did not reply.

'But you know I will come out with it at some point. I always tell you what really happened, you know I do.'

He heard her put down her glass.

'That's true,' Bird said at length.

'Antonio Nerida had not forgotten me.'

'I guessed as much,' Bird said.

'He knows where I live. Who I'm married to, and that I'm no longer practising as a surgeon.'

'Did he tell you that?' Bird asked.

He had sat down at the desk.

'What does he want with me?' said Sofia.

'What do you think?'

'What am I going to do?'

'Come home,' Bird said. 'Right away. Today. You can get a plane from Bilbao to London. There are at least ten flights a day from Stansted to Oslo Airport. You ought to be on one of them.'

'I have the urge to be here in the autumn,' Sofia said.

'I guessed as much,' Bird said.

'Suddenly I feel so calm.'

Bird looked at Monet's garden again. He regarded the flowers, the grass, the pale-green slope running down to the water's edge, and the way the reflections sparkled among the trees. He observed Monet's style. He had spent a lifetime mastering it and suddenly Bird found himself gasping for breath, like a sprinter on the starting line.

'Come home Sofia. Please. Otherwise I'm going to have to come and get you. Simen has already asked me to.'

Sofia did not answer.

'Are you going jogging?' she said.

'Yes,' said Bird. 'First thing tomorrow.'

9

According to Sofia: when she no longer had the strength to lift the scalpel, and when her arms withered, her suffering became chronic. She dropped the coffee cup, the bread and the jam dish. All of a sudden there were no well people. Living became an ordeal, a healthy mind in a healthy body seemed a Utopian ideal, tests carried out in laboratories would one day reveal certain genetic dispositions. Suddenly, for Sofia Linde it became a matter of getting to grips with future illnesses. Life became an illness. It made her ill. She could live for a long time, but she would feel ill. And she did not mean to do anything about it.

'It's embarrassing,' Bird muttered to himself the next morning as he was putting on his running shoes.

The snow had melted when the rain started.

He had lain awake, listening to the rain pouring down, but when he got up the autumn air was cool and clear.

The thermometer outside the kitchen window read five degrees Celsius, and he ate two biscuits and drank rose-hip tea while getting his track suit and leg warmers from the drying-rack.

The leg warmers smelled of sweat, even though they were newly washed. He tightened the drawstrings and got ready. As a sprinter, his calves were his weak point, but ever since a ballet dancer had taught him to wear leg warmers, he had had no problem.

He rubbed Oriental oils into his calves and every creak from his ankles was carefully noted. Before leaving the flat he placed two bananas on the kitchen worktop, spooned protein powder into water and stirred it round, and placed it on the top shelf of the fridge, closest to the ice-cube compartment. He rummaged through his drawers, looking for his hat, the grey woollen hat that Sofia had knitted, but could not find it. It was the first time that autumn that it had occurred to him to wear a hat, but it was cold outside, he could tell, it would be windy up around the lake and he did not like the thought of the headwind on his forehead when he picked up speed.

He felt a bit off-colour.

Behind his left temple, close to his ear, he could hear sounds; his neck was stiff, he felt a twinge in his left lung when he breathed, but his shoulders were loose and on the way down in the lift he was filled with the urge to run. He did not know why he ran, or why he had always done so. He was, however, sure that it was just about the only harmless thing he did.

He went for a run three mornings each week, never more; never for more than two hours and only a hundred metres at top speed. Five years earlier, the first time he had sensed that he was not as young as he used to be, he had strained a ligament, and he did moderate weight training to build this up.

He really loved to run.

When he ran, he did not think. Occasionally he would go so far as to admit that those seconds at top speed were tantamount to sheer joy, and he had mentioned this to the other joggers. He was happy to know that his reflexes were almost as good as they had been twenty years earlier. Every autumn, in the middle of September, he did three timed trial runs on the track and it surprised him to find that he was only two seconds slower than when he had been at his peak. He took the first five hundred metres at a stroll, did not run, felt joints and calves loosening up,

According to Sofia

he never pushed it, but waited until his reflexes were as they should be. After that first stage he raised the tempo on the uphill stretch. He liked the uphill stretch. He had been using it as a warm-up for years. The hill, known as the 'Little Killer', was a gradual, gravel-covered slope on which his rubber studs could get a firm grip, but it was three hundred metres in length and steepest towards the top. He jogged to the top, strolled two hundred metres, covered the next three hundred metres at a steady trot, jogged for two hundred then slowed to a walk for at least five minutes. Everything was functioning.

This was one of the three high points of his week.

He always smiled with satisfaction when he felt his shoulders loosening up. And by the time he reached the tarn he was ready for the first test of the day. He walked for fifty metres on his toes with his arms dangling by his sides. A waiter at The Stables had told him that he always walked home from work on his toes, that it was the best remedy for varicose veins.

He readied himself. His calves made no protest. His knees were fine, as always. He was warm now, but breathing easily, nice and steady, and Bird was pleased. He jogged contentedly along the bank of the tarn, the water was black in the shadow of the mountain beyond the benches, beyond the big rock where the swans sought shelter in stormy weather and again he was conscious that his calves were supple, his knees strong and his heart beating steadily, rhythmically. A thin film of ice spread around the water lilies along the water's edge; the water was clear, almost transparent and he could see right down to the sandy bottom at the spot where he normally waded in when he swam here in the summer. In the lee of the gully there was hardly a breath of wind, it was early in the morning, quiet, no joggers other than him had been along the gravel path. He stood quite still for half a minute. Then he attacked the steps, running the whole way up the 'Big Killer', the flight of steps built into the gully out of huge slabs of rock and natural steps in the cliff face. He had never counted how many there were, but he guessed it had to be a couple of hundred steps to the top, and he ran smoothly up them, keeping his shoulders loose, letting his thighs and his feet do the work. He ran fast, a bit too fast he found when he reached the top. He realised that his heart was pounding, pounding way too hard; he stopped, his breath whistled in his lungs, but only for a moment: after half a minute he felt his pulse subsiding and his heart pumping as it always did.

The tough uphill stretch was not his favourite part of the run, but he had to do it in order to check whether he was still in condition. Sprinter that he was, he ought not to do it, it was too punishing, or certainly would have been had he done it too often, but he was getting older, he was not as limber as he had been, not as supple, and his calves still needed massaging, so he felt it was necessary. Sometimes he managed to convince himself that it was, in fact, vital, even when he had to prop himself up against a fir tree until the grip on his lungs gradually slackened.

Afterwards he walked down the hill.

He jog-trotted along the path skirting the mountain, past the signs for the ski trails running through the forest to the marshes, past the clubhouse, past the pond, he could feel his thighs quivering, exactly as he had hoped they would: pushed to their limit, but not beyond.

He ambled slowly along the path under the oak trees for some minutes, waiting until he was totally composed. On the other side of the pond lay the gravel track, almost two hundred metres long, and he gathered himself, started off nice and easy, gradually accelerating, then accelerated a little more, still taking it nice and easy, and he gave the ghost of a smile as he noted that his hips were at the right angle and that his arms, thighs and calves were doing their work. It had taken him time to learn all this. He was not, in fact, a born sprinter, but he had learned, through perseverance he had learned, through perseverance he had discovered how the brain and the body reacted, how he had to remember to lower his shoulders until he found his balance, and how he had to wait until the cooperation between his brain and his feet had become second

According to Sofia

nature. So he was happy when it worked, and he savoured the feel of the wind on his brow and his chest, running at top speed now, not for long, no more than eight seconds, then he slackened his pace, gradually, with the wind and his blood rushing in his ears.

He looked at his stop watch: a little slower than expected, but not bad, he thought, considering that he had been feeling a bit off-colour when he left the flat.

The last hour of the training session was given to warming down.

He let his arms hang loose as he ambled, jogged and trotted down the paths through the grove of trees, cutting off the main trails on to the smaller tracks leading down to the old ski-jump hill, still with traces of the night's snow lying around the tower at its top.

As a boy he had jumped almost thirty metres on that hill. He had hurt himself when he landed, broken his ankle, he had given up ski jumping after that. He ran up to the old castle where he had played as a boy. He remembered the way they used to yell as they charged down the slope brandishing wooden swords and shields. He saw the sunlight flickering between the fir trees, felt hardly any warmth from it when he stood still. His heart was beating steadily, his breathing was regular, his calves as supple as they ought to be, and he loped down to the hill overlooking the beach. He ran past the red bothy with the last water-temperature reading written up on the board, and he was feeling a little off-colour, no doubt about it.

On the other path, five metres below him, where there was always a trickle of water from the tarn running out of the wall, he saw the leader, a young woman in a snow suit, walking at the head of a bunch of kids waving woolly hats and buckets. Bird smiled when he heard their cries, placed his hands in the small of his back, kneaded gently, starting at the base of his spine and working upwards, and suddenly he realised he was on his knees, bent double, and as he was wondering why he was doing this, he passed out.

Bird was woken by a small boy pouring blackcurrant squash over his face, and he did not understand why, but the boy asked whether he was sleepy. He then called out to the young woman, who dragged Bird on to the path, some metres away from the water's edge. She worked swiftly and silently and knew what she was doing when she turned him on to a stable side position, pulled off her snow suit, slid it underneath him, stroked his face, laid Bird's head in her lap, pulled her mobile from her bag and spoke into it quickly, but softly, and Bird passed out again, possibly from fright, he tried to explain the following day, because his heart had suddenly changed pace and he could hear the sound of galloping horses approaching the finishing line.

'It was horrible. I wonder whether maybe I preferred to pass out just to get away?' he told Dr Vige, who brushed his hair back from his forehead, nudged his spectacles further up his nose and read the case notes while smiling at Bird.

'You're an old warrior,' came as a completely abortive attempt from the doctor. He had steady hands, cleared his throat again and again and said: 'You were lucky.' Dr Vige had been Bird's bridge partner for years and he told him again that he had been lucky. Because the young woman had had a mobile phone they had been able to get to him only ten minutes after he had fainted. 'Otherwise you're in great shape. I envy you,' he said, pursing his thin lips. 'Sometimes the heart gives a double beat. It's nothing to worry about. I don't think you're suffering from arrhythmia. But if you are, then you're going to have to take it seriously,' was his first pronouncement. Bird lay in bed in the hospital, feeling rather done in, but mostly confused, and he inhaled the sterile odours of ether and floor wax. He knew he was going to be told to take things easy and he did not ask for how long.

'Do you want to go for a run?' Dr Vige asked. 'Now?' he added, smiling. 'Couldn't you wait a while? Couldn't you lie quietly in bed? At least until tomorrow. You're in excellent shape.

According to Sofia

I'm impressed. That will stand you in good stead in the weeks to come.'

Bird knew they would have him sedated to the eyeballs and he asked if he might not manage without that, in fact he insisted upon it, but Dr Vige prepared the syringe, explained to him that this was something to calm him down, to take the edge off, it was quite safe, the most popular drug within this branch of medicine. 'Why are you so sceptical?' He simply wanted to know whether the double beats would stop. Whether the symptoms would disappear?

'I think it's all just symptomatic.'

Fifteen minutes later Bird was feeling absolutely fine. 'I don't feel dizzy any more,' he announced. 'I've been having dizzy spells for weeks,' he said. 'For months,' he added, and he had been feeling strangely spent. He was drained. About as drained as when he had propped himself up against that fir tree at the top of the 'Big Killer'.

'It's rather like having a chronic dose of the 'flu,' he endeavoured to explain to Dr Vige, who nodded, made notes, checked his pulse, waited while Bird admitted that he had been feeling awful for the past six months. But he was always at his best in the winter, in those ice-cold, clear, white winters of long ski treks across the high moors. 'Are you writing this down?' he asked Dr Vige. 'The winters have been the best.' The doctor listened again to Bird's heart and declared that after fifteen minutes the heart was pumping normally, that the symptoms of influenza appeared to have disappeared, that he did not feel dizzy.

'Is that correct?'

Bird eventually owned that it was. He had not felt this good in a long time. 'I can see more clearly,' he announced in amazement and the doctor nodded discreetly and said that he would be on hand for the rest of the day. 'I can see you quite clearly,' he said. 'It's a long time since I saw anyone so clearly.'

As far as Bird was concerned it really did not matter one way or the other. He noticed that he had two cuts on his right hand, and while he was trying to figure out why, he fell asleep.

That first afternoon, Bird dreamt of lions, of prides of lions, and that he had lost a finger. He had lost the ring finger on his right hand and when he was talking to the lions, and to one sedate lioness in particular, he spoke of this loss. The lions were lying motionless on a yellow knoll and he hunkered down and regarded the finger which was no longer there. He squinted at the lion, which blinked lazily at him, rolled in the stiff, tinder-dry grass, growled, a long-drawn-out growl, slid her claws out of her paws. Then she stretched her back, lifted her tail over the yellow, sun-scorched grass, rolled over on to her back and went to sleep beside him under the tree.

He slept for a long time.

Now and again he tweaked the lion's ears, and when he heard the deep thrum in her throat he snuggled up against her back. He had dreamt of a girl in a green coat whom he had never had the nerve to speak to. The green coat had hung on its hook outside the classroom and now and again he had run a hand over it, although he actually denied doing so. It was embarrassing. Until he was twenty, just about everything had been embarrassing. Now he was lying in a hospital bed, he was rested, a little woozy, a little far away due to the sedative, and he tried to forget that he could not remember the girl's name. Instead he thought of Sofia down in the Basque country, of the heavy rain, the televisions in the stone houses, the echo on the streets, the smell of olive oil, of Therese Somoza who was a famous pianist and had written a dissertation on McCoy Tyner, one which had won respect from the acolytes of jazz and could be accessed at any time on the Internet. Bird read it often. He was proud of her. Although he did not really know why. He did not know her, or at least only slightly. Then he dozed off yet again, went back to the lions whom he trusted. His right hand was not as it should be and this troubled him. 'I don't like this,' he told an older woman who was washing the floor under his bed with a mop. 'I don't understand this thing with the lions. I've often thought about lions, it's true. They're beautiful and I know them.'

She finished washing the floor, leaned against the bed, smiled at him and said that it was probably best to leave the lions in peace.

10

I'll have to make do with this old banger to start with, Leon thought when he bought the Toyota for two hundred dollars. 'You don't know a thing about modern finance,' he said in Norwegian and smiled at the brilliantined owner in Beni-Saf, who believed he had done a good deal with a guy who looked like a dwarf. Leon was only a head shorter than him, but he had an impressive roll of dollar bills in his pocket. He cradled the roll in the palm of his hand, looked at the owner, twanged the rubber band round the dollar bills and generally acted as if he had just won every war going.

This made no lasting impression on the owner of the garage.

Leon consoled himself with the thought that no one knew he had also worked as a motor mechanic.

While studying at the Conservatory, whenever he was strapped for cash he had done evening shifts at Olsen's Autos. He rented a bedsit on the floor above the workshop; at night he lay in bed and listened to the sounds of two stolen cars being welded together to make a new one; he heard the drone of deep, metallic voices in the workshop and the slap of bankrolls changing hands. When the boss bawled up the stairs to him he climbed into the green boiler-suit with 'Olsen's Autos' on the back, and when

According to Sofia

Olsen was down in Jutland, rounding up cars, Mrs Linda Olsen would come for Leon.

She dished up more than just beer and warm smørbrød.

She was fifteen years older than Leon, maternal, kindly and she laughed with surprise when she had an orgasm. When he entered the bedroom she never switched off the light, but she did shut the window. She swept the flecks of tobacco off Olsen's snow-white pillow, chattering away to herself, rolled over on to her back and breathed through her nose. He recalled the smell of a perfume with accents of sage and sweet deodorant, and suddenly she lay perfectly still and he crawled over to her, felt his way, and was not upset when she laughed at him.

Before marrying Olsen and Olsen's Autos there had been times when, so she told Leon, she had had to earn her living on her back. Leon, who did not find it odd that he was her favourite, was astonished to hear her giggle when she taught him a new move and sometimes she became so flustered and so flabbergasted that he would ask her to go to the kitchen and have something to eat.

Linda Olsen was the only person whom Leon thought of every day.

He had not forgotten how to change a brake band, and the sand-yellow Toyota was only going to be driven 125 miles and none of those miles through the desert. He placed the money on the desk among battered ring-binders and oil-spattered papers and said yes, please to the tea which the owner poured from a tin pot. Leon noticed how the stream grew thinner when he announced that he was going to drive across the desert to Colomb Bechar. 'Not in that wreck,' Leon said, and shook his head when the owner offered him a cigar that reeked of hemp. 'I'm going to drive it along tarmacked roads to the nearest Toyota garage where I'll sell it for four hundred dollars. It is one of the great mysteries of North Africa that you can get twice as much for a clapped-out jalopy if you pass yourself off as an American, wear a tie and have a roll of dollar bills in your pocket.' He saw the owner of the garage look up. He scented a friend who understood that money is a handy means of postponing the inevitable. 'The catch being that you buy a more expensive car from a dealership. You know that. Have you never given it a go?' Leon asked and tasted the tea, which smelled of dates and mint. He tried to conceal the shudder that went through him, but the owner was on the alert; he picked up the tea glass, poured the tea down the sink and asked Leon if he would like whisky or brandy. 'I wouldn't mind a cola if you have one?' Leon asked. He waited placidly for the next question, drinking cola and eating wafer-thin ginger biscuits. 'Which garages did you have in mind?' the owner asked. They shook hands, and he confided his family name, pronouncing it with so many proud vowels that Leon smiled. 'Well,' he said. 'There are lots of such places in the backstreets of Algiers. If you know what I mean?' he said, happily helping himself to another biscuit. 'You can drive out of a garage with a full tank of petrol,' the owner said. 'I'd be interested to know which garage you foreigners use. Can't you see that?' Leon mentioned the four names of as many garages and while the owner nodded and scribbled down incomprehensible symbols, Leon tucked the roll of dollar bills into the one pocket which no pickpocket would ever consider going for.

Afterwards, Leon was tempted with the offer of a visit to the man's cousin's restaurant, for genuine Berber cooking and porno films in the back room, but he politely declined, saying that he had to get going. There was something about the garage owner that he recognised and liked and he felt sure that a prolonged stay in Beni-Saf was a possibility. And besides, he liked the clatter of tools on the cement floor in the workshop, the smell of oil, rust, common swindling and blowtorches, and the owner observed this, spread a newspaper over one of the chairs, pointed, and they talked about Ford Mustangs. 'It has to be a red Ford Mustang,' he said. 'That goes without saying. If we're talking veteran cars, then we're talking Mustangs.' This particular car, the growl of the

According to Sofia

engine, phlegmatic pistons slumberously ticking over, was, for both men, the stuff of boyhood dreams.

They sat for some time at the green plastic table, amiably discussing the smooth glide of the Mustang gear stick under the hand. Afterwards, they sauntered out into the shimmering heat of the car lot, and the owner grumbled about the heatwave which knew no end. 'It's worse today than it was in the middle of August,' he said. 'I hate this heat.' It was so hot that Leon shut his eyes, but the petrol tank was filled to the brim and while the salesman changed the oil and the filter, Leon was given promises of undying friendship and fidelity, and prayers for Allah to be with him. 'I might well need that last one,' Leon hissed as he heaved on the gear stick, which reluctantly allowed itself to be coaxed out of reverse. He drove off with the windows open, the cushion under his backside making him feel like a fool. He was so short that he had to crane his neck to see, and as he gazed at the sea of sand and the date palms outside of the town he rattled off his thoughts on North Africa, French colonies, lazy louts, Berbers and the heavy stench of corruption, spices and decay. He was alone. Totally alone with the sun and the sand. Alone in a car with a view from the hills of both the sea and the desert. That, in itself, made him feel more cheerful, in the face of the warm wind wafting from the interior. 'Nobody can get the better of me here,' he said to himself and started to worry. 'Nobody. Just let them try.' He was sure it was not healthy to talk to yourself. Certainly not when driving a clapped-out Toyota on African roads. He decided to exchange it for a car with four-wheel drive, a cool interior, capacious petrol tank and plenty of spare parts. It helped a little: the thought of a Japanese take on a British jeep was a happy inspiration. Suddenly he found himself humming a few bars from 'Alice in Wonderland', and just as suddenly he found he understood the labyrinthine passages behind LaFaro's bass when Bill Evans played that particular chord, and he felt confused, anxious almost, and yet pleased, no happy, he thought as he listened to the great LaFaro, and he had the urge to play, preferably in a dimly-lit restaurant, and he caught a whiff of cigarettes and cheap whisky, beer and vodka. For his own part he would, as always, be sober when he ran his fingers over the keys. 'You're done with that,' he told himself. 'You're completely done with that. You have redeemed yourself,' he said, with so little conviction that he surprised himself.

And against his will he noticed the soft, cool shadows thrown by the sand dunes, the vibrant light, the heat haze hanging over the dark-grey tarmac, and at one of the water holes he saw two camels striding majestically out into the murderous desert. They marched unconcernedly across the hot plain, scarcely bothering to raise their heads when he tooted his horn. Leon thought of an ocean with waves of sand and he pursed his lips, but managed to persuade himself that he had not felt this good in years. He smiled at the yellow light outside, at the date palms, at the camels, at the Berbers, at North Africa and thought to himself that he ought to be howling. 'Onward to the bloody oases,' he said out loud. Onward to all my enemies in Colomb Bechar. I'm back. I'm looking forward to seeing them, he thought. But he was not sure who he was talking about. He had no idea where they were, or whether they were alive. It was complicated, but funny, when he thought of LaFaro and Bill Evans, and he hummed and improvised in the yellow light. He went on like this for some time, close on half an hour, and he thought: this is me. Or a little piece of me at any rate. I can't believe it. At long last. Here in the desert. And because it struck him so suddenly he stretched his back, forgot about the cushion under his backside; the thought of Sofia crossed his mind and he hummed because everything fitted. Once he started to play like shit he made money. Lots of money, everybody wanted to hear him, because he played like shit. 'They adore that crap,' Sofia said. 'They buy it. It can never be bad enough. If you want to get rich you mustn't give them anything new. Don't you see that?' Sofia kept me at a distance, at a safe distance, even when she was sitting up in bed, naked and eating a cheese and ham sandwich, he thought. Leon felt how the grip on his stomach

According to Sofia

loosened when he thought of Sofia. She has her own moral code to contend with. It's tough on her at times. Simen knows that, he accepts it, lives with it, and at this very moment, as the position of the sun over the sand dunes attested, he is sitting at the computer, writing the leader which the apparatchiks will read tomorrow morning. Leon kept his eyes on the camels for a long time. He pulled into a bus lay-by, rested his head on the wheel and watched the camels striding off into the dun-coloured desert, and the driver riding easily in the brown saddle, letting himself be jounced along.

11

Bird had had enough of the lions. He refused to be treated with injections and tranquillisers, and with his heart pounding in his chest he turned on to his right side and heard the blood rushing in his left ear. He tried to apply what he had learned of breathing techniques, only to find that his sports training was of little use here.

His heart was beating at a pace all its own, according to new rules.

He clung to the bed, grunted and saw the wall in front of him turn inside out, and he started screaming, not because he was afraid, but because it was so unpleasant that he had to put his hands over his eyes. Just at that moment he had no idea what he was defending himself against, or for how long, but it was on the point of becoming interesting, he told Simen two days later.

When the nurse went ahead and stuck another needle into his backside anyway, he spread his fingers as conscientiously as any pianist and tried not to think about the lions.

Simen stood beside the bed clutching flowers and chocolates. He started looking at the clock as soon as he entered the room, and he grinned at Bird, who was feeling fine now. He was so doped up that he was not sure whether he could be bothered to open his eyes when he blinked. 'What happened when you were sprawled there on the ground?'

'Dr Vige was there,' Bird said.

'What did he say?' asked Simen.

*

'You might as well resign yourself to it,' said Dr Vige. He flicked the syringe with his index finger and lifted it up to the light. 'This is quite safe. I'm going to have to give you more than I'd like, it's true, but it's quite safe. Over the next three days you will be given substantial doses of sedatives. I think your running shoes will have to stay at the back of the cupboard for a while. Don't ask me how long. But it will be longer than you'd like.'

'What did you say?' Simen asked.

'Did I say something?' said Bird.

'Yes,' said Simen.

'When did I say something?'

'You lifted an imaginary syringe and said that this was quite safe, even in large doses. You were speaking like Dr Vige, about running shoes lying at the back of the cupboard.'

'Really?' said Bird.

Simen did not answer.

'Did I say that?'

'Yes,' said Simen.

'Know what?' said Bird. 'This morning. No, yesterday, I think, I was talking to the cleaner about lions.'

'That must have been nice.'

'It was nice,' said Bird.

'Was she good-looking? Was she really? Did you follow her with your eyes when she was here in your room?'

'Who?'

'The woman who was washing the floor?'

'I can't remember,' said Bird. 'She wiped under the bed with a mop. But the lions were beautiful. We were lying on a knoll. A yellow knoll covered in tall, yellow grass and there was a smell of dung.'

'I think you should come off the drugs,' Simen said. 'It can't be right. You can't handle it. You can hardly handle taking an ordinary aspirin. You run it off. Or you used to. Always,' he added. 'You're going to have to stop all that. Running isn't good for you. Not at your age anyway.'

'Is there anything else I shouldn't do?'

Simen smiled at Bird lying there in the bed. There was not a pick on him, his face was white as a sheet, and he looked as though he had not run so much as twenty metres in the last ten years. 'Is there anything I can do, Bird?'

'If you can think of anything that would be great,' said Bird.

'The problem is . . .'

He had turned to face the window.

'The problem is . . .'

Simen saw that Bird was almost asleep. 'The problem has always been that you never do anything wrong. You're perfect. And that can be disastrous.' Simen crossed, as always, to the window, gazed out at the trees in the park, at the leaves which were still clinging to the trees, and the sun which was only just managing to make the grass steam.

'It's frosty,' he said. 'In October. It's not to be borne, but it's frosty.'

'Are you feeling the cold?' Bird said.

Bird shut his eyes before Simen could give him the chocolates. He turned over on to his side and returned to the lions. The big lioness gave a little growl, but Bird, who was feeling dizzy, hunkered down on the top of the knoll, scratched the lion behind the ear, murmured soothingly to it and said that there was a smell of dung and drugs.

'What did you say?' said Simen.

He dragged himself away from the window.

'Nothing,' said Bird.

According to Sofia

'You said something.'
Bird made no reply.
'Should I go?' Simen asked.
'Yes, maybe.'
'Shall I come back tomorrow?'
'That would be good,' said Bird.

He liked the sounds the lions made when they ate. He liked the rough crunch of jaws on meat, and he liked the flies around the lioness's nose, the ants swarming about in the grass and the way slanting bars of sunlight fell through the leaves.

He was not hungry, but he was a little sleepy, and when he opened his eyes the wall in front of him turned inside out, and he lay still, waited, shook his arms, dropped his shoulders, slowly crouched down, placing his feet in the starting blocks and both hands on the right side of the chalked line, and when he heard the pistol shot in the distance he ran for the finishing line.

12

Bank manager Ted Fichter, one of Linda Olsen's loyal clients, called while she was standing barefoot in the kitchen, frying bacon. She moved the new Teflon pan over on to the zinc worktop, picked up the mobile phone and padded across to the chair by the window and the morning sun. 'Good morning, Ted,' she said when she saw the number on the display panel. 'Are you sick, or does the little woman want you home early today? It's Tuesday and I've got the night off.' Ted Fichter, lean, wealthy and freshly showered, with light brown skin which smelled of malt, had, in his youth, had two shameful fantasies which he acted out in Linda Olsen's arms.

'There's no need to take on so,' she comforted him, when he had grown too old for a certain bizarre practice. 'It's not you that's the problem, the fact that you can't manage it, it's me that's got too fat for the old routine. It takes it out of you, you know,' she said. 'I eat too much,' she consoled.

Ted had reconciled himself to this, but he went on coming to see Linda. They often ate catfish dipped in Bacardi and always crème caramel. Afterwards they took a taxi to see the horses at the trotting track. They owned two horses, Alexis and Dinn, both mares, which had been showing a decent profit over the past two years.

According to Sofia

But on that particular day, after the board meeting in the nut-brown office which smelled of stencils and old oak, chills had begun to run up Ted's spine and all he wanted was to go home to his wife and a warm fire. It had been an unpleasant morning, with his subtle chairmanship skills being thwarted by junior members of staff with contacts on the stock exchange. They apologised, repaired to the back room with their mobiles and made money. Which was exactly what he was trying to do at the office, but things were not moving fast enough for the errand boys in Armani suits. He found the beeping of their pagers bothersome, too, and when they left the room, all deference and boyish smiles, he forgot what he had actually said and was thrown into confusion. 'As you know, I'm a coward and I pee my pants when I'm stressed,' he complained to Linda, who was studiously frying bacon in the Teflon pan.

Before he could drive home to his wife, rose-hip tea and a warm fire he had to advise her that Leon had sent her a check from Africa for ten thousand dollars. Ted Fichter yawned. 'I think he sent it from Beni-Saf in Africa.' Normally, Leon sent two hundred dollars on the first Monday of every month, but the sum had suddenly risen to ten thousand. 'He must be off his head. What am I supposed to do with ten thousand dollars?' said Linda Olsen as she drank filter coffee. She had known Leon for seventeen years, ever since Olsen the used-car dealer was carted off to jail, was gone for three years, showed up again, then went away for good. 'I hope you'll come,' she said. Ted cleared his throat, felt suddenly pleased with himself, his voice steadied as he listened to the sounds of Linda in the little kitchen, and the thought of bacon made him forget the junior members of staff. Linda grew mellow when she thought of Ted's thin moustache, trimmed, tended, his beautiful hands, his smile and the smell of malt. 'Who would ever have thought I would have done so well for myself?' she was wont to confess to the butcher when buying bacon and sausages. She thought of Leon. Of his shoulders and the back of his neck. When he hobbled into cafés it did not surprise her that the voices around the bar fell silent. Linda knew it would never do to allude to the fact that he only came up to her breasts.

'Beer and Polish vodka,' Leon breathed to the waiter. He drank a half-litre of beer and a glass of vodka every day. Never more. 'It's the closest I get,' he said to Linda, who was not sure what he meant.' 'I never drink more.' Linda was genuinely fond of him. 'He's a genius,' she whispered confidentially to Ted, who had lost faith in geniuses when his sexual fantasies turned to dust. 'What's happened to my bloodstream? It used to run to my groin. Now it's gone all to hell.' The thought of Linda Olsen did not arouse him as much as it once had. Ted's life had been reduced to figures, nothing but figures. 'I can't even remember how it felt,' he complained when they were sitting at the table with the crème caramel in front of them. By this time they had polished off two bottles of French wine, which Ted neatly chalked up to the bank's expense account. 'I can still get what you might call aroused when Alexis or Dinn trots past the grandstand. I'm sorry, I'm harping on. There's nothing left, you see. I'm good with figures. Nothing else. I'm a multi-millionaire. I have everything. A boring job, a villa, a Mercedes, a dodgy prostate and a wife who plays bridge with other millionairesses. Between rubbers they swap stories of intimate ailments and otherwise confide only in chiropractors, primal therapists, colonic irrigators, masseurs, acupuncturists and other such con-artists. They are like me, the only difference being that I can turn ten kroner into twenty by dint of a couple of quick deals on the stock market.

'Am I boring you? I'm a boring person. I suffer my boredom in silence. In emptiness. What good to me is a world in which I have everything at a safe distance? What good to me is refined silence? I'm not going to starve to death, I'll be bored to death. Actually, it's an art, you know. I like being bored. I'm never happier than when I'm sitting in a leather chair by the fire. Is there anything more tiresome than a warm fire? Is there anything more ridiculous? It reeks of the past, of fear, forefathers and Neanderthals. If I sit by the fire for an hour I burn fifteen

According to Sofia

kroners' worth of birch logs. I drink Irish whisky that costs forty kroner a glass. I eat only foods which cause heart attacks. I am rich, difficult and notorious among those who know me well enough: the very people whom I find the most boring. I'm not interested in talent, art, science, economics, politics, astronomy or biographies. In the circles I move in, all the losers love biographies. They read about Freud, Bismarck, Bohr and Nansen. About all the winners who really took risks. They, on the other hand, went to the right universities and have never taken risks. They have led their sheltered lives and become experts on wine and food, entrenched inside villas with beautiful women, dogs and gardeners. They have never done anything really dangerous. Made a choice that could have ruined everything. They have never fallen flat on their faces. Exactly like me. If only, just once in my life, I had done something really dangerous. Something disastrous. It wouldn't have mattered what I believed in, as long as I knew that I believed in it. A little bit, at least. For a few months. A year. I could think back on it as I sit by the fire, drinking Irish whisky. I like Leon, for sending you money every month. Why does he do it? Does he have fantasies too?'

'McCoy Tyner,' Linda Olsen replied. She gazed glumly at the bottles which they had finished. But Ted was adamant. One good bottle of red wine each. Never more.

'He's Leon's fantasy,' she said.

'Who?'

'McCoy Tyner.'

'Who's McCoy Tyner?' said Ted.

'I don't know,' said Linda Olsen, picturing Leon in Algiers. 'He's fine,' she said out of the blue. 'He's never been better. I bet you anything.'

And Linda Olsen thought of Leon hobbling across the little square with the fountain in the middle. She heard the tinkle of the tortured jet of water. She had two pictures from Algiers in the drawer and she knew where he was staying. 'The little midge,' she said out loud to Ted. 'He has everything that you don't,' she said and was aware that she was growing anxious. Now and then she simply had to call him. He didn't like it, but she did it anyway. She had heard Leon hiss with rage and had never forgotten it. At this very moment, she knew, he was massaging his fingers and getting ready for the evening's gig. 'What's he doing in Algiers?' asked Ted, who did not open his eyes. 'Playing the piano,' Linda said. 'Why?' said Ted. 'Give me one good reason. All I want to do is sleep. I want to eat and sleep and work just hard enough to become a millionaire. It's not particularly difficult when you've had a wealthy father.'

Linda Olsen smiled at Ted. 'McCoy Tyner,' she said.

'Right. I'll try to remember that. It's an odd name, but I'll do my best, I really will.'

He opened his eyes.

'I'm dying,' he said and looked at his hands, which were trembling. 'I'm all frosted up inside,' he explained.

Linda pulled the travelling rug from under the sofa.

'Of course you are,' she replied. 'You've got into the habit of dying every Thursday. You've been doing it every Thursday for seventeen years. To be honest, I think I quite like it. It's not a bad thing for a bank manager. I'm fond of you. It has taken time, ingenuity and patience. I love your hands. Right now they're trembling. It's hardly surprising. You've led a sheltered life, barricaded behind figures, books and laws. You're a coward and you lambaste everybody who has taken risks. You are my best friend. You had a domineering father who filled your mind with his growling neuroses. It's so banal that it's actually quite reassuring. You have been protected by the humdrum round of university and the bank. You took over a small family estate with cows and geese. You could run crying to the doctor every time you had a bit of a sniffle. I like you because you act like a child, but always have things under control. You have never teetered on the brink of the precipice, lost a good night's sleep, clung to someone, been beaten up, shaken in your shoes at the thought of all the things you knew you were capable of. Be glad of that. Dear Ted, be glad

According to Sofia

of that. Because it's not easy, I'm telling you. But your hands are trembling. That's not good. You've led such a sheltered life that your hands are trembling. I have to see Leon. I miss the orgasms. I just do. I have to breathe. I have to breathe on the back of his neck when he's asleep. Do you understand? Will you pay for the plane ticket? I'll have to stop off in Bilbao. I can't be bothered explaining, but they'll be expecting me.'

Ted did not ask who would be expecting her.

'I'll spend two nights at the Hotel Conde Duque. No special offers for me. You know that. They have the most fabulous jacuzzis in the bathrooms. I'd like to stay in room number five. The one we stayed in last year. I want a room that costs a hundred euros a night. It's expensive. Are you awake?'

Ted looked at her. 'Linda,' he said, and pulled the travelling rug up to his chin. He did not open his eyes.

'Is that okay?'

'Of course,' he said.

13

'Bird. Do you hear me? We almost lost you,' said Dr Vige. 'Now you're going to do as I say and take your pills.'

Bird nodded. The ceiling panels in the ward were a pale grey and the room was filled with the sweet smell of the biscuits and flowers on the bedside table.

'What happened,' Bird asked. 'At the finishing tape? I don't know what happened. But I saw the timekeepers.'

'I can well imagine,' said Dr Vige.

Bird heard the drip-drip of water from the tap into the sink and he turned over in the bed, glowered at the drips, smiled at Dr Vige, then at a young woman doctor with bronzed skin. He felt unwell and rolled slowly on to his right side, gingerly, tentatively. The woman perched on the edge of the bed, took his hand, but did not smile. 'My name's Gerda,' she said. 'I'm Danish. I'm from Copenhagen and I do locum work here at the hospital in the winter. Do you remember what happened?'

Bird nodded towards the sink.

'Could you get that tap to stop dripping?' Her hand felt warm, dry and sinewy in his.

She stood up, crossed the freshly waxed floor, turned the tap, waited until it was no longer dripping, then came back to the bed. She moved so smoothly that Bird could feel the stillness all

According to Sofia

around her. She dropped her pen on the floor, picked it up without bending her knees, put the top on it and slipped it into her breast pocket. She was lithe, not skinny, but thin, and her fingers were long and slender. She perched on the edge of the bed with lowered shoulders and he observed the way her arms rested on the duvet.

She looked at him.

'You overdo things,' she said.

Bird made no answer.

'Do you always do that?' she went on.

'I was just out running.'

'For long?'

'The same as usual,' said Bird. 'My usual run. I do it three times a week.'

'All year round?'

'Do you do any sports training?' Bird asked.

Still she did not smile. 'Handball,' she said.

'In sports halls?'

'Yes,' she said. 'Where else?'

'Often?'

'Occasionally,' she said.

'Do you like sports halls?'

'Not really?'

'Do you always give one-word answers?' said Bird.

'Do you?'

She did not smile.

'Not always,' she added.

Dr Vige looked at Bird. All at once he was breathing easily. He looked at the pills in the dish, then changed his mind when Bird heaved himself up on to the pillows, retreated to the window, waited, tugged at the hair at his temple, crossed the room and went out.

He knew they had not noticed.

'Really train?' Bird said.

She nodded.

'Proper training, several times a week? You look as though you cycle sixty miles a week. Do you?'

'I played handball for Denmark. Five years ago. Then I stopped.'

She was finally smiling, Bird saw.

'Why did you stop?'

'I wasn't good enough to play professionally. I had hoped I would be, but it wasn't to be.'

Bird did not answer.

'It just wasn't to be,' she said.

'That's too bad.'

'Maybe,' she said.

Bird looked up.

'I don't know, really,' she said. 'I wouldn't mind turning pro. I make no secret of the fact that I had hoped to make money out of it. There was one club that tried using one of those glitzy advertising agencies. They came up with this PR stunt. We were to play in the nude at the sports hall. I liked the idea. I wouldn't have minded doing that. It sounded like fun. The money wasn't bad either.'

Bird tried to raise himself on to his elbows.

'Easy does it, Bird,' she said. Bird noticed that she pronounced his name softly and naturally. 'There's more than one meaning of professional, as you know. In the modern sports world, at any rate. There was a time when I was willing to pay the price. I had considered most of the options, including those that no one talks about, to win a permanent place on a first division team.'

'Abroad?'

'For example,' she said.

'What are you doing here?'

'I'm sitting on your bed,' she said.

Dr Vige entered the room. He cleared his throat. 'Couldn't you . . .?'

'No,' Bird broke in.

'Couldn't you try?' said Dr Vige.

According to Sofia

'I'm a psychiatrist,' she said.
'Are you?'
'A psychiatrist.'
She was laughing now.
'How are you feeling?'
Bird clutched her hand.
'Not that great,' he said.
She gave a big smile. Bird noticed that her teeth were a gleaming white and her breath smelled of menthol. The skin of her index finger was a pale yellow and the nail neatly clipped. She's a smoker, he thought. Before driving to the hospital in the morning she smokes a last cigarette, scours her fingers and rinses her mouth with menthol.

His neck relaxed as he looked at her.
'Do you often try to run yourself to death?'
'I keep myself fit,' Bird said.
'It looks more like self-destruction. Ever thought of that? There are lots of ways of doing it, you know. I've come across the most ingenious methods. You must have thought of that.'
'No,' said Bird.
'Do you always try to cure arrhythmia by going for long, boring runs?' she asked.
'Do I have arrhythmia?'
'What do you think?'
'No, said Bird. 'I'm fine. It's a virus. I'm sure it's a simple dose of the 'flu.'
'Why do you keep passing out?'
'I don't know,' said Bird.
'Why do you think you do?'
'Simple anxiety. Rather too much stress over rather too long a time. It's perfectly common,' said Bird.
'But you still go running,' she said.
'Jogging isn't boring.'
'Really?' she said. 'I hated it. It's one of the most boring things I can think of. I like walking, though.'

'Do I have arrhythmia?' Bird asked.

'No,' said Dr Vige. 'But you're well on the way to it. Could you not be sensible and take the pills in that dish?' He nodded towards the bedside table on which sat a glass of blackcurrant squash and a pill dish.

'Okay,' he said to Dr Vige. 'Could you just stay sitting there on the bed?' he said to Gerda. 'What's your last name?'

'Hansen,' she said.

'Couldn't you try to give more than a one-word answer? Just try,' said Bird.

He eyed her in amazement.

'Hansen's almost as dull a name as Leif. Does it say Leif in my case notes?' Bird asked.

'Naturally,' said Dr Vige.

'Would you be kind enough to correct it?' Bird said to Gerda Hansen. She had brown hair that glowed in the light falling on it from behind. He was now holding her hand in both of his own.

'Bird,' said Dr Vige. 'Stop that.'

'Stop what?'

'Bird,' said the doctor.

Neither Bird nor Gerda was looking at him.

'That,' said Vige. He nodded in the direction of Bird's hands, which were now tucked between Gerda Hansen's thighs. He was looking at her as if he wanted to pull her under the duvet and keep her there for ever.

'Why are you doing that?' Gerda asked, laughing down into the face on the pillow. 'Does it help?'

'It seems to,' said Bird.

'Well, that's all right then.'

Dr Vige tried not to smile. 'Where is your sister?' he said.

'In the Basque country. She ran into an old acquaintance who is a lawyer and rescues her from all the fixes she gets herself into. I'll bet there's no holding him back.'

He could tell from Gerda's shoulders that she was laughing.

'Do you know her?' said Bird.

According to Sofia

'I've heard of her,' said Gerda. 'Everybody talks about everybody else in this hospital. You know that.'

'Did I almost die?' he asked.

Bird could tell by the silence which hung between the doctors that he had almost died. Dr Vige cleared his throat. 'You have been very careless.'

'Not really,' said Gerda, placing Bird's hands and her own on her thighs. 'But something happened which we don't really understand. We are in the process of analysing it. We'll know more in a couple of hours.'

Bird shut his eyes.

'Don't go,' he said to Gerda.

'You are so fragile,' said Dr Vige.

'If you say that one more time, I'll scream,' said Bird. 'I'll roar my head off.'

'The same could be said of just about anyone,' said Dr Vige. 'You have the heart and lungs of a young man, and yet you have these dizzy turns. It doesn't seem to fit with everything I have learned. You are fragile.'

Bird tried to scream. He took a deep breath, opened his mouth and realised that this was something he really should not do. He clutched Gerda's hand, and he heard her laughter: deep, distant and coloured by Danish vowels.

'I'll be here when you wake up,' she said.

Bird saw her hair silhouetted against the window. He squinted at the light, shut his eyes, slowly, and was not sure whether what he was hearing was the sound of shoes or lion paws moving across the floor to the door. 'Is he asleep?' said Dr Vige. 'He's dreaming of lions. All day yesterday he dreamt that he was living on the savannah. It's odd that he should be dreaming about African lions.'

'I don't think so,' said Gerda Hansen.

By then, Bird was asleep.

14

When Leon arrived at the hotel in Algiers he complained that the room stank of rancid dates, and that the previous guest had left their underpants on the water cooler. Also, the air-conditioned room was about as cool as a Roman bath. Leon treated an equable desk manager to a lecture on Berber fecklessness.

Then he told him who he was.

Leon knew, of course, that the desk manager had been informed of his identity. The vast room in dove-grey marble had been booked by busy men from the city's famed entertainment agency. It was the best room in the hotel, not a suite but a cool room with a sleeping alcove. Leon had a reputation for being difficult, but he was invariably sober. Added to which, the agency's men comported themselves like modern Muslim undertakers and discreetly slipped a banknote into the desk manager's top pocket. He poked between his gold teeth with a toothpick, eyed Leon up and down and glanced through his papers. He had spent twenty years behind the reception desk, he had heard every complaint going, and he knew that it drove people crazy when the heat carried on into the autumn.

He decided to like Leon.

They were about the same height, and when he saw Leon's shoulders, his arms inside the blue shirt and the pugnacious look in his eyes, he told him about a studio where the brotherhood was in the habit of meeting to practise the local version of Tai Chi. 'I see the crest on your tie-pin. How can you stand to wear a tie in this heat? I beg your pardon, but I have been bathed in sweat for four months,' the manager explained. Leon raised his hand to his lower lip. He was taken aback.

Rarely did anyone speak to him. No one, until now, had ever insinuated that he was a snob for wearing a tie. Nor found it funny.

'For a midget like yourself to be accepted at the studio you have to walk through the door without ducking your head,' the desk manager told him. 'You are so small that it will be no problem for you. I can get in, but only just,' he added. The brotherhood, otherwise known as the athletes, had the studio to themselves, with no referee and confined by the standard rules of Tai Chi, but they used felt-covered staffs. 'The point of the exercises is, after all, to expose tricks, learn new ones, compose oneself, enjoy the silence and never lose the head.'

The desk manager smiled at Leon. 'You're going to have problems there. The man you are going up against knows exactly what he has to do. To show that you are chronically bad-tempered,' he added. 'Which is not good for the blood sugar.'

Thereafter, he recited the creed which forbade anyone in the studio from being under the influence of alcohol or drugs.

'This you know. But I am obliged to mention it.'

They were not permitted to be professional, hungover, sick or smoke tobacco. No one wore gloves. It was not necessary. 'You do not have to worry about your precious fingers,' he said with a yawn. Leon nodded. 'I've never tried it with sticks. But I've read about it. Is he Chinese?' This last was greeted with suspicion. The desk manager flicked through a folder on the desk, playing for time. 'Is he Chinese?' Leon asked again. 'What do you mean? Don't tell me dwarves have started discriminating? Well, there's a new twist – I'll have to remember that.'

Afterwards, in reception, the desk manager came close to betraying the fact that there were still American bohemians living in the lean-tos of the city's shanty town, but instead he took a deep breath, lifted his head and looked at Leon again.

'We are about the same height,' made an impression on Leon. 'Today is a holiday,' made Leon look round. 'I've been thinking of going to Colomb Bechar,' prompted the desk manager to remove his glasses. 'Do you really have to?'

It was so hot that they sat down at a round table under the fan and the manager bellowed to someone in the kitchen to bring them tea. While they were waiting, the manager was made a present of Leon's mobile phone. The manager bowed, thanked Leon, then Allah, and finished by raising his eyes gratefully to the greyish-yellow mosaic on the ceiling. The reliefs were a reminder of Allah's chronic presence and of the fact that gifts were a blessing. In exchange, the manager undertook to show Leon where genuine Kelims dyed with henna and indigo were sold. 'None of that synthetic rubbish,' Leon said.

He took the phone out of the manager's hands.

'Just one last call.' He tried unsuccessfully to call Linda and Ted. 'Either they're asleep or they're at the trotting track,' he remarked to the manager in Norwegian. 'They've had dinner and now they're lying peacefully under the travelling rug.'

He then called Ted's mobile number and was asked to leave a message after the tone. During the two minutes when Leon was on the phone, the manager fell asleep, his mouth gaped, his teeth followed suit, exposing the roof of his mouth. Leon, who was suddenly reminded of Berber toothlessness, looked away. The manager had not been born in the city, then, but in one of the oases and had lost all his teeth by the time he was twenty. When every meal for years consisted of nothing but sweetmeats, resistant bacteria invaded the oral cavity and attacked the sinuses. This was a dangerous state of affairs and only the smart ones got themselves to a dentist in town in time.

He woke up, nudged his dentures back into place with his thumb and bowed his head.

'Was it touch and go?' Leon asked, pointing to his own teeth. The manager shrugged. 'Are you from around here?'

'I lived in these parts,' said Leon. 'A long time ago. Far too long ago. What's your name?'

Flies buzzed over the table. The silence became awkward. Suddenly Leon could hear the fan on the ceiling. At the reception desk, two polite German tourists were poring over a map. The place smelled of tea and sweet cakes. Leon sat quite still, studying his shoes.

At last the manager smiled. 'You're not supposed to ask such things. Not yet. You'll have to wait a few hours. Preferably a couple of days. Remember that. I realise it's a long time since you lived here.'

Leon blushed.

He inclined his head.

'I beg your pardon,' he whispered.

They drank tea. Ate. Dozed in their cane chairs. Woke up. Dozed off again and were woken by the sounds of a family walking past on the street outside. They were complaining of the heat, of thirst, of the bus and a dreadful meal. The manager stretched and pulled out his keys, opened the brown cabinet, took out the grey dropping bottle and measured ten drops into Leon's tea to begin with, paused and eyed him inquiringly. Leon held up five fingers. 'You're taking a risk,' the manager said. He measured five more drops into Leon's tea and regarded him with interest.

Leon dived into a sultry world of fathers who measured children, animals, racetracks, newspaper buildings and the distance to the moon. They used gold folding rules divided into four equal sections, then the felt for tiny spears employed as toothpicks by baboons and sprinters. He put both hands to his head and fixed his eye on the manager. 'Do you take this stuff every day?' he whispered. 'If you keep very still for ten minutes, it will ease off,' the manager replied. 'You had best not get up from that chair,' was the stupidest thing he could have said.

Leon promptly got up from his nice, safe seat at the round table with the glass top.

'I tell you this much,' he declared the next day to Bird in his hospital bed. 'It was like floating on the flying carpets of the Orient. All of a sudden I was lying in a pool full of lukewarm water.'

'Lukewarm water?' said Bird.

'I was still in the hotel lobby,' Leon continued. 'I could feel my body glowing, but my head was a block of ice and I waded around in the pool with a teacup in my hand. I screamed a bit. Howled is probably closer to the truth. In any case, it feels weird to have had a trip on a flying carpet.

'The manager assured me that everything was fine and said I ought to eat some thin soup with noodles at the home of a friend who held cockfights in his backyard twice a week. I was soaking wet, lethargic, happy, angry and hungry. And I was feeling dizzy. I'm not a pretty sight with my clothes plastered to my body, you know. I felt exposed,' he told Bird.

There was silence up above, somewhere between the Earth and the Moon. All Leon could hear was the crackle of the satellite.

'What are your plans for the rest of the day?' Bird said at last and felt the receiver sticking to his ear.

'I'm gearing up for a stick fight.'

'For what?'

'A stick fight.'

'What's that?'

'The brotherhood holds fights almost every day here in Algiers. There are a lot of us here, you know,' said Leon. 'We have to keep ourselves fit to face a world of giants.'

'What brotherhood?'

Bird heard Leon lower his voice in a way that said he was smiling: 'Of midgets,' he laughed. 'Of all the dwarves who have

According to Sofia

learned to defend themselves. We demonstrate our ability to thump one another. With or without sticks. We use every dirty trick in the book while at the same time learning how to survive. We compare notes on the latest techniques for beating dissenters into silence. You need to be aware of this. You've known me for over thirty years,' he added. 'I'm feeling a little sleepy,' said Leon. 'It's probably the manager's drops. I wasn't prepared for that.'

Bird, who had just been given a sedative injection, raised a hand in greeting to Simen. He entered on tiptoe, carrying bananas this time, and he closed the door gently. He stared in bafflement at Bird, who was yelling into the phone.

'You must be a right idiot, knocking back drops from a grey bottle. Are you out of your mind?'

He boosted himself into a sitting position. Smiled and propped his back up with pillows. 'It's Leon,' he whispered to Simen. 'He swam in a pool in the lobby of an hotel in Algiers.'

Simen peeled a banana, picked up the extension, tucked his left elbow into his stomach as he munched on his banana.

'Hi, Leon. How are you doing now?'

This particular question was stifled by another break in the signal. Bird sighed, lying there in the bed. Simen did sometimes lose his grip. He told Simen at his bedside and Leon in Algiers that he had never believed in this close spirit of brotherhood between midgets.

'Do you mean dwarves?' said Leon. Simen stopped munching and set the rest of the banana down on a dish.

'What brotherhood?' he said, the journalist in him instantly to the fore. They laughed much as they had in the old days. Everything was much as before. When the three of them were together everything was actually the same as before. On those days when, with Simen rambling on and Leon and Bird setting the world to rights, they skipped school, sneaking out of the grey brick building that could still make Leon quiver with fury.

'Come home, Leon,' was a remark from Simen that bounced straight off.

'I'm suffering from arrhythmia,' from Bird made some impression.

'Really ill, with a drip on a stand and everything?' came the quickfire response from Leon, in a voice which betrayed that he was worried. 'You have to look after yourself, Bird. I need you right now. I know you don't like me very much. But I'm the closest thing you have to a friend. Don't spoil it. You have a way of spoiling things. You're one of many who spoil things without meaning to.' Bird looked long and hard at the receiver while Simen drummed on his forehead with his fingers.

'What do you mean?' Bird asked.

'If it's never occurred to you before then that's just too bad for you,' Leon said.

Bird regarded the drops dripping from the bottle and down the tube, drop by drop, and through the cannula in his arm to the vein. He was so still inside that he shut his eyes.

Simen gave his shoulder a shake. 'He doesn't have arrhythmia. His heart gives the odd, harmless double beat and he's feeling a bit under the weather: pull yourself together,' said Simen.

'Who's to pull themselves together?' asked Leon.

'Both of you,' said Simen.

'I'm fine,' said Bird.

'What do you know about your sister?' Leon asked.

Simen made no attempt to conceal the fact that he found this embarrassing.

'She's in Vitoria. She's under the protection of some lawyer. One of those celebrated Basque lawyers,' Bird said.

'Just as well, probably,' said Leon. 'With Sofia in the Basque country life will be even more dangerous. She'll make it look like a Greek tragedy with Creon playing the lead.'

'Who's Creon?' said Simen.

'Later,' said Bird with a wave of the hand.

Leon chuckled, as he always did when Simen displayed his ignorance. 'Look after yourself, Bird,' he said again.

'Are you all right now?' Simen said.

'Maybe. I'll have a better idea of how things stand in a few hours' time.'

'How do you mean?'

'I'm going to the studio. Tai Chi, you know.'

'No,' said Simen. 'I haven't the foggiest. As usual, I've either forgotten or I never knew.'

'It's sort of like Chinese shadow boxing. Here in Algiers they practise a local version of it. I've read about it and I'd like to try it.'

Simen fell silent. Soundlessly he mouthed the name Tai Chi as if it were a resistant virus. He sighed, glanced into the bag of bananas, then at Bird who smiled at him.

'I've no idea what was in that dropping bottle,' Leon said. And Simen, now wearing a new suit, a Burberry coat with a matching belt and a hat with a turned-down brim, ate the rest of his banana, drank Bird's coffee, unwrapped the sugar cube and nibbled it, and listened to Leon who was describing the view of the plain. 'Of the desert,' he said. 'From where I'm sitting I can see the treacherous sand. It's not golden, but grey and swarming with scorpions. I honestly did not realise that I had been missing it. It's like a disease. Like being drunk,' he added and drained his glass.

'What are you drinking?' Simen asked.

'It's odd,' said Bird. 'Why is nobody where they should be any more,' he roared. Startled by the loudness of his voice, he tried to lower it. 'Who decided that we can only talk to one another on the phone,' he roared again.

'Don't shout. It does no good,' said Simen. 'I've eaten nothing but bananas today,' he added. 'I hate bananas. Come home, Leon. Please.'

Bird was feeling better. The walls were not turning inside out before his eyes. It was quiet in the hospital room, but he missed the pictures of Monet's garden. He had been reading an article on aggressive bees when Leon called. Now Bird could hear Leon snoring down there in Algiers.

'He's asleep,' he said to Simen. 'He'll sleep for ten hours, at least. Here we are in a hospital in Norway and we can clearly hear Leon snoring in an hotel in Algiers.'

Simen crossed, as usual, to the window. He looked out at the rain, took off his coat, shook it, pursed his lips, eyed Bird, considered the temperature chart and Bird's colour. 'Have you eaten?'

Bird did not reply.

'You have to eat.'

'I'm trying,' said Bird.

'Have you tried muesli?'

'No,' Bird said, in a way that prompted Simen to brush invisible flecks from his shoulders.

'I think you'd better go now,' Bird went on. 'I think you should quite simply be getting back to the office.'

'It's been raining,' said Simen. 'We're going to have four months or more of rain and snow. The thought of snowflakes in the rain is just unbearable.'

Bird shut his eyes.

'I think I'll take a trip up to the mountains,' Simen said. 'Go hunting. I've been thinking about the cottage since I woke up this morning. It might not be raining up there. What do you think?'

15

'What do we do now?' Bird said.

Gerda Hansen opened the menu. Bird eyed the bill of fare dubiously, ran his fingers over the tablecloth, considered her at length, rubbed his chin with his hand, cleared his throat and waited.

'We're going to eat,' she said.

'Dinner?' Bird asked.

'A slap-up meal,' she said, laughing. 'I'll be keeping an eye on you. I'll be keeping a close watch on you all evening, so there.' She was still smiling. 'All the way up until ten o'clock. Nobody here would know you were ill.'

'Am I?' Bird said.

'Of course you're ill.'

Bird placed his hands on the menu: 'You know,' he said. 'I've never heard you talk as much as you're doing right now.'

Gerda Hansen looked at Bird as if she had no intention of ever being surprised by him. She gazed into his face so steadily that Bird realised he would have to get used to her. 'That's to get you to eat,' she said. 'You haven't eaten. Not for two days. I've smuggled you out to a restaurant with white tablecloths and candles on the table. Here's the menu.'

'I like steak tartare,' she said. 'Proper steak tartare. Without the egg yolk. But I have to have freshly ground pepper and sea salt.'

'Sounds awful,' Bird said.

'You know,' she said, and took a long pull on her cigarette. She spent a long time looking at her lighter. She stared at her lighter for so long that Bird clasped his hands.

'What do I know?' he asked.

'I've stopped.'

'Stopped?' Bird repeated, regarding her cigarette.

'Doing most things.'

Bird closed the menu.

'Just about everything,' she ventured.

Bird tried to beckon to the waiter. He didn't like her confiding anything whatsoever to him.

'You don't like confidences.'

'No,' he said.

Hansen the waiter emerged from the kitchen. He stood by the door and followed two women with his eyes. They weren't sober, but quiet and he walked up to them, took their coats and led them to the table behind the pillar. He observed how they could not sit down quick enough, so eager were they to hold hands under the table. He waited, got them seated, eyed them placidly, smiled politely, lit their candle and moved the flower so they could see one another.

'What were you saying?' Bird essayed.

Gerda Hansen smoked and took pleasure in it. Bird noticed how her face grew calm when she looked at him and this unsettled him; he glanced at the menu again before laying his hands on the table.

'What do you do when running does no good?'

He ran an eye round the restaurant. Hansen the waiter was handing the new arrivals' coats to the cloakroom attendant. He had his back to Bird.

'What do you do?'

'Nothing,' said Bird.

Gerda followed the smoke from her cigarette with her eyes. He could tell that she liked both the smell and the colour of the smoke and that she didn't care about anyone else in the room.

'I meditate it away.'

'Where?'

'On the floor,' said Bird.

He heard the two women at the table next to the pillar start to giggle when Hansen the waiter filled their glasses.

'At home?'

'Yes,' said Bird. 'On the living-room floor.'

'Alone?'

'Yes, of course.'

'Are you always alone?'

'Almost always.'

There was silence over by the pillar when the waiter left the table and in the yellow candlelight the women's faces were soft, and he could tell from their hands that they could not help touching one another.

'Do you drink?'

Bird shrugged: 'It's better than it was,' he said.

'In what way?'

'There's no point,' Bird said. 'There's no longer any point,' he added.

'Doesn't it help?'

'Hardly at all,' said Bird.

'How much damage have you done so far?'

'How do you mean?'

'Who?' said Gerda.

Hansen the waiter had caught sight of Bird. He walked over to their table as if he had just received a piece of good news. He had already observed that Bird was restless. He was still not done reading the menu and he hunched his shoulders.

'Do you want to eat?'

'I'd rather not.'

The waiter stood by the table. He was pale, he coughed discreetly and looked at Gerda Hansen. He just managed to note that she was good-looking, slim, bordering on skinny, a little grey under the bronze teint, as if it were synthetic. She worked too hard, he decided. She gets home too late in the evenings. 'My name is Hansen,' he said. They chatted as if they had known one another for ever.

Bird had been known to bring women to The Stables, but they were usually colleagues, he was inattentive and did not keep his eyes on them when they talked. The waiter bent down and whispered in Bird's ear. 'Was it your heart?'

'Whatever it was, it wasn't pleasant,' said Bird.

He did not know what to say.

'I've missed you, you know. I don't like your flat being in darkness.'

Bird bowed his head. He tried to read the menu, but the old waiter pointed to the Dish of the Day. 'You like that.'

'Are you sure?' Bird asked.

The waiter looked up from his pad. He stared for a long – far too long – time at his pencil before saying: 'You've hardly said a word.'

'No,' said Bird.

Hansen the waiter left them. Bird could tell from the waiter's back that he very much wanted to talk to him. He wanted everything to be the same as before, but something had changed and he did not know why. He felt like staying by the table and simply being nice. He felt like being close to Bird, but refrained because of the woman. He turned in the kitchen doorway, raised a hand to Bird, straightened his back and pushed open the brown swingdoor.

'What do we do now?' Bird asked.

'Sometimes I eat strawberries.'

'Do you really like desserts?'

'You're not exactly entertaining,' she laughed.

She stopped Hansen on his way past the table, ordered a bottle

According to Sofia

of mineral water, a jug of iced water with slices of lemon, steak tartare with freshly ground pepper and sea salt.

Bird noticed how Hansen the waiter relaxed. He placed a hand on Bird's shoulder and brushed Gerda's arm. He liked her and made it plain to Bird that he had been won over. He did not write anything on his pad and he smiled the same smile he wore when watering the petunias in the window boxes. He tilted his head back a little and laughed softly, but affably. Bird noticed that he looked more at Gerda than at him.

'Do you often come here?'

Hansen the waiter brought the iced water. 'I sort of look after him,' he said with a smile. 'I call him up and tell him when we have something he likes.'

'I'll do that,' she said and filled a glass almost to the brim, drained it, smiled, lit another cigarette and poured half a glass.

'Is this where you drink?'

'I am actually a little bit hungry,' Bird said.

She sat back in her chair and gave a real smoker's cough.

'Would you like something to eat?'

It was a bit sudden. He put on his glasses, peered down at the menu, ran his index finger down the page and did not look at her.

'Well, what would you like then?' she repeated.

The pianist lifted the lid of the grand piano. He had spoken to the head waiter and the two women sitting next to the pillar, nodded to people he knew and moved as slowly as he could. He had made the women laugh, and the head waiter smiled with satisfaction. He had got there with ten minutes to spare and drunk coffee from a mug. No one had noticed his twitching fingers or the fact that he had not showered. Bird, who still had not looked at Gerda, smiled at him, shrugged, put a hand to his chin, and Gerda knew without a doubt that the pianist was dreading having to play. Hansen the waiter immediately set a glass on an occasional table beside the piano and the three of them looked at one another and smiled.

'What's all that about?' she asked.

'He's having a bad day. He's been having rather too many bad days lately and he ought not to have any more. He knows it. All the regulars know it. He used to be very good, but not any more.'

'You must have been very frightened.'

Bird made no answer.

'When you passed out.'

'Yes,' Bird said. 'Of having an operation,' he added. 'I am afraid of that blue light when you lot wheel me in. I don't like the idea of people cutting into me with scalpels. I don't like the smell or the sounds. I'm afraid of the injection that makes me feel as if I don't care, when I'm actually terrified.'

The pianist attempted to play 'Round Midnight'. He made two mistakes almost before he'd begun and Bird, who lowered his eyes each time, moved his napkin and his glass. He tried not to hear the way the pianist's fingers blundered over the keys. He looked down at his hands, at his white fingers, at the glass from which he blew invisible dust. He took a deep breath, shifted restlessly, pushed the menu away from him and slowly exhaled.

'Do you find it painful?'

She nodded at the pianist.

'Yes,' said Bird. 'I don't understand why he always has to try such tricky pieces when he's tired. He's just asking for trouble. And that is exactly what he gets. Can't you hear it?'

'For me it's simpler,' said Gerda Hansen. 'I grow mellow,' she continued. 'I prefer to listen to Frank Sinatra. He's deceitful and commercial. I like Frank Sinatra because he is one of the great liars. One of the greatest. His lies are not convincing, but they're beautiful.'

'That makes it bearable.'

She dabbed her mouth with her napkin, smiled at him, refilled her glass and gazed down into the jug. It was almost empty and she set it down gently behind the flowers. It was so quiet round about her that Bird heard her cigarette being crushed in the ash tray.

Bird sat back in his chair.

According to Sofia

'A little calmer?'

Bird put his finger to his lips.

'Is that the whole point?'

'I don't know what the point is,' Bird said at length. 'According to Sofia,' he added, 'there is no point. We are tracked down. We don't find her. She finds us. It can be unpleasant, but that's how it is. She rounds us up. We don't even realise what's happening until it's too late.'

Bird sipped his iced water. 'That was quick,' he said.

'What was quick?'

'It's not often that anyone talks to me. It hardly ever happens. Apart from Sofia,' he added.

Gerda laughed when he said Sofia's name. 'She's found herself a lawyer down there in the Basque country. That was quick, too.'

'Yes,' said Bird.

'Does it happen often? I mean, does it happen as often as they say at the hospital? Her upping and leaving, is what I'm trying to say.'

Bird did not answer.

'More and more often?' she said.

The mobile phone rang in Bird's pocket. He took it out, looked at the display panel, pressed the button and said: 'Is that you, Linda? Are you at home, did you say? Was it Simen who called? No? Ted, you say. Is he asleep under the travelling rug? Is he doing any better? He still can't manage it? No? And he refuses to go and see his usual doctor. I can well imagine. No, no. I'm at The Stables. Yes, yes, I'm fine.'

Gerda poured the rest of the iced water into her glass.

16

Above all else, what drew Leon to the cool studio was the silence. He found the building behind the third palm past the police station, an enormous, whitewashed edifice, hexagonal, well-kept and, most important of all: in the shade of the mosque.

Leon had not asked about the formalities, but had had them explained to him, so he walked into the entrance hall, showed his card to the caretaker and proceeded into the changing room.

Although the test was not necessary, he had to pass through the door which revealed how small he was.

The door was a sandy yellow and decorated with archaic symbols, almost square and used solely to measure the height of the brotherhood's members. There was a hand's breadth to spare between the top of his head and the lintel, and the master, a courteous dwarf with white skin and tattoos on his back, bowed from the hips, raised both his hands and presented his palms to him, whispered a welcome, asked him for payment, preferably in dollars, but otherwise in pesetas, pounds or euros. 'My apologies, but fewer and fewer people request my services.'

Leon liked him.

He liked the smell of leather and vegetables in the studio, which was actually a converted café with a hatch in one wall. It was so quiet in the room that Leon could hear the murmur of the air conditioner. No fans on the ceiling. No draughts. The room was cool. And Leon could tell that this brick building had been cool for a long time.

The master peered at Leon, smiled; he stood quite still, waiting, Leon fumbled with his stick, the dwarf twirled his and Leon felt the rush of air through his hair as it swept over. He crouched down, swung to the left, ducked his head and stepped slowly backwards.

He was taken aback. This was one manoeuvre he had never come across before. He had visited studios in Paris, Damascus and Cairo, but had never been so swiftly disarmed. He fumbled, failed to find his centre of gravity, fluffed his grip and the distance between himself and his opponent became hard to gauge. In the studio, the stick was never used as a weapon. Ruthlessly it exposed one's opponent's reflexes, more clearly than in boxing, and Leon did his best to stand quite still, facing him. The master watched him, intently, silently, almost soundlessly, but Leon could hear the resin on the soles of his shoes. Each movement was so gradual that it might have been planned.

'Who do you think I am? Muhammed Ali? Or what about Jersey Joe Walcott?' Leon said, smiling at the dwarf.

He had gentle eyes, rather too gentle, rather too many evenings spent alone with his books, ascetically, with tea and sweet cakes, and rather too worked up to go roaming the hot streets alone.

'Who is Joe Walcott?'

They circled one another, slowly, modulating every movement, indicating with a flick of the hand where they could have struck, raising their arms, their right legs, standing motionless for minutes on end, only their eyes moving, and Leon, who was out of condition, felt his shoulders quivering. He proceeded with the classic exercises, these being obligatory, but when he could remain motionless no longer he took two steps to the left, then to the right, the master mirroring his actions, then once more they held still, silent, courteous, their sticks never lifted above their knees, and Leon felt himself slowly rolling over on to the outer edges of his feet.

'Your breathing is fine. Your midsection is a little stiff, but just about acceptable. Ten minutes almost without moving. That is not bad,' he heard.

'Your eyes flicker when you are tired. That is a bad sign. Your reflexes are not up to scratch,' the dwarf said. 'Do you drink? You have done better than this in the past,' he continued, demonstrating with his stick how he could have tapped Leon's left ear. 'I will go easy on your ears,' he said. 'You had best not leave this room with your ears ringing.'

The dwarf circled rhythmically round Leon, his eyes fixed on him, on his arms especially. 'You have very good arms. From the shoulders on down. Not too long. You are not a dwarf, but you are small,' he said, but Leon did not let this upset him. 'That is often worse. Being small. You are not a dwarf. You have hardly any of our handicaps. Nor any of our advantages. There are some advantages to being a dwarf, you know. But you are merely small. Much smaller than you think. Almost a dwarf,' he said and lowered his gaze. 'But I am not here to lecture you on the subject of your arms. I am going to show you what sort of state your reflexes are in,' he said, and made Leon aware of the point just over his liver.

It happened so fast that Leon had no chance to react. He scarcely felt the stick graze the skin just over his liver. He felt totally wasted. Exposed. He stood there, bewildered, unable to do a thing. The dwarf was really fast. 'You take a drink every day. Not much. But still too much. A little brandy. A little wine and beer. You have a few too many sleepless nights. You really only concentrate when you have to, not when you ought to. It takes it out of you. You frequent places where there are too many voices and too much smoke. You ought to stop doing that. You have lost the notion for it. Are you feeling unwell?' he asked and could have tapped Leon's knee.

According to Sofia

'Surprised?' he said, so softly that Leon snarled. 'You should be. Five years ago you would have parried that,' he said as Leon started to sweat. 'You are sweating. I can smell it. Do you spend your days in air-conditioned rooms?' he said, so slowly that Leon could not mistake the mocking note in his voice. He took a step to the master's left. 'You're at your weakest when I come at you from the left,' Leon said and received a friendly flick from the felt-covered stick in reply. 'You're quick. I've never met anyone as fast as you are. Where did you learn to move so fast? In China?' They did not touch one another, moved as slowly as they could along the lines marked out on the floor, did not stop, did not look at one another, moved in circles, ever decreasing, ever narrowing circles, until they came to a point where they stood stock-still.

'It is said to be ecstasy,' the dwarf said; he remained motionless for so long that Leon lost his balance. 'To some extent I understand you. But only to some extent. It's like jazz,' the dwarf said. 'John Coltrane?' he continued, swirling the felt-covered stick above his head. 'The one you've been stealing most from for years. Relax. There's hardly anyone listening. Do not lose your concentration. You do not see my moves coming. Your reflexes have become blunt. You could have been a goner by now. You know that, don't you? Have the courage to use your own reason.' This last was a quote from Horace. Leon decided not to reveal this fact. 'Allow more of a distance. Keep them at a distance. From everyone. From everything. Arrogance will get you nowhere. Not yet. That comes later.'

After half an hour Leon knew more about what sort of condition he was in. He was pleased, but not entirely satisfied.

Ten years earlier, on his best days, he had seen every move coming, and had needed merely to make the suggestion of a counter-move. That was all. That and a little feint which said that he had spied other openings. He sweated as profusely as when he played the piano. 'You find this abhorrent,' was really such a commonplace remark that it had no effect on him. 'It is actually a kind of ballet,' was unnecessary. 'What is it like to be famous?' was annoying, but devoid of impact. 'I hear you are some sort of philanthropist, sending dollars to his friends,' left him completely unfazed. 'It's not particularly original, sleeping with the boss's wife,' was embarrassing. 'Did she switch off the light when you entered the room?' was a considered pronouncement. 'Working as a mechanic, did it never worry you that you might damage your fingers?'

'Are you as good as they say in the jazz magazines?' was a fresh attempt. 'I know you used to be much better,' was in no way offensive. 'I think you're overrated,' sounded ridiculous. 'I think I know why you want to go back to Colomb Bechar,' came as a laconic follow-on to another marking of his vulnerable liver. 'You really are very vulnerable,' made Leon smile.

'What is her name,' on the other hand, led him to drop his shoulders. 'Why did you run off? Do you often do that? Is she as beautiful as they say?' Leon raised his stick above his knees. 'Why don't you sleep with her?' Leon snarled, lowered his head, advanced on the dwarf, looked into those gentle eyes, thought better of it and stepped back.

'Satisfied?' he asked, lowering his arms.

The dwarf smiled. 'Do you wear contact lenses?'

Leon nodded.

'You should change them. You can do better than this. You're pulling a little to the right and you're not steady on your feet. I know a good optician.'

With his stick Leon outlined the move the dwarf was about to make. 'Not bad,' the latter admitted. 'Do you take notes?'

'Never,' said Leon.

'So it's all improvised,' the dwarf said and showed him where he could have jabbed him on the shoulder.

'Always,' said Leon.

He knew that he had been at this for over an hour. His knees were starting to stiffen up. The back of his neck hurt. His calves were cold, but he had stayed cool, watchful, silent. His muscles were starting to ache. 'Why don't we circle one another,' made the dwarf smile. They backed off until they were five metres apart and Leon, who was panting heavily, followed every move executed by the dwarf – slowly, with such gruelling slowness, each step and each lift of the arms was halted, emphasised, examined; Leon could hear the muscles in his neck creaking, and the more slowly he dared to carry out each move the more it hurt, at the back of his neck especially, and with the sweat pouring off him he carefully closed his eyes, he could have completed the rest of the routine blindfold.

'It's time you went,' the dwarf said. 'You cannot take any more. You can come again, but not for another two days. What is her name?' the dwarf finished, stepping back with a smile. 'She must have a name,' was an exaggeration and in truth a warning of sorts. Leon turned his back on the dwarf. This, too, an unmistakable warning. They barely glanced at one another, bowed, first with their hands pressed together, then with their palms facing forward, took two paces backward and walked off to separate changing rooms.

Leon took a long shower. He washed his hair with Spanish shampoo with no odour or perfume, dried himself well with two towels, changed into fresh clothes from his holdall and tied a knot in the plastic bag containing his soiled practice clothes. The blue silk shirt had only been worn once then cleaned, the collar was soft and comfortable, the tie dyed with henna, the suit purchased in Switzerland, but not in some trendy boutique. He loathed Armani, those fine Italian leather shoes were too suave, too soft, all the rage with Nordic fops; Zegna suits were the finery of choice for all those who were into copies, Calvin Klein underpants were for people who had been born old. Leon had his suits made by a tailor in Bern. They were tailored to fit him, charcoal grey, they made him look taller, slimmer and on those occasions when he was able to walk without crutches he enjoyed the sense of being anonymous, snappy and dependable. This last made him laugh. It took him almost an hour to get dressed. He did not look in the mirror. And when he was done he paid the caretaker five dollars to deliver the soft leather holdall to the hotel.

17

For Leon, who was not to be convinced, not even by Tai Chi Chuan, it had been a quiet morning.

He breathed slow and deep, and as usual after a stint in the studio he was warm to the very tips of his fingers.

'Crook,' he whispered at the master's blue changing room. 'You may have gentle eyes, but you're a master of disguise,' he said, raising his voice.

'The usual crap,' was muttered mainly to himself.

He stepped out on to the street, nipped into the shade; the heat beat down on him from the white walls of the buildings. He ambled along on the shady side of the street, heading towards the old square, the one which the modern-day barrow-boys had forgotten or overlooked. He knew exactly which path to take through the narrow streets, and the alleyways smelled of rancid olive oil and boiled chicken feet. 'It hasn't changed,' he muttered to himself. He was freshly showered, briskly towelled down and smelled faintly of Spanish perfume.

In the square, ancient Berber superstition and African tradition stood patient watch by the stalls. The shadows of the awnings fell impotently over the crates of fruit; it was so hot that he sidled from stall to stall and from the minaret of the mosque he could hear the monotonous cries to the greatness of Allah. That guy praying up there in the minaret is not without talent, Leon thought to himself, that guy means what he's saying, he calls so mellifluously, so melodiously, it might almost be a tedious cantata. He glanced up towards the top of the tower, but Allah's man had taken cover behind the pillars, that his prayers might be answered in the shade. Not even up there, in the hazy sky, was there any sign of a wind from the sea. Most things were decided by the heat from the desert. The torrid air vibrated. Shimmered. It squeezed the salt out of the pores. Filtered the senses. Rummaged around in the labyrinths of the mind. Steam rose from the dark men's hair, from their backs, their shoulders, their thighs, and from the women's armpits. Impetuous boys sat in the shade, biding their time, their eyes on a football. There was no chance of a game until darkness fell. They felt let down by Allah, their fathers, their mothers, by the sun, their urges and the desert wind. A few women, virtuously black-clad, hurried from stall to stall, the heat of October was their punishment: incomprehensible, naturally, justified, naturally, but a burden which relentlessly forced out of them all the hope they had once cherished.

And yet they made no effort to conceal themselves from Leon.

They walked around him at a respectable distance, paraded, peeped, assessed. He was the unknown, the man of the moment on the square: small, but rich. The black-clad women were in no doubt. They lingered a little too long at the stalls; with a smidgen of hope the eldest lifted their eyes to the minaret of the mosque. The younger ones looked at Leon, not at the mosque. The monotonous warnings from the man of prayer showed no mercy. 'Hey, you up there in that dun-coloured tower, wailing on and on. Why don't you just shut up? We know you. We've felt your hands on our bodies when no one was around. You've tried it on. We know into which bed you tumble when you've been granted absolution for the day. Lamb meat is expensive.' They giggled warily at the stallholder as they pointed at the reddish-brown bunches of carrots. They flicked away insects with their shawls. The turnips were no longer edible. They turned their backs on the

According to Sofia

tower. 'Why can't you leave us alone? We're here for you, you know. Anytime. You don't so much as doubt it. Not a man in this square doubts it. Nonetheless, I rather fancy that little man in the expensive suit. He's bold. He's boiling. He's sweating. He's red-hot. We can tell. His arms are good. He fears none of you. That, too, we can see. Do you think we learn nothing during all our years behind these veils? We have learned to observe. We can listen. The silence inside our tent. A whole life lived behind the veil. We are every bit as isolated as any dwarf. We too, like that little man, are chronic exhibition-goers. And sometimes we stand naked in front of the bedroom mirror. No one knows for how long. No one knows what goes through our minds.' The women listened to the word from the man up there in the heat haze. Heard how every note settled over the marketplace.

'I really do fancy that little man,' thought a young woman in black robes and dug a sharp elbow into Leon's chest. She leant forward and bought tomatoes. In the sunlight the tomatoes glowed like balls of fire. Steam rose from the mound of potatoes, flies buzzed around the dates, the artichokes were imported from Almeria, the almonds were very pricey. Leon bowed. He regarded the woman who had elbowed him in the chest. She addressed the street vendor in a string of soft gutturals. Leon smiled at her. Not with his lips. But with his eyes. He went on smiling for a long time. Just long enough not to be seemly. She lifted her face, allowing Leon a glimpse of her chin. A soft, young, oval chin. Thereafter, with discretion and the skill born of long practice he discerned her teeth, her mouth and the soft down on her upper lip. She knew that Leon would not forget this. Not today. Not tomorrow. But in a week it would be forgotten. Not tonight, though. He would remember it when he lay in bed and could not sleep. She bought root vegetables with names unknown to Leon. She bought a green vegetable. Then another of the same. She slipped them slowly into a plastic bag. Pointed to a slightly too red tomato and exchanged it for another. She stretched a hand across the young turnips, pressed her foot down on Leon's Italian shoe, long and hard, while complaining to the street vendor that he was trying to sell her rotten tomatoes. In all the markets of Africa there was not a worse salesman. He was a skinflint. Her gaze flitted across Leon's as she paid, whispered that she should never have bought a vegetable at that stall and turned away from Leon.

'Beat it,' the stallholder said. 'See that man over there by the pump? He is that woman's husband. He owns her. He has seen it all. It is hot today. He will skin you alive. The wind from the desert is so hot that the lawyers will view it as an extenuating circumstance if he should kill you. Where are you from?'

This last he could not help but ask. It was too tempting. A small foreign man inducing a newly wed woman to touch his shoe. An age-old trick. Even with the cries to Allah from the minaret ringing in her ears. Even with her husband looking on. He was rather impressed by the little man in the charcoal-grey suit.

'What circumstance?' Leon smiled.

'You should not mess about with married women when the wind is as hot as it is today. Surely you know that. You're just asking to be killed,' he said and pulled a fresh cigarette paper from the pack, the previous one having come apart in his sweat-soaked fingers.

'Who's been messing about?' Leon asked.

The street vendor rolled the sodden paper into a ball which he tucked into his pocket. He pressed both hands to his chest in a way which confirmed that Leon was living dangerously.

'I realise that,' Leon replied in the local dialect. 'Of course I know that. I wouldn't mind a little rendezvous. Isn't that sort of foolishness usually settled outside the city wall? I would happily go a round or two. And today would suit me just fine. What do you use? Swords? I like swords,' he smiled. 'I really wouldn't mind that today. Who did you say it was? Is it that man drinking water from the pump? The one with the belly like a pregnant camel?'

According to Sofia

The stallholder sighed. He retreated into the shade.

'The heat has gone on for too long this year. Far too long. The wind is too dry. The heat has seeped into our brains.'

He looked at Leon. Closed his eyes.

Take yourself off as far into the desert as possible, was not said, but understood. As if we didn't have enough on our plates today, what with that one wailing from the top of the minaret, and with the flies, those bloody flies that have been over every single date, every vegetable, every apple and all of the artichokes that my cousin smuggled in from Almeria. There's the haulage to be paid and the palms of the Spanish customs people greased. Half a box has to be set discreetly in the harbour-master's anteroom. He sat down on his stool, considered both Leon and the damp cigarette. 'Do you smoke?' He placed a yellow plastic bag on top of the mound of potatoes.

'No,' said Leon. 'Is that tobacco?'

'It is hemp,' he said, not even bothering to smile. 'Common hemp, brought in every Friday along with the apples. It is really good.'

Leon shook his head. The stallholder seemed to have given himself up to the drug, so little interest was he taking.

'I'm thinking of going to Colomb Bechar,' made him open his eyes again.

'To . . .?'

'Colomb Bechar,' said Leon.

'Today. What is wrong with you? Aren't things bad enough here?'

Slowly Leon took off his jacket. Perhaps that was what did it, that action. Him taking off his jacket. He had taken off his jacket in the hotel room in San Sebastian. She had been sitting in the chair by the window, drinking a Tom Collins. The room smelled of aloe vera. It smelled of powder. It was raining. He was cold. He had played so badly that evening. He missed her. He missed her today. Why not just admit it. Admit that and all of the other things you were not supposed to do. He had promised himself never again to stand in an African square. He had promised never to hear the cries from the street vendor by the box of dates, from the mosque, the soundless cries from black-clad women, from poverty, from the deep shadows along the walls, from motionless men; he looked away and his eye lighted on the European brunette. He started. For as long as she had her back to him, showing only the nape of her neck, he could be mistaken. She looked like her: the handsome brown hair, the taut, jeans-clad backside and the way she tilted her head back when she laughed. Leon watched the way she picked out oranges from the crate, inspecting every single orange. He looked up at the sun, turned, hid behind the awning of the man selling vegetables, it stank; he swore, the stallholder laughed, that look was one he had seen before. 'Is that her?' was so superfluous that he did not expect an answer. Leon studied her shoulders, her arms, her back and the hand on her hip. He lowered his shoulders, knew that it was not her.

'Well?' the stallholder said with a shrug. When he received no answer he looked as though he had been cheated out of sex. 'Do not leave today. I would not recommend it.'

Leon made no reply.

'Sweet potatoes,' he said and pointed to one of the crates. 'I can barbecue them here. Why do you speak our dialect?' he asked when Leon shook his head.

'Don't go,' he went on. 'Another fifteen minutes and I'll be going over to that café,' he said, nodding in the direction of another stall. 'You can have whatever you like.'

Leon put a hand to the back of his neck. The stallholder stubbed out his joint; the cries from the man at the date stall were all that was needed to make him beat a retreat, the square fizzled with desert light, like neon. The light that rolled down the boulevards of Hollywood. The old Hollywood of fake stars. It was all a mirage. Optical illusions. Fabricated fantasies. Stage-managed horrors. Stuntmen in free fall. Neutral. Why was it so unpleasant to be as small as a dwarf? He was really only the majority in disguise.

18

Paul Fichter tucked his briefcase under the plastic table. That done, he looked up at the departures board and saw that the plane to Sandefjord was one hour delayed, and as he squinted into the white light of the lounge at Stansted he slipped his laptop into a soft calfskin bag .

'Yes, I'm still in London,' he told Linda Olsen on his mobile phone. 'I've no idea when I'll be there. I have to go to Oslo first. Maybe to Bergen. After that I don't know where I'll be going. Is Dad asleep?'

He knew that Linda would tell him the truth.

He was also in the midst of sending an internal mail to the woman at the table by the window.

She was about forty, he guessed, fair, straight-backed, well-dressed and English, and on the table in front of her she had one of those little electronic gadgets which discreetly pick up all e-mails within eyeshot.

Paul Fichter bought all the latest electronic gadgets.

He sent her his name, phone number and a coded indication of his interest. A gaze deep into the eyes of a husband clad in a brown Harris tweed suit followed her glance at the display: evaluation, analysis, then the little gadget was popped into its case.

The man in the Harris tweed suit paid the waiter and the

woman walked past Paul's table without making eye contact.

A good sign. As good as in the bag, he decided and poured cream into his coffee. 'What did you say?' he asked Linda in English.

'Speak Norwegian,' Linda replied. 'I feel like a kid when I speak English on the phone.'

Paul Fichter was fond of Linda Olsen. To be honest he was a little too fond of her. He bought her presents. Usually small gold figurines which she put in her safe deposit box. She occasionally referred to these as her stock-in-trade. She patted the box and hummed.

'Dad just pretends to be asleep, but it's nice of you to fuss over him,' Paul Fichter said. 'It does him good to be with you. I'm worried. Well, you know that. I'm always worried about him. That something will happen to him. Because then I'll have to take over,' he said, suddenly whispering. 'I'll have to take over everything that he and the family have scraped together. I'll have to take care of all the things that my greedy friends work themselves to death to attain. To win,' he added. 'I can see it in their eyes. The longing. I'll bother you with the longing later. Poor Sofia. I wonder how she feels when she senses their eyes on the back of her head. Am I boring you? It's Tuesday today. Isn't that Dad's usual day for dying?' he went on, while eating a prawn and dill sandwich. 'Norwegian prawns,' he told Linda, who sighed.

'It's raining,' she said. 'I can't be bothered going out when it's raining. I was meant to be popping down to the butcher.'

Paul Fichter would inherit the family estate: traditions, tractors, fields, geese and all. He mopped his mouth with his napkin, feeling bored. He was bored when he shaved, laughed, ate, flirted and worked. He neither smoked nor drank. 'Nothing is going to get the better of me. No bloody way,' was the terse remark from Paul which Fichter senior liked best.

'Reassuring,' Ted Fichter explained.

At that particular moment he was lying on the sofa under-

According to Sofia

neath the travelling rug, ascertaining that his son was speaking to Linda from London Stansted and that he had spoken four hours earlier to colleagues in Bonn, Paris, London and Copenhagen. 'Is Sofia in Spain? Has she run off? Again,' he added. 'I didn't know. Did Bird call from the hospital? I didn't know that either. Simen on his way to the cottage? That I knew. He told me he had spoken to Leon. In Algiers. Give me one good reason for being in Africa. In the autumn, when just about everybody has been driven half-mad by the summer heat. Leon was sitting in a hotel room, polishing the soles of his shoes with resin. Don't ask me why. He seemed to be absolutely fine down there.'

He propped himself up on his elbows. 'I can't believe that this is actually me, lying dozing on your sofa for hours on end. This doesn't seem like the same man who was in the bank three hours ago. You're so blessedly restful.'

'What's that, dear?' said Linda.

She hears every word I say, thought Ted Fichter. Today she has poured gin into the vinegar bottle. I can smell it. But she never drinks more than two dram glasses of it. She becomes heavy and unmanageable when she takes a drink. She laughs when she should be acting sexy. Age takes its toll, as do sausages, old habits and boredom. I felt the first signs of a cold today. 'Do you think I should call the doctor?' most certainly went unheard. So he thought of all the things he had never had the guts to do.

He thought of Leon.

Leon with no surname. Leon. Ted tucked the blanket up around his sore throat. He curled up on the sofa, feeling drowsy.

'I could lie here till my dying day and simply watch the world through the pattern in this rug,' he whispered. 'That would do me just fine. Instead I have to join the modern-day rat-race of stock exchange and bank. It's making me ill. I've got it into my head that it's making me ill. Five days a week I have to attend board meetings that are becoming more and more idiotic,' he said to Linda who waddled off to the kitchen. The smell of baked potatoes and parsley. Of sage. The scent of bacon. The scent of how it used to be. He shot a glance at the door to Leon's bedsit. He tried to forget how Leon had hobbled along on crutches until he had the operation at that English hospital. The surgeon was said to be a genius, as well as a nice man; little, a little Iranian immigrant, copper-coloured and distinguished. It had cost a fortune, blood money, paid by him, Ted Fichter, although close inspection of the accounts would have revealed that it was actually the bank that had shelled out. The bank and Olsen's Autos. 'It never occurred to me that stolen cars stood for twenty per cent of that bill. I wonder where Olsen is now?' he murmured into the warm blanket. He was feeling better. 'A bottle of red wine really does a lot for the self-confidence,' he said.

'What're you saying now?' Linda asked. She came in from the kitchen smelling of gin and bacon. 'You've been at the fridge, pinching bacon,' he said, plumping up his pillow. 'I pay for quietness. I would give just about anything to be free of all the noise in the bank.' It was so quiet in the flat on the second floor, screened by trees, money and the caretaker. 'We made money on the horses this year. Over two hundred thousand,' made no impression on her. She stood next to the fridge, screwing the cork back into the vinegar bottle. Why do I keep shying away from the subject of Leon? wondered Ted. I really don't feel up to thinking about him. 'Grand lad,' was a remark which made him feel stupid. 'He's got guts,' would do at a pinch. Sometimes he imagined that he could hear the sound of Leon coming up the stairs. After the operation he could climb the stairs without any problem, without hobbling, without resting, but his hips pained him in the winter. 'He should have been my son,' he said. He had been feared at the stock exchange. By the brokers. By those who do nothing but move capital about. By ambitious men of power.

He could have made millions,' Ted concluded. 'He could have been a government minister. Minister of Finance. The world's smallest, but wealthiest. Instead he's charging about the world, getting all steamed up about McCoy Turner. Do you understand it? I don't know the first thing about music. And certainly not

According to Sofia

about McCoy Turner,' prompted Linda to lower the racing column of the morning paper. She had come in from the kitchen and seated herself in the chair by the window. 'You can forget the fifth race,' she responded. 'I'm sure it's fixed. I've always thought that little jockey with the moustache looks like Olsen the garage owner. One's as unreliable as the other. They have the same smile. I've learned never to put money on Olsen or that jockey. Another couple of years and he'll be in the clink. Take it from me,' she continued.

'It's so quiet,' Ted said. 'True silence is found only here. In your living-room. At your table. In your bed.'

Bank manager Ted Fichter tended to become melodramatic when he drank Spanish wine and ate crème caramel.

He made another attempt to think about Leon. He rolled on to his side. He rested his hand under his cheek, thought of nothing, but noted that the skin of his hand was crinkled and smelled of malt. He felt suddenly old, but at the same time that he was not going to die, or at least not today. When he told Linda this she replied that they would have to steer clear of the fifth race. 'A sure loser. An open mares' race. No doubt about it. I wouldn't bet one *krone* on that race.' Ted was never sure why it was so difficult to think about Leon. 'I miss him. I eventually got used to the sound of him,' Ted said. 'The little midge,' said Linda, in that voice which three years earlier had made the hair on the back of Ted's head stand on end. She had seen on the television that the temperature in Algiers was over forty degrees. 'He can't stand the heat. He's liable to do anything in that heat. God, I'm so worried.' She put her hand to her mouth and thought of the presents in the safe deposit box. Amulets, crucifixes, small nuggets of gold and figurines of small men fighting like giants.

Ted Fichter remembered a time when Leon's world had been in pieces. He had been unable to walk more than three hundred metres. He had stomped along. Made no complaint, just stomped. He would hobble along for a while, then have to rest. He roared in fury, never in pain. Ted began to feel uneasy. He pulled the blanket up to his nose, sniffed, cleared his throat, only his eyes visible above the embroidery. Linda glanced up warily from the racing column, studied Ted, sighed and tried again. 'The fifth race is fixed,' she said and could hear that it didn't sound right. 'What's the matter now?' did not help any. 'Ted, dear, why don't you think about the horses? About the races? About the excitement in front of the grandstand when a good jockey finds an opening and you don't know whether we're going to win or lose. The crucial difference recorded by a photo-finish. You've bet too much and you can feel your throat tightening. The jockey yelling at the horse. Do I really have to tell you again that everything in this life has its price?' said Linda Olsen. 'That's just how things are.'

Here we go again, thought Ted. The same old story. All the things we've gone over before. I hear it everywhere I go. On the radio. On the television. I read it in the papers. I simply feel it. I've felt it for months. The new aristocracy which is to rule our everyday life. 'Just like before,' he said. 'They mean to rule the day-to-day existence which I prefer to observe through the pattern in this rug.' At the stock exchange they're out to rule the everyday life which the television news department refers to as the real world, he thought. It's more or less the same aristocracy as ruled everyday life in Albania. The life which Linda regulates with Bols gin, cigarettes, bacon and sausages. Bank manager Ted Fichter thought about the youngsters who knocked about the nut-brown conference room, and the fact that his only wish was for everything to be as it used to be. Long ago. When everything was a lot worse. What a right old mess.

'It's not that long ago,' he said with a shudder. Back then I could still get my arms round Linda, he recalled. 'What's happened?' he asked out loud. 'Nothing has happened. Linda has merely discovered that the fifth race is fixed. That pretty much everything is fixed. Everything is set up by doctors, vicars, prelates, not to mention the political priesthood. They're the

According to Sofia

worst,' he concluded. 'They don't just decide what I ought to feel and think, but also what I ought to know. And then, as if that wasn't enough, they tell me the price to be paid for it. I've never had a price on my life,' he whispered into the pillow.

'Well, you should think yourself lucky,' said Linda Olsen, putting another cross on the coupon.

'Can you hear what I'm thinking?' Ted Fichter asked.

'Of course I hear what you say. Every word. You're feeling uneasy. You were uneasy when you got here. Don't you see? You began to feel uneasy in the conference room. When the meeting was over, I mean.'

From this Ted Fichter understood that he had actually been yelling that there is no price on life. You work all your days, and all it comes down to is keeping death at bay. He could tell from Linda's face that he was yelling.

'Why don't you pull yourself together,' she said. 'The fifth race,' she repeated.

'Is fixed,' said Ted Fichter. Nearly every race is fixed,' he whispered into the pillow. But not all. There are a few races that aren't fixed. I can't help thinking about Leon. He doesn't cheat. I wonder why not?

He regarded Linda, who raised her eyes from the racing column again. She set the betting slip down on the table in front of her, moved the vase of flowers, slid the silver box across the tablecloth, regarded him and said: 'Don't you ever learn? I've been telling you the same thing for I don't know how many years. Don't spill ash on the tablecloth. Your son bought this in Japan. It was a Christmas present to me five years ago. I'm very fond of this cloth. I don't care if it's ash from your most expensive cigars. I hate filthy manners. Can't you get that into your head? I know most people have their doubts about me because I used to be a whore. For two years. That's all. But I really do hate filthy manners. Flimflammers!' she cried suddenly. 'It makes me ill. Ted, you have to help Leon,' came as an order. 'He doesn't cheat. He's a genius. He can't hobble around on crutches for the rest of his life. I've heard of a surgeon in London. He's both notorious and renowned. And he's very good, but it will be expensive. Extremely expensive.'

19

Leon sighed when Simen held forth on cheating in journalism, when he had to listen yet again to complaints about cheating among politicians and when Bird testified to Ben Johnson's cheating.

'Everything is a cheat, that fact should form the very basis of every leader I write,' Simen announced.

'It's no longer funny when Ben Johnson cheats,' Bird said. 'The coffee I drink is nothing but chicory and cheatery,' Sofia complained when she was feeling forsaken. 'It's all a bloody cheat and I act accordingly,' was the refrain from Paul Fichter. 'The stock market is just one big cheat. The whole thing. The price of shares is a cheat, all the stocks, bank bonds, industrial bonds, even the capital certificates are a cheat,' he said.

Paul Fichter did not cheat when he was playing with and adjusting electronic gadgets.

Linda Olsen had been known to cheat with her exotic orgasms. 'For form's sake,' she explained to Sofia. Not always, you know, but it had been known. 'How can she have an orgasm when she's eating popcorn?' was a problem for Ted. 'I have been known to be aroused by it,' he marvelled. 'It's taken me time to learn how to spot the difference. But more often than not it's the real thing,' he admitted to Leon. 'Then I feel like a perfectly normal man. She'll survive. I don't know how it came to this. I assume it takes time and energy to become a survivor. There's an explanation, obviously, but I wouldn't be able to understand it. Not yet. I tell myself that in some sort of way I'll grow from this and sometimes I forget that I'm a worn-down bank manager. It's a little triumph. A real triumph,' he corrected himself. 'Linda is truly splendid,' marvelled Ted Fichter and knew that he was right in this. It was actually hardest on Leon. He did not cheat. 'It's an awful nuisance with all those orgasms. Not that it's ever bothered me. Never,' he told Ted. 'But why does everybody get in such a sweat about it?' For Leon it was simple. He had to watch his fingers. They were every bit as sensitive as advanced electronic equipment. When he was welding stolen cars in Olsen's workshop he wore gloves, but in the chilly garage, with the constant draughts: 'Shut the door,' he would yell, and despite the warm overalls, woollen sweaters, green, thick and lovingly cared for by Linda, from the hips down his joints stiffened up. 'Lie still and let me do the work,' Linda would say, sitting on top of him. He lay quietly in bed and traced the pattern of the Japanese lampshade on the ceiling.

'I'll be as careful as I can,' she went on and was so gentle that Leon forgot the aches and pains in his back and hips.

'I don't know how he manages it,' Paul Fichter confessed to his father. 'That guy has it all. He can turn his hand to just about anything. Even mathematics. And he can give me step-by-step instructions over the phone on how to fix a carburettor.'

Most people said Leon had it too easy: reported to be a genius, difficult and admired, and yet he dropped out of his studies at the Conservatory.

Six months before his finals he realised that it would be best for him to leave the workshop and his bedsit on the first floor. Olsen was tight-lipped and morose when he returned to the garage with the cars. His trips to Jutland were lasting longer and longer. Receipts disappeared. The accountants complained when Olsen showed up with coffee-stained scraps of paper in a

According to Sofia

shoebox. The profits dwindled. Olsen was taking more and more risks. He did not sleep at night. When he thought he was alone he spoke Polish. The bundles of banknotes were no longer so impressive. Letters from the bank arrived every day. The stolen cars had to go by a roundabout way: first by ferry to Poland, then transported to Sweden by a young haulier who smelled of perfume, malt whisky, peppermint and Estonian mud baths. The cars which Leon welded together were no longer small vehicles that changed owner fast, but expensive Mercedes' and BMWs. They stuck out like a sore thumb in the little backyard workshop.

'Go,' Linda said. 'Today. Or he'll drag you down with him.'

Leon packed his bags. He was gone within two hours. 'He got everything he owned into two suitcases,' Linda murmured, remembering how he had waved from the back seat of the taxi.

Leon had gradually come to understand that he should not worry about Olsen, Bird, Sofia, Simen, Linda, Paul or Ted Fichter. He had to think of himself. He had to find a quiet flat where he could sit for weeks at a newly tuned piano.

He got the taxi to stop and called Ted from a phone box. The latter responded quickly, efficiently and generously. Leon was installed in a soundproofed flat in the centre of town with a view of the hills, hazy in the morning mist, bluish-grey, weighty and Norwegian. Leon was going to write music. 'Preferably something Norwegian,' said Uncle Ted. When Leon sat down at the solid oak table to have breakfast he lived among and looked out upon wealth, old money, solid stock holdings, elderly men who discreetly looked the other way when the dog was peeing on the council trees. It was here, in this tenement flat that Leon was to begin upon his opus. Was it really an opus, though? He was not sure. It was not often that he felt so unsure for so long, but he was not sure. 'I think it's a perfectly ordinary fad,' he told Bird, who usually popped into the flat for a shower after his run. 'I was afraid of being found out. I was afraid of being sent to prison.' Olsen had paid him generously out of the bundles of notes and

Leon had taken the surplus to Ted Fichter. 'Buy shares. The sort of iffy shares that you buy yourself.' Bird realised that he would do well to stay out of the way. He took to running different routes and did not speak to Leon for almost four months. 'He went off,' he told Simen and Sofia. 'I don't know what he's up to.'

No explanation was ever forthcoming. Leon never mentioned it. An unsolved case. A stupid venture, time-consuming, was the only reason Leon gave. To Sofia, of course. Only to her. She sat quite still and listened to what Leon told her, never gave it away, not a word to Simen or to Bird. 'A four-month nightmare. A daft attempt to write music for a symphony orchestra.' He left it at that. Sofia did not ask. But later, whenever he was tired, he would go to her, take her hand and place it on his right cheek. He wasn't interested in cheating. He made no attempt to hide it. It was so intimate a gesture that Bird felt his fingers tingling, felt himself gasping for breath.

20

For Leon, who only slept five hours a night, they were four restful months. He had the flat to himself, he never went out, ate at the kitchen table; his shopping was brought to the door by a grocer who thought he was sick. He lived on canned food, sardines and liver paté, crispbread and cheese.

His neighbours were so refined that they tiptoed to the lift, he never saw them, never heard them and sometimes he wondered whether they even existed. In the warm hush which stood guard over stocks and shares and old money the stairs were washed by Pakistanis from an agency, but the caretaker was freckled and discreet.

When Leon whispered that he was not at home to callers, not to anyone at all, the caretaker understood that he did not really exist. He left him in peace.

The flat had been renovated for a Norwegian violinist: young, gifted, he was forging ahead in his career with the British Symphony something or other. Leon surveyed the seven photographs on the mantelpiece, soft-focus pictures of a man in tight trousers with an effusive smile, narrow shoulders, pullover and tie. In five of the pictures he was posing with men in full evening dress, trousers a little too tight, Englishmen with little or no chin, a clear sign of breeding and the fact that they were enjoying being in their thirties.

Leon took a deep breath when he saw pictures of what he knew were referred to as fun people. He could tell at a glance that they lived in stone-walled country houses with rather too many stiff tulips in the flower beds, ivy-covered walls and old Rovers in the gravel drives. Brass, Leon thought. 'A raucous roar from the brass,' he said to himself at the breakfast table. 'I will address my complex relationship with the tuba.' He munched crispbread and scribbled down ten descending intervals which were picked up by five tubas groaning with delight. He imagined how it would sound from the bridge in Vigelandsparken. A right royal howl from the Norwegian mountains that would make Japanese tourists drop their cameras on the stone steps. It was this howl that occupied his mind. This indignant sigh from the heartland. The stream of fresh accusations from Northern Norway. A deep moan from the oil state of Norway. Runaway tubas to blow in a new millennium. The image of the Oslo Stock Exchange. Politicians in the make-up chair before going into the television studio. The king's face, wise and rueful. Leon thought of the buzz of complaints from Norwegian fishermen, farmers, brokers, doctors, politicians, bishops and prelates. He got a little too carried away by it. He admitted it. A little too caught up in the process of getting it down on manuscript paper or napkins: squealing brass, chromatic, unbearably slow and hazy as the hills in the distance and yet immediate, rhythmic and rock-solid.

'This is the stupidest thing you've ever done,' he admitted as he opened a can for dinner.

He poured the contents into a pan. Coley fishcakes in brown gravy, that was his favourite. He took a glass of water from the tap, tasted it as if it were wine, talked to himself and drew up a plan of campaign for the evening. The hours at the piano when he scribbled down possible passages in the tuba register. He had no intention of keeping a single tuba reined back behind the man pounding on the kettledrum. He meant to give them their head, in a sort of madcap gallop, a salute to the mountains, moors, meadows and frolics in the summer pastures. 'This is silly,' he cautioned himself during the four months he spent in the flat. But it was fun. He could not remember when he had last had so much fun. A bit of nonsense, he thought in bed when he could not sleep, with no obligations. He could have called Ted for some sleeping pills, but he did not dare. No beer. No vodka. And no sleeping pills. The police might suddenly come hammering on the door. He did not ask himself why they should do this. He did not really know what he was afraid of. He had not actually done anything wrong. Olsen was safely behind bars. His shares were in the care of Ted Fichter.

'Insight,' Ted explained. 'Insight and a firm grip on the guys at the stock exchange. And experience helps. Because the money's there. In the bin. In that big Norwegian bin that's managed by my lads.'

Leon had made money. 'Nigh on a million,' he whispered into the darkness. He knew that the money had been laundered, rendered anonymous, then invisible, resurrected and recorded, but still anonymous. All but gone. Little figures in a column. A small, intricate detail. He was a tiny entry in the Fichter accounts. He had been young Fichter's silent rescuer. His degree in mathematics had been stage-managed by Leon. Such things were not forgotten. He sat in bed, propped up by pillows. It was raining, rain that turned to ice when it hit the ground. His back and hips ached. He hissed in fury. He always hissed in fury when his back ached. And he fancied he could hear the deep drone of the tubas among the sculptures in Vigelandsparken, and he thought to himself that worse collections of sculptures, so much sublime rubbish, so much superficial crap, were to be found elsewhere under the sun. And yet he thought he could hear the tubas among the joggers puffing through the park and he pressed his hands against his hips, lifted his face, looked up at the white ceiling, at the little stucco cherubs. Playing with themselves and minding their own business.

'It'll pass,' he said. 'Scream if you like. No one will hear you. The joiners have done an excellent job. The place is totally sound-proofed. Not a single note can escape from this dungeon.'

Often he would be at the piano at four in the morning. Banging away. 'You feel sorry for yourself because your back is not pain-free. It's against the law. According to Sofia it was against the law. According to you it's against the law.' He knew it sounded hollow, stupid and self-centred. But he also knew that it would pass.

It passed. Suddenly, one morning at the breakfast table, he saw the hills in the distance quite plainly. The sky was ice-blue, the weather was dry and cold, the air clear. He could just make out the mountains marching away behind the hills, but they were of no interest to him, his back did not hurt, his hips felt new and supple and he tucked the tub of painkillers away at the back of the cabinet. He had not taken a single pill. Not because he was afraid of becoming hooked on them. But he had to have a totally clear head, in case anything should happen. He wasn't quite sure what. As far as he could tell the only thing he had done wrong was to get paid cash-in-hand. But it was the thought of being exposed. 'As what?' he whispered. To save answering this he called Sofia. It was six in the morning and she was in the kitchen drinking coffee as usual. He listened to that deep voice, a little husky from the night, a little too flat for her to be having a good day.

'Simen's not here. I'm alone. It hurts to be alone today. I wish you were here.'

During his four months in the flat Sofia was the only person he called, he confided three months later. He said he was writing for tubas. 'Tubas?' Sofia repeated. Is it particularly wise to be writing for tubas? If you were ripping off Benjamin Britten I couldn't be more surprised. Then again, who knows? It's a bit sudden, that's all. You know?'

Leon heard her cross the floor, pour coffee into her cup. She

According to Sofia

cleared her throat emphatically and often, a little too often, and declared that she had no intention of giving up anything whatsoever. She was going to carry on smoking as before. And anyway, she had to be at the hospital in three hours' time. 'Just a routine operation. Gall bladder. I dread each new day. That's the worst part.'

The encouraging smiles in the corridors to patients who would soon be ashes. The nurses wheeling the newly operated into the lift. Arrogant doctors. Gifted surgeons. 'They get better and better. I've taken to dreading things. Almost everything and almost all the time,' she added and laughed that laugh which prompted Leon to remember every line of her face. He remembered her hair and, most of all, her eyes. He spoke to her for an hour. Afterwards he sat down at the piano and for the first time considered leaving the flat. He thought of Sofia. Not often, but he thought about her when he was eating. He thought of her more often than he liked to admit. He thought of her when he was mashing his potatoes into the gravy from the fishcakes. He thought of her when he stood at the window, gazing at the hills. Why do I talk to her like a sister? The way I confide in her, anyone would think we lived in the same house. She's the only person in whom I confide. Why can't I think of her as anything but a sister? He smiled at the fishcakes, glanced out of the window to check that the weather was still cold and dry. Because then he would sleep at night. Six hours maybe. If he worked through the afternoon and evening he might start to nod off by the fire and it would be warm and cosy under the duvet. He was looking forward to it. After dinner he crossed the room to the piano; hunched over the keys, with his coffee cup in his left hand, he picked out a simple scale with his right: slowly, without getting excited, and he detected the potential for supple improvisations on the piano. He raised his hand to his mouth. At such moments he wondered why he had walled himself up within this carpeted luxury.

'What is it that's happened and why?' he asked, looking at the phone. Sometimes he thought of Stravinsky. Of the blaring horns. Protesting brass. 'Why do I have the feeling that the police are suddenly going to come hammering on the door?' He had accepted invisible money from invisible bundles of notes which had been rendered anonymous by an expert with a bank at his disposal. It was very silly to wall himself up inside this sound-proofed flat. It was unnecessary. Playing at being the artist, intriguing in his isolation. The solitary composer. 'A smart move on the part of dead-beat artists,' he said. Leon played his best on a stage in a smoke-filled restaurant. He always had done. He missed having an audience.

And gradually, as he sat in front of the glowing fire, pain-free at last, almost cheerful, it dawned on him that he was living in the flat to save having to speak. There was no one there to speak to. No one spoke. He did not need to answer. He heard no words. He did not have to utter words. There was no need to make any sounds except the ones he scribbled down on the manuscript paper. When he woke in the morning, he shuffled across a floor strewn with white sheets of paper covered in notes. There was not a single opinion to be found on any of those white sheets of paper, no confidences, no doubts, no regrets. The sheet music formed a path from the kitchen door to the fireplace and was very, very quiet. He wanted to get back to a wordless life. As a boy in Colomb Bechar he had not spoken. For five months he had refused to speak. At school in the whitewashed stone building on the outskirts of the shanty town, the Spanish teacher had allowed him to sit undisturbed at the desk closest to his own. Leon remembered those five months for the smell of ink, dust and dates. The teacher, a reed-thin Spaniard who played the flute, did not fuss, did not ask questions, did not tell on him, just waited until it passed. In the afternoon they would sit wordlessly on the bench outside the school while the teacher played sentimental songs from La Mancha. It was then that his mother, the missionary's virtuous woman, placed a hand on the boy's head,

According to Sofia

smiled, narrowed her eyes, poured a drop of brandy into a fluted milk glass and announced: 'To hell with it. You'll only hurt yourself with this. That's the worst that can happen.'

And when at last he got round to remembering that, the smell of the brandy that his mother drank only very occasionally, when she was sick or afraid, he got up from the chair in the luxurious flat, poured himself a vodka and a beer and stretched his hands out to the warm fire. At last he knew what he really wanted to do. It had taken time. And he realised that he would have to stay on in the flat for some weeks yet. But if he was patient, waited a few weeks and did not speak, he would hear the silence. He splayed his fingers, could still discern the marks of grazes inflicted by the expensive tools at Olsen's Autos.

'I could have ruined my fingers,' he said. 'I could have ruined more than my fingers. Actually I don't quite know what might have happened, but it was a near thing.'

21

Simen tried not to get annoyed when the new telephone receptionist answered the phone. She did not recognise his voice and Simen could hear the rustle of a pack of biscuits. 'This is the editor-in-chief. I'm still visiting at the hospital and I'd like to speak to Inger. She's my secretary,' was answered with a cool: 'How was I supposed to know that?'

Simen was standing in the hospital corridor. Bird was asleep. 'No, how were you supposed to know that?' he said to the young woman. 'I'm sure you're young, single, live alone in a bedsit and are actually having a pretty good time of it.'

This last was uttered after he had studiously switched off his mobile phone.

Simen was actually quite happy, but he missed the heat. He missed the summer. He did not miss Sofia, Bird, Leon. He stopped there. Was there anyone else? Did he have anyone else in his life besides Sofia, Bird, Leon? He was so taken aback that he stopped at the hospital newsstand, bought a copy of *Time*, sat down at a white plastic table, opened the magazine and read that Chelsea Clinton was on her way to the film studios in Hollywood. She was all set to become a new goddess of the camera lens. Nice layout, he thought to himself. Good piece of work. I wouldn't mind a week on Crete. On my own. With no computer.

According to Sofia

No mobile. I wouldn't mind a week on a beach under a Minoan sun that would light up that spot in the brain where depression is stored. It's the sun I miss. He sneaked a glance at the people at the next table. No one was looking at him as if he was a senile man, talking to himself. So he must just have thought it, not said it out loud. Chelsea Clinton believed that American hackers had more power than the members of the Senate. They could alter any announcement, all reports, opinions, break into newspaper editorial desks, government offices or the UN, and know everything there was to know about the pope's menu and his prostate. He had the impression that these hackers could black out the moon. Simen put the copy of *Time* down on the table. Bird, the only person in the newspaper office who liked computers, had gone back to the lions. He was out on the synthetic savannah, wrestling with his own concerns. Two tranquilising injections and back he went to ants, silence and lions on a yellow knoll. 'Today you've had enough,' Simen muttered to himself. 'Sofia has beaten up a waiter in Vitoria. Leon is in North Africa. He thinks he hates Beni-Saf. He has put on his best suit, complete with handkerchief in the breast pocket, tie and tie-pin. Leon also thinks that I'm sitting at the computer as usual, polishing tomorrow's leader. Fortunately, the newspaper's leader doesn't have to deal with the really serious issues. I just have to voice an opinion on something. Not much of one. Just a little one every day. Simen,' he ventured. 'You're a notorious editor-in-chief, but your teeth have been drawn.'

He noticed the shoulder of the man at the next table twitching. Message received and understood: Simen pushed back his chair, stood up, wove his way between the tables, turned back, picked up the copy of *Time* from the table and found his way to the exit.

He was conscious of the eyes on his back.

He walked slowly. A little too slowly. 'Keep your head now.' He reached the car, unlocked the door and got in, breathed and felt as if he was almost home. He could have said: 'What's happening?' But he knew what was happening. Twenty years of hard slogging, *that's* what was happening. Twenty years without a proper holiday. For thirty years his ambitions had just kept piling up. He started the car and reversed, got his driving glasses out of the glove compartment. 'Easy now,' he cautioned. 'It's happened before. Everything has happened before.'

At the lights he noticed the box of chocolates. He had forgotten to leave them on Bird's bedside table, and he tore off the cellophane while he waited for the lights to turn to red again. 'I've eaten four bananas today,' he muttered. 'Now here I am, stuffing myself with chocolates.' He sniffed exhaust fumes, switched off the soundless fan, more chocolates. He nudged his driving glasses further up his nose, the window steamed up, the traffic remained stationary as an ambulance raced past, siren blaring and lights flashing. He clenched his back teeth against the shrill wail. While he waited he punched in a code on his mobile phone and received an OK in reply. He had now switched on all the heaters at the cottage. He had to sit through two green lights before getting through the junction. There she was. That new female reporter on the newsdesk. She was young, ambitious and attractive. No more than that, he thought. She played handball and talked to Bird about sprinters.

He swung out, pulled into the lane leading out of town, into the sticks, to still mountain lakes, hushed pine-barrens and what had, for years, simply been referred to as 'the cottage'. The family cottage. Straitjacket. Temple. Mausoleum. Where Simen pottered about.

'It's pure relaxation for Simen, pottering about up there. Doing odd jobs,' Sofia would say when they went off to the cottage. Simen knew it was true. He bought tools. He looked through all the catalogues. He still got a kick out of buying new rechargeable drills, nails, roofing felt and doors. He liked the staff in the shop. He liked the smell of the place. He could chat about the fireplace he was going to build next month or next year. He could scoff at the latest nail gun. The latest glue gun. He had to pull into the side again. He looked down at his thighs on the seat.

According to Sofia

'God, they've grown so thin.' He waited, drove ten metres, waited. Iversen, the old editor, would be taking care of the leaders. Simen had a break from writing for three days. For three days he would not have to voice an opinion about anything. Inger dealt with all the day-to-day problems. She only called him if she really had to. He checked the time, breathed, more chocolates. He closed the box, eventually located the button for rolling down the window and closed up on a semi-trailer with a mud-spattered number plate. Patsy Cline's quiet conviction that, sad to say, one can fall in love with anyone at all, drifted out to him from the trailer-truck's loudspeakers. According to Sofia this observation was quite correct. Simen did not disagree. He rolled up the window, nodded, and the love fell silent. He drove slowly for another fifty metres, stopped: diggers, ditches, deep pits, men in orange work clothes, diversion signs. He rolled down the window again and asked where to, and again – from the trailer-truck – he heard that Patsy Cline was still convinced, but that lovin' was often in vain. He did not disagree with that either. Pine-barrens, he thought. Pine-barrens where nothing has stirred for fifty years. Or better still, seventy years. Dappled sunlight on light-brown between the tree trunks; paths running towards the mountains; inky tarns, their banks fringed with a film of ice, the smell of snow and sheep, still out this early in the winter.

He opened the chocolate box. Ate another chocolate and tossed the Kong Haakon box on to the back seat. The automatic gearbox gave a pleasant little kick and the trailer-truck was left far behind him. Patsy Cline went on lovin', alone; she was tired of being alone.

Simen was not sure. He was not sure what he was tired of. There were several possibilities, he admitted it. Most people were worn out these days. 'We slog away at unnecessary tasks,' he admonished. Therese Somoza had her ambitions to contend with. Bird was trying to run himself to death. Leon, whom everyone was worrying about, was safe with people he knew. The problem seemed to be that he knew them too well. Simen breathed. He drove fast. And for the first time in ages he was conscious of feeling tired – no, sleepy, he decided. He'd have to stop at the shop for bread, margarine, steak and Clausthaler.

The usual old guard of stolid worthies were hanging about under the pent roof, looking out at the sleet. They were smoking dog-ends. He had always wondered where they got all the dog-ends. He said hello, went inside, grabbed a trolley and wandered up and down the aisles, past coffee, tea, sugar and light bulbs; he had forgotten to remove his driving glasses, he stuffed them into his pocket. Was he feeling calmer. A little calmer? Or was it his imagination? The chocolates were coming back on him, and yet he was hungry. He bought a steak. An enormous steak. Then several runs up and down the shelves: coffee, bread, margarine. He had remembered the lot. He nodded to the woman at the check-out, paid by card, popped the things into three carrier bags and hurried out to the car. What's your hurry? He was feeling calmer. Out on to the main road. He noticed that the automatic gearbox seemed to be kicking down more often than usual; two cars flashed their lights, but when the third car, not one he recognised, flashed twice, he realised that the police were sitting in the lay-by on the straight stretch. They always sat at that same straight stretch, brandishing their radar gun.

'You're here to potter about and do odd-jobs,' he essayed. 'You're going to eat, sleep and potter about.' He spotted the policeman with his camera in the lay-by, and he took it nice and easy, cautiously even, for the next few kilometres. Slivers of ice floated on the puddles on the road through the forest to the lake; long, dark shadows from the pinewood and shreds of mist drifted over the lake. Who was Antonio Nerida? Was he rich, eccentric, mad, or merely a lawyer? What was he really up to? Therese Somoza was Sofia's daughter. Bird read about her in the newspaper. He read about her in *El País*. Sitting at the computer at home he had visited her website and read an article by her. About McCoy Turner. Bird hardly ever mentioned it. Sofia never spoke about her. The lake was like glass. He could make out the cottage

According to Sofia

on the other side; it was actually a reddish-brown cabin, cobbled together over three generations. Grandad. Dad. The first had done as much work as possible with as few materials as possible. Simen's father had left it to the professionals to build an extension and put in electricity. Simen did not really care one way or the other, he simply pottered about, did odd jobs. He used as many materials as possible and left it to the tools to do the work. And the result? He shuddered. A house crammed with conflict. He locked the car, put on his warm boots, loaded the three carrier bags, his rucksack and briefcase into the rowboat. The fringe of ice crackled as he undid the rope and pushed off with the oar. There was not a breath of wind. Not a sound. Not a soul around. He sat down and slowly rowed across the lake. The mountains. He scanned the horizon. How often, he wondered, had he watched the darkness come stealing over the mountains? Actually, though, what he liked best of all was the sight of the bluish-white winter light gradually having to give way to the darkness that engulfed the landscape. At such times he would stand on the back steps in woolly hat and sweater and wait for it to become totally dark. It got so dark that the sounds changed. They seemed to go down an octave, the ice on the water began to grumble – the still trees, not a murmur from them, and the rustlings of creatures he never saw.

He rowed the last few metres to the shore through thin floes of ice. It was always a couple of degrees colder out on the point and he poled the boat in, lifted the oars over on to the jetty, made the rope fast to the post with two half-hitches, hoiked up the carrier bags and rucksack and stepped ashore dryshod. Nothing had changed. Everything was just as it always was. Constant. There were patches of ice on the path; he stepped carefully around the puddles, across the bridge over the stream, which he had built himself when it was still summer, and: stain, he thought.

'I'll need to give the bridge a coat of stain,' he said, so loudly that he glanced round about. No one to be seen. The beaver was asleep in its heap of twigs down on the point. Not a single ripple of fish on the lake. He stamped his feet on the steps. Went in. The cottage was bright, warm, and just as he had left it. He got the fire going before emptying the carrier bags; there was a note on the table, a memo in his own hand, reminding him of the need to check the main fuses. He opened the cabinet, made sure that everything was as it should be. Closed it again. Opened the fridge and put the Clausthaler and the steak on the bottom shelf. He beheld the idyllic sight. The rag rugs. Three rugs: white, blue and pink. Sofia's contribution. Her only one. The warm light. That cottage smell. The darkness gradually creeping across the lake. He poured just the right amount of water into the coffee machine. Opened the bread bin. He removed his hat. He took it all in. Took in the cosy living-room. Again and again. The fire crackled. The living-room was reddish-brown and quiet. So quiet. Nothing happened. Simen thought: What am I doing here?

22

Ted pushed himself up off the sofa with his elbows and cleared his throat so loudly that Linda woke up in her chair.

'You're so restless,' Linda said. 'It's not a big problem. But you're too restless. I don't know how you do it, but you manage to wake me when I'm in the middle of a dream. I miss Leon. I was with him when you started clearing your throat.'

Ted Fichter pointed to his ears, indicating that he could not hear.

'I know,' Linda said. 'D'you think I'm senile or something? No, of course you don't. You know I'm smarter than you are. Not many people know that. I can take it,' she said. 'I'm the type that can take it. It's water off a duck's back to me.' She was, however, not certain exactly how much she really could take. Ted fell asleep. He slept virtuously, with his hands on top of the travelling rug.

'I don't know why I am so fond of you. Maybe it's because you shower every day and don't smell of diesel.'

She waited until he was asleep before going through to the kitchen. She stood at the kitchen bench, gazing into the mirror. She looked as she had done for the past five years, and she actually liked what she saw. She had a placid face, pink cheeks, she was blonde and she ate too much. The only thing she could not control was her craving for meat. When she woke in the morning she thought of the butcher on the corner. Her thoughts would go to the carcases in the slaughterhouse with their rank, sharp odour, and she remembered the sounds from the abattoir when they dragged the cattle for butchering into the slaughter hall. When she got to the shop the butcher chatted in high-pitched tones about fillet and loin, minced beef and stewing steak.

In the forenoon, three hours after listening to the news on the radio, she fried the beef in a Teflon pan. The radio sat on top of the bread bin and she did not switch it off until she went to bed at night. She browned flour for sauces, boiled oxtails for stock and chopped exotic herbs from the pots on the kitchen bench. She could spend the entire afternoon in the kitchen making a plain, ordinary beef stew. She preferred to eat alone, with no one to see.

She did not know why Ted was always so worried. When he fretted about falling ill she would take herself off to the kitchen to stop from smiling. She could not think of a single reason for worrying about anything at all. And yet she felt uneasy. She wanted for nothing, but still she was uneasy. She decided that that would have to do for today. She sighed heavily and shut the bread bin. That would have to do.

Regret brought Linda out in a rash. It looked rather like German measles and she had long since stopped going to the doctor. Sometimes, when she felt regretful she went to church. Always alone. Always in the forenoon when the churches were empty and the vicars in their offices. She would sit in one of the pews up beside the pulpit with her hands folded. She did not think of anything. This was the only place where she did not think of anything. And in the winter when it was cold outside, and if the church was warm, she could sit for ages just watching the way the light filtered through the stained-glass windows.

It was here, seventeen years earlier, that she had heard the brisk clump-clump of Leon's crutches. He had come to adjust the

According to Sofia

organ pipes and when she stood up he was taken by surprise, eased himself down on to the toolbox under St Luke the Evangelist, turned and smiled.

'That's right,' Linda said. 'It's me, the one that works nights at Lolly's. I've seen you playing the piano.'

Leon made no reply.

'I just sit here,' said Linda.

He made no reply, hobbled up the steps, two sharp taps with the crutches, then he picked up the grey rucksack containing his tools, made off round the side of the sacristy, towards the back stairs leading up to the organ.

'I heard the sound of his footsteps and the clump-clump of the crutches and felt hungry. I don't think I've ever been so hungry. I had a notion for cabbage, or plain, ordinary cauliflower, and I don't even like cauliflower.'

She told Ted about this. 'I felt hungry in a different way, if you know what I mean,' she went on. 'I thought of a Swedish herring buffet. I thought of beef broth. I even thought of spinach. I sometimes wonder if this was when I started to put on weight. I've been thinking about food ever since. I'd rather not think about the mountain of meat I've eaten since I met him. And while he was up there among the organ pipes he played "The church is an old house". I sat quite still in an ordinary Protestant church and listened to a hymn. I couldn't understand it, and I don't think I'll ever understand it, but I noticed the difference. There's no point in asking me what difference, but he made absolutely everything seem different. For the first time I realised that things could be otherwise. I've never forgotten it, because at that moment new possibilities presented themselves to me. In tuning the organ pipes he washed the hymn clean and I sat there motionless, listening. It was as if I had been waiting for this to happen, but never believed it would. Nothing would ever be the same again, but nothing would change either. It was the first time I really heard what music can be. It was a little bit special, but on the whole it was perfectly normal. Suddenly the church was an old house and I knew why I had gone there on that particular morning.'

She sat there for two hours while Leon knelt on the floor, adjusting the organ pipes, and she heard the way he swore, loudly and profusely when he couldn't get the reed knife to go in. Leon was so small that he could crawl under the largest pipes, she could hear him tapping them with a small rubber-headed hammer and the echo rang in her ears as the sound reverberated around the church cupolas. She never forgot that sound. 'I can't get over it, Ted. It's odd, but the one forenoon I cannot get over is that forenoon when Leon tuned the organ pipes. He lay under the organ the way he used to lie under the stolen cars and he could adjust a carburettor as precisely as he tuned an off-key organ pipe. I was flabbergasted. A little frightened. I sat absolutely still and waited. The fact was that I couldn't help but wait. And it's been the same ever since.'

Once Leon was finished in the organ loft, Linda was sure that he would speak to her. 'Where shall we eat?' he said. He spoke so gently to her that she arched her back.

As always, at the table in the restaurant she placed thumb and finger on the cloth, swivelled her hand and waggled her little finger, and Leon looked up from the menu and said: 'Do you always do that?' He ordered a sparkling mineral water.

'Are you an organ tuner?' she asked.

He did not try to hide his crutches, but laid them neatly under his chair. Linda noticed the care with which he handled the crutches, the way he made sure that they did not topple on to the floor.

'Do you take so much care with everything?' she said and immediately regretted her words.

She blushed.

'I have perfect pitch,' Leon said.

According to Sofia

'What's that when it's at home?'

'I recognise notes,' Leon said. 'I can tell exactly which note is being played on an instrument. I can tell right away. It's a bit like being able to pick out individual letters in a book. I can identify a note when I hear it.'

'Is that a good thing?' Linda asked.

Leon placed his gloves on the table. 'For an organ tuner it is.'

'Can you make a living from it?'

'No,' said Leon.

'Is that your job?'

'One of many,' he replied.

The waiter slapped his pad against his palm impatiently. 'I'll take number four and coffee,' Leon whispered. He got up and walked to the toilet without the aid of crutches. He did not look back.

'Did he speak?' the waiter asked.

Linda looked at him.

'Did he speak?' the waiter repeated.

'Of course he spoke.'

'How did you manage it?'

Linda eyed the waiter. 'What's the matter?' she said. 'Do you want us to move tables?'

'No, why would you do that?' the waiter said.

He smelled of hair oil, onions and toothpaste. In the light from the window he looked quite dashing with his brilliantined hair, thick pencil moustache and a smile which gradually spread to his eyes. On evenings when the light in the restaurant was dim and the diners drunk he knew he looked like Jack Nicholson.

Linda shifted in her seat. 'I wish you'd stop that. It's a real pain to have you standing behind my chair, peering down at my breasts.'

'Why?'

'It's distasteful.'

'Really?' he said. He smiled, as if suddenly remembering a time when she had not minded it at all. He also did his best to conceal the fact that there were other women in the restaurant waiting for him.

'Yes,' she said. 'I don't like it.'

'You don't like it?'

'No,' she said.

'Are you unwell?' the waiter asked. He bowed to a guest who was pointing to a table by the pillar which had not been cleared. Anyone would have thought it was the guest who had made a mistake, and Linda wondered how the waiter did that.

'I'm fit as a fiddle,' she smiled.

'Have you met someone?'

'I might have,' she said.

'Yesterday?'

'No, today. This morning. I'm not telling you where, you wouldn't believe me anyway.'

'Does he have money?'

Slowly, Linda turned to look at him: 'Is that the only reason you can think of? Can't you ever come up with anything better?'

'I'll think about it,' the waiter said with a smile. 'I'll think about it today, tomorrow and for the rest of the week. I'll try to come up with a better reason. If I come to some other conclusion I'll let you know.'

'Do that,' she replied.

The waiter clapped his hands and a busboy walked over to the table where the guest was still standing by his chair. The young boy was ordered to take away the dirty cutlery, but the waiter did not take his eyes off Linda: 'Am I distasteful,' he asked in an undertone. 'Am I really so distasteful that you forget all the benefits of knowing me?' His eyes were on Linda, but still he managed to keep track of everyone who came and went. 'You eat here more or less for free. I see to that. On the quiet,' he added. 'And yet I'm distasteful?'

Linda sat quite still with her hands on the table. She gave him a long look, caught the scent of male cologne. 'That's right,' she said.

According to Sofia

'What's come over you?'

'I don't really know,' Linda said.

The waiter slipped his pad into his pocket.

'Have you left that garage owner?'

'No,' said Linda. 'Why do you ask?'

'It sounds like you have.'

'Suddenly I felt like a whore,' Linda said. 'Ever since this morning I've been feeling like a whore.'

'Really?' the waiter said. 'Never before?' he all but whispered. 'That must have been a strange discovery to make.'

'I didn't understand.'

He did not answer.

'Until today,' she said.

'You don't say.'

'Yes, I do,' she said.

'Does it hurt?'

It was all he could do to smile at her.

'Yes,' she said.

'That's a turn-up for the books,' he said.

Linda had tried to forget it, but there had been no derision in the waiter's little smile. He showed how things were, what she did, with whom, and that she could not get over it.

She told Ted about it later, when she was sure he was asleep. And she tried to tell Olsen the garage owner, but couldn't. She fumbled with knife and fork as she ate pickled herring, felt awkward and regarded him disconsolately. Olsen lowered his eyes, scraped his plate with his fork and went on reading the paper. He tried not to look at her.

Another thing she realised at that moment, sitting at the table with the waiter behind her, was that she had put in her last night at Restaurant Lolly.

'The thing is,' Linda told the waiter. 'The thing is that you never grow up. You've never got past puberty. It's still smouldering away in there. It will never pass. It's like some nameless disease. It will always bother you, and it will bother the women you meet. The women you live with would rather not know about it. But it will come out. It always comes out. The whores are actually the only ones who know that some people never get over it. That is what we learn. It takes time, but we learn. It's embarrassing. And we do our best to steer clear of men like you.'

'My heartfelt thanks,' said the waiter. He tapped his pad with his pencil peevishly and at length. 'You really are so helpful and so grateful. You have been a joy and a comfort.'

Linda looked down at the tablecloth. She looked nice in the glow of the table lamp. All at once her shoulders began to quiver and the waiter realised that she was beautiful when she laughed, and he felt self-conscious and tapped his pad again.

'It must be tough,' he said. 'It must take it out of you, attaining such great wisdom.'

'Yes,' she said. 'It is tough.'

He pretended to write on his pad. He gave away the fact that he was an old hand at waiting tables when he turned towards Leon. He knew when a guest was approaching the table and he raised his head: 'Do you know him?'

'A little,' she said.

'Does he speak?'

'Of course he speaks.'

'This is the first time I've ever heard him say a word. This is my table, you see. It's never happened before.'

'He plays the piano at Lolly's. Sometimes he's still at the piano hours after closing time. The restaurant closes its doors, but the manager allows guests to stay on at their tables. I don't know why, because nobody buys any more than another beer or two. We have a nice time, and he's the only musician the manager doesn't shout at.'

'Why not?' the waiter asked.

Linda blew through her mouth. She blew loudly and clearly and felt her laugh catch in her throat.

According to Sofia

'Is he one of your clients?' he asked. He looked at her as if he intended to repeat the word 'clients'.

'No,' said Linda.

The waiter gazed at the ceiling. He heard the sound of Leon's footsteps and propped the crutches up against the unused sidetable.

'Is he bothering you?' Leon asked, saying this so loudly that the waiter could not help but hear. Leon swept breadcrumbs off the table and turned coolly to the waiter: 'Sod off,' he hissed.

The waiter glanced down at Leon's shoulders, then at Linda, who smiled, and she did not know why, but suddenly she realised she was hungry. She pointed to the menu and eyed the waiter's back.

Leon reached up with his head and gingerly curled it forwards. He knew he was betraying the fact that he was in pain. He pointed to his hips.

'Is it?'

'A form of rheumatism. I don't feel like going into detail.'

'Is there anything you can do for it?'

He edged his chair closer to the table.

'I suppose so.'

'So why don't you do it.'

Leon did not feel like answering.

'Is it a matter of money?'

'It often is.'

'Where do you live?' Linda said.

'In a basement flat.'

It was the busboy who set Linda's herring before her. He served Leon pasta with prawns, dill and a sauce which smelled of seaweed. They ate. Slowly. They hardly looked at one another. Linda, who was slim, bordering on skinny, with blue eyelids, noted that Leon ate delicately, hesitantly, as if assessing every single piece of pasta.

'Do you live alone?' Linda asked.

'Yes,' he said.

'Do you like living alone?'

'Yes,' he said.

'What do you do?'

'I play the piano. I play night and day. My landlady's stone-deaf. That's why I live there.'

'Even when your hips hurt?' she said. She drew back in her chair after saying this.

'It's okay, I don't mind you saying,' Leon said.

He ate his pasta with a spoon. He cut it into small pieces, mixed it with the sauce and raised the spoon to his lips with long, fastidious fingers.

'You should take vitamin pills,' Linda said. She spoke so softly that she felt herself blushing. It was so unusual for her to blush that she stared in confusion at the tablecloth.

Leon lifted his face to hers. 'Should I?'

'Yes,' she said. 'To be on the safe side.'

'There's nothing wrong with me. My hips hurt, but I'm never ill.'

Linda tried not to ask.

'I'm a student,' Leon said. 'Of music.'

Linda did not know what to say.

'I make music. Sometimes it's fun, and sometimes it's no fun at all.'

'Would you like to come and stay with me?' Linda said.

Leon laid his spoon gently on his plate.

'We've got a bedsit on the first floor. A small flat,' she ventured. 'Two rooms and kitchen. With its own toilet.'

She spoke quietly to Leon, who went on eating. 'Our bedroom, Olsen's and mine, is across the landing. He goes to Jutland a lot. You could come over whenever you like when he's away.'

Leon looked at her.

'For free,' she said.

23

When Leon moved into the bedsit on the first floor above Olsen's Autos, Linda stopped working nights at Restaurant Lolly altogether.

She went to church so often to think about nothing that the vicar, a grizzled man who would never make dean, asked if she was looking for comfort. 'I might be,' said Linda.

She smiled cannily.

'But I'm not looking for the sort of comfort you vicars imagine.'

She looked up at him.

'Or have in mind.'

The church became her refuge. Suddenly she was hardly ever to be found at home in the kitchen and Olsen, who welded and produced cars in the backyard workshop, began to wonder.

'I'm following Leon,' she explained. 'I want to see what he gets up to. He always seems to know what he's going to do next. He's the only person I've met who has no doubts.'

'About himself?' Olsen said.

'I've no idea. He just gets on with things and doesn't talk about them.'

Olsen ate eggs, rollmops and toast. He wiped his mouth, looked at Linda, switched off his mobile phone and poured filter coffee into his cup. He always studied his nails when he did not feel like answering.

'I wonder what he's defending himself against?' Linda said.

Once Olsen had finished inspecting the black lines under his nails, he said: 'Defending himself?'

'Yes,' said Linda.

Olsen sprinkled salt on his egg. He did not usually have cucumber for breakfast, but he cut slices of cucumber with the cheese slicer, slid them on to a slice of bread with his knife, munched and looked at Linda.

'You're spending too much time in that church,' he said. 'You sit there gawping at those beautiful stained-glass windows. The way I see it, it's very simple. Which is not to say that it isn't difficult. But I believe that Leon has come to terms with the fact that he has to hobble around on crutches. He understands this and he doesn't try to run away from it.'

'You think he's defending himself?'

'Of course he's defending himself,' Olsen said. 'Everybody does. We all have to. If we're on crutches, at any rate.'

'What is he defending himself against?' Linda asked.

Olsen chewed steadily on his cucumber.

'Honestly, what do you think?' Linda said.

'Honesty is overrated,' said Olsen.

He ceased chewing. 'You say: what. You mean who.'

He regarded the grey rollmop on his plate. 'What you really mean is who? Isn't it?'

He scraped butter on to his toast. They ate breakfast and listened to the buzzing of flies against the kitchen window. It was so quiet that they could hear the clatter of tools on the cement floor down in the workshop. He stirred his coffee and Linda kissed him on the cheek. 'You're no fool, Olsen. Not that I ever thought you were. I'll try to get to the bottom of it.'

'So you see,' Linda said, some years later when she eventually spoke to Sofia. 'It was the most peaceful summer I can ever remember. Nothing happened.' Olsen, who refused to be a poor mechanic, had finally been given his big break and there was no holding him back. He produced cars for the Estonian market, which was corrupt, insatiable and ruled by unseen Mafia bosses. At the breakfast table he spoke on the phone to his partner in Tallinn. He was Olsen's contact, actually Swedish, but born in Karelen, a mobile man and gifted linguist who followed the money. 'For they shall inherit the earth, and right now that means the market,' Olsen said at the peaceful breakfast table. 'It'll stay that way for a few years and then other folk with other theories will inherit the earth. It's a bore. The same old story, again and again. And we can only wait for it to pass.'

He ate his rollmop with the egg, looked at the trees outside in the yard and was really quite content with that.

'It suited Olsen down to the ground,' was Linda's opinion. 'A flat done up by professionals,' she continued. 'He liked soft rugs on the floor, an old piano that gathered dust, ornaments on the window-sill and rollmops for breakfast. As long as he could keep the creditors at bay he was happy; he said they were a pain in the neck and he was glad when they weren't around. He paid for his luxuries by picking up stolen cars in Jutland, transporting them to Norway, taking them apart and welding them back together again. All that so that he could eat rollmops for breakfast,' Linda laughed. 'When the tin was empty he drank the brine,' she owned. 'He talked to his partner in Finnish, sometimes in Swedish, don't ask me where he picked that up, but he never had to search for words and he spoke fondly of the yellow plains between Tallinn and Perno and the smell of salt as he neared the sea. He spoke of the farms, once run as collectives, now more like haunted castles. Said that they were well-tended, past their sell-by date and all but invisible in the fog over the Estonian plains.'

'It's not to be borne,' he said. 'Collective farming. How stupid can you get?'

Linda explained that the wads of notes in the grey safe deposit box were laundered at the race track. But his mood was stable, his stomach was in good order and he could still drink coffee. 'That summer, Olsen drank two litres of coffee a day, didn't smoke, didn't drink, and didn't lay a finger on me. Not once. But he didn't spend his nights on the town. I didn't miss him. That surprised me. He discovered that it was possible not to be who he really was and naturally he got confused, not scared, but a bit surprised because the money kept rolling in. He bought whatever he wanted and then spread his presents out on the kitchen table and gazed at them in amazement.'

'You see?' Linda said to Sofia. 'Olsen, a harmless mechanic, born to be a mechanic. He became a garage owner and that he should never have done. That summer he bought his first pair of hand-sewn Italian shoes. He ran his rough index finger over the soft leather and smiled to himself. A tailor made blue suits for him and he swapped an old Volvo for a gold Swiss watch. He thought it would last. He thought it would never end. It lasted for almost three years. Olsen thought he had discovered an Olsen who neither smoked nor drank nor took his pick of the housewives and students who worked at Lolly's. Only when he put on his green overalls did he become the old Olsen again, the mechanic. I tried to stop him, but he laughed, shook his head and didn't touch me. It was embarrassing although I could not have said why.'

'Why it was embarrassing?' Sofia asked.

'Yes, of course.'

'I don't understand,' said Sofia.

'Be thankful for that. I mean it. Be thankful that you don't understand.'

'Tell me about Leon,' said Sofia. 'Tell me what you know about him.'

Linda told her that she had bought a bike that summer. She had not been on a bike in ten years and when she cycled along the bicycle paths through the park in short, tight trousers, men whistled after her and a few women followed her with their eyes.

According to Sofia

She followed Leon from his bedsit to the bus, saw how he swung himself up on to the platform: with a crutch on the pavement and one hand on the door he would haul himself aboard with a twist of the hips. It was quickly done and hardly anyone remarked on it. The driver made no attempt to help with the crutches and Leon sat at the back of the bus, looking out on to the park. In the bus he ate bread and cheese. Linda cycled along the gravel path through the park and caught up with the bus again at the lights. On the first day she was surprised to see Leon get off the bus and hobble across the street to the library. She ate an ice cream while she waited, and as she was chaining her bike to the rack along came Ted Fichter, whom she had only met in passing, and when he halted and cleared his throat she was aware, for the first time, of the exclusive aroma of malt.

He was tall and lean and he carried a soft leather briefcase, and when he asked if she needed a hand, Linda said:

'With what?'

Ted Fichter felt embarrassed because he could not conceal the fact that all he really wanted was to talk to her. So he bowed from the waist, nodded in the direction of the library and asked if she worked there, and when he took a deep breath Linda smiled at him. 'Not me,' she said. 'But I think I know someone who does.'

'You think?' Ted said.

She blushed.

Ted did not laugh at her. She pushed the bike into the rack, locked it and regarded him as he said: 'Are you following him?'

'Yes,' said Linda. 'In actual fact I am.'

'Is that particularly wise?'

'No,' said Linda.

'Then why do it?' asked Ted.

'I don't know.'

'It all happened so suddenly,' Linda explained to Sofia some years later. 'I knew that *this* I would remember. Olsen at home in the workshop, dismantling a Ford. Leon in the library. Ted fumbling with the bike lock. The buses trundling past. The sunlight slanting through the leaves in the park. The pungent scent of petunias in the flower beds. I felt clammy. Hot. Bewildered. And I was sure that nothing would ever be the same again.'

Fichter the bank manager bowed so courteously that Linda thought he must be a little drunk. He was wearing a charcoal-grey suit with a stripe which only showed up in sunlight and he wanted to touch her, stroke those tanned shoulders, and she was pleased – no, I was so happy, she said – when she laid her hand on his arm. Ted running his ring finger over his narrow moustache.

'It was simple. Suddenly it was all so simple. Do you have any explanation for that?' she confided to Olsen when she returned home with fillet steak and asparagus. She did not tell Olsen that she had gone into the library, up to the counter, and there at the desk was Leon, whispering to an elderly lady who wanted to borrow a book on Persian olive oils. She was explaining that she always used Persian olive oils to soothe stiff ankles. She saw the look Leon gave her and she told him that she read everything on the Indus Valley, the ancient kingdom, the people, their meals and their habit of drinking olive oil for breakfast. 'I'm not mad,' she told Leon. 'I'm poor, I can't afford to be mad. I'm only a little bit mad.' She placed the tips of her fingers confidentially on Leon's hand, smiled into his gentle eyes and said that sadly she was getting too old. He took the elderly lady over to the history section, found the book in which she was interested and escorted her to the door like a rather obsequious major-domo.

'Leon made her day,' Olsen said as he waited for the fillet steak.

'Everything's going to be okay, Olsen,' she said. 'They won't get the better of you,' she lied. She told Olsen that he ought to go to the library more often, she liked the synthetic hush and the smell of paper. She had read a book about swans, whooper swans. She read that the noise made by these waddling birds was forced up through their throats, filtered. She read this word twice: filtered, she repeated, and again she had the feeling that every-

According to Sofia

thing was so simple. Leon walked on crutches in such a way that his workmates forgot they were there. At twelve o'clock he finished work at the library, swung down the big flight of stone steps; the bus drew up while Linda was unlocking her bike and it was all she could do to keep up with it, following the tramlines up the hill. Only then did she notice that Leon was carrying the grey toolbox he used when tuning instruments. She pedalled and pedalled, spotted him entering a large villa. He stayed there for an hour and when he stepped back out on to the pavement he slung the toolbox over his shoulders by means of two straps. Thereafter, he took the bus to the Conservatory where he stayed until five o'clock. It was all so normal, so simple; so she really was not surprised that when Leon got back to the bedsit, he pulled on his green overalls, went downstairs to the workshop and changed the water pump on an old ford Consul. He lay under the car, whistling. Linda heard how he improvised, how he never faltered, just as in church when he played the organ, and she sat contentedly in the office drinking coffee. For the first time it occurred to her that she was not thinking of him as someone who walked on crutches. 'I think he accepts those crutches,' she said. 'He's not happy that it has to be like this, but to be honest it makes no difference to him either way.'

It was meant to last for ever, Linda complained to the stained-glass windows in the silent Protestant cathedral. 'What a bloody swizz,' she hissed at St Luke the Evangelist and the spot where Leon had set down his tool box the first time she met him. Nonetheless, she was reasonably happy, a little on the plump side, it was true; she had put on weight over the past three years. 'Would you believe it?' she whispered slowly to herself. 'Olsen had only three years as Olsen the affluent. For three years he ferried cars to Estonia. He took a room in a hotel near the square in Tallinn.'

'It's comforting to wake up in Tallinn,' Olsen said. 'I can persuade myself that there's no hurry. I take my time shaving, have a good long shower, brush my grey suit and have breakfast in a little dining room. On the wall are pictures of hunters and still mountain lakes. Two elderly women in aprons sit behind the counter, knitting. Their knitting needles clickety-clack and they keep their voices down because they know I speak Estonian. From the window alongside my table I can see the old square. I like the buildings with their pointed gables and the old bank on the corner with its threadbare sofas and the smell of wool. I like the queue in front of the teller's window, the sceptical clerks, the sharp glance and the transactions in the office with the green plush chair seats. It takes time, but I can convert all the currency I have. I get ripped off, of course, but no more than I can bear. I think it was the Hanseatic merchants who laid out the square. It certainly looks like their work,' he told Linda, who did not ask who the Hanseatic merchants were. And it was on one of these mornings, when he was sitting at the breakfast table extolling the virtues of Tallinn, that he went back to being the old Olsen, the mechanic. As he was talking about the veil of mist over Tallinn harbour, with the lights of Finland in the distance, the stalls in the main street selling woolly Estonian mittens and Bohemian glass, and saying how much he missed the intimate little restaurants so reminiscent of Hanseatic times, at that very moment a police car pulled into the backyard.

He took it well.

'It was bound to happen,' he said, popping his Rolex watch into the flour tin, the wad of notes into the bag of sugar; but the key to the safe deposit box he tucked into the blue bowl of sticky raisins. He stroked Linda's breasts for the first time in months, spread his arms wide, displayed his empty hands and treated the policemen like old friends.

'Goodbye, Linda. Thanks for everything. It's been a blast. You're the only person I know who understands how to keep the worst at bay. I see that now. You've been wonderful. You are wonderful,' he cried, stuffing his silk shirt into his trousers as he sauntered across the yard to the police car.

According to Sofia

'A play-actor to the last,' she admitted to Sofia. 'Ready with his exit line. It's odd, though, because he's actually a shy and rather timid man.'

*

'Tell me about Leon,' Sofia said again. 'I won't give up. I want to know as much as possible about him. Please. Don't ask why.'

'He didn't speak.'

'He didn't...'

'Speak,' Linda finished.

Because early that summer Leon broke a welding rod while working under a Mercedes and the flame, bluish-white against the skin, nicked his throat, nothing too serious. Linda drove him to casualty and while they were sitting at the lights she confessed that she had been following him.

'I know that. D'you think I'm stupid?' said Leon, pressing a towel to his throat. He gave her a look she would never forget. The doctor: young, keen, but overworked and with nicotine stained fingers, described the burn as nothing but a scratch.

'Under a Mercedes? How did you manage to break a welding rod?' he wondered. 'The wound will hurt for a couple of days. Come back if the pain doesn't let up.'

The doctor yawned, gave him four Panadeine and yawned again. He was surprised to hear that Leon did not want a sick note, he eyed him up and down, slipped his business card into his breast pocket. 'No sick note, you say? So you work cash-in-hand too, do you?' He smiled at Leon. 'I'm heavily into old British cars. It's an expensive passion. I've three Rovers at home in the garage. I pay cash,' he said. 'And I wouldn't tell a soul.' The last thing Leon said that summer was:

'I'll think about it.'

'It's so simple.' Linda could not forget how Olsen had always maintained that it was so simple. 'You have to get up every morning before seven and have breakfast at a cloth-covered table set with the jam dish, liver pâté and nice cutlery. No mugs. Don't forget that,' he'd cautioned. 'You have to eat slowly and not fuss about.'

He informed Linda that much gloom and despair could be dispelled by freshly laundered bed linen, bacon and eggs for breakfast, fresh-brewed coffee and some sort of order. 'Preferably superficial order.'

Olsen considered her at length, as she wandered around the flat in her dressing-gown. 'Get dressed,' he said. 'Put on the blue blouse I bought in Bonn. You look lovely in blue. You don't make the most of yourself, swanning around in that orange dressing-gown.'

Linda turned to Olsen. She was not used to him being able to talk like a play-actor. 'Where are you from, Olsen?' was dismissed with a shrug. 'Where were you born?' with that laugh which put an end to any conversation. 'Why don't you stop before something goes wrong?'

She thought of this as she watched his solid back disappearing into the police car. 'I'll be locked up for three years at the most,' he called to Linda. 'I'll take my punishment,' he grinned at Linda. She stood bewildered and barefoot among the petunias she had planted two weeks earlier. 'I got careless in Tallinn. A little too big for my boots. I could handle the cash, the gold watch and Italian shoes to begin with, but I never got to grips with the success. It was too much for me. That's the sort of thing that shows us for what we really are,' said Olsen. 'I was stupid, recklessly drunk, full to bursting, and that can be dangerous. But I didn't try to flee my past. That would be too crass. Too stupid,' he added. 'That I have never done. Not for a day. Not for an hour. Almost everyone does it. Because it's so easy. I'm not ashamed of a single, solitary thing. I'm not afraid of anything. It's crazy. I know. Leon is exactly the same. He has accepted it. He has accepted the crutches,' he added. 'He's not running away. He's not fleeing the past, the crutches, his setbacks or Sofia. He won't ever do that.

According to Sofia

Look after Leon,' he cried as the policeman shut the back door. 'Take him under your wing. He deserves it.'

'I had no idea there was so much of the play-actor in Olsen the mechanic,' Linda told Sofia. 'It was almost like nodding off in front of a play on television where the director really hasn't understood the piece at all. I kept expecting Olsen to come stumbling on to some lurid stage set. It was so boring.'

'Why didn't you tell me this earlier?' Sofia said. 'We've known one another for eight years. I wouldn't have told anyone.'

'I didn't understand,' Linda said.

'What didn't you understand?'

Linda stared down at the frying pan. 'How should I know?'

'Leon didn't speak, you say.'

Linda took a deep breath, scrubbed the frying pan, rinsed it in warm water and put the washing-up brush back on its holder. 'So? Haven't you ever been in that position?'

'No,' said Sofia.

'You've been lucky, then. You've led a sheltered life. You've been shielded by the fact that everyone wanted to sleep with you.'

'Linda,' said Sofia. 'You knew.'

'I knew in the same way that you know. The way you know it today.'

'What do I know?' said Sofia.

'All you can think about is a man on crutches. I don't know why that should be.'

Sofia hesitated before answering. 'Is that right?'

'It's simple,' Linda said. 'There's far too much prejudice, cowardice and stupidity around. Why is it so often the case that we don't realise what really matters until it's too late?'

24

Bird was in no doubt – as he stuffed his blue pyjamas into a plastic bag and said goodbye to the cleaner, who was familiar with his spells among lions – as to what he should do.

'Peace,' she said. 'Go in peace,' she repeated. 'I was born in a village in Ethiopia, where we wish for peace when we have been ill. It's common superstition.'

'Almost everything comes down to superstition,' said Bird.

He stepped slowly into the corridor, called for a taxi and asked the driver to take him to his flat. The old driver glanced at him in the rear-view mirror, hesitated, then asked if he should come up with him to the flat. Bird shook his head and said that his stay at the hospital had been purely routine. He had passed out, lain in a bed for three days, felt bored, read magazines, eaten and been given tranquilising injections.

'It was the heart,' he said.

'The heart,' the driver said, removing his woolly hat. 'I thought as much. Aren't you the chap who works on the newspaper?'

This could not be denied. Bird had not thought of his office at the newspaper for four days and, thinking of it – the computer with the yellow notes on the screen, the telephone, the coffee cups and the morning meetings – he stepped into the lift.

According to Sofia

'Today I'll take the lift,' he told the driver.

He paid the fare. And as the driver walked off towards the main door, Bird smiled at the sort of trouser seat only seen on drivers.

Dr Vige had explained to him that he must not stop taking the Valium, instead he should gradually reduce his intake, and because the doctor had said this, Bird opened the hatch of the rubbish chute and chucked the yellow tub down among all the other trash. 'Without the Valium, your demons will assail you from all sides,' the doctor had said, handing his papers to a nurse. 'They'll show no mercy. I'm sorry, but they sneak up on you. They'll turn up when you least expect them. They'll tear you apart. They'll make you accept all the things you don't want to know. Do you understand?'

Bird, who would have agreed to anything if it would get him out of the hospital, had nodded and announced that his heart was beating exactly as it used to do. 'No pain. I haven't passed out in two days,' he lied. 'No double beats. There's nothing wrong with me. It was an accident.'

The flat smelled like a summer cottage in the country. He paused by the kitchen table, opened the windows, walked through to the living-room and stood there, at a loss. As usual, he had tidied up before going for a run, the mug containing the dregs of his sports drink still sat on the table. As he tipped the brew down the sink he felt the first pulse beats at the back of his head.

He hunkered down.

'Easy now,' he whispered.

And crouching there like that he wondered how many others were sitting just as he was doing now. Hunkered down, he thought. We hunker down and wait for something to pass. Now there's a novel exercise. A project for some eager-beaver statistician. 'When you feel as if you're going to faint, sit down on the floor right away,' Dr Vige had told him. 'Don't think you can escape it. I know you, Bird,' was exactly what he did not want to hear. It was still light outside, but the street lamps were lit and he stayed perfectly still for fifteen minutes, until he felt the grip on the back of his head loosening. He breathed as he had been taught. Slowly, steadily, from the stomach. He was completely done in. And he missed Simen. 'We who hunker down and wait for something to pass.' A serviceable idea for an article in the Sunday supplement, he thought to himself. On the sense of impotence incurred by seeing Norway sliding towards the far right. He had respect for impotence. He was afraid of superstition. He did not find it hard to see that earthquakes, volcanic eruptions, hunger, thirst and common persecution bred panic. And that refugees could discover that it was only a short step from there to magic. Where else were they to find comfort and safety of a sort, he thought as he crouched there. He could not have said why he suddenly remembered that the Hopi Indians had been in daily contact with mathematicians from an unknown galaxy. 'The Hopis stood on the top of their sacred mountain and pissed on the moon,' he hissed. The Incas brought the calendar of eternity with them from outer space to Machu Picchu. The Pyramids were built by the forefathers of the Hittites. Goebbels lived out his life as a clerk in Brazil. Clairvoyants predicted the coming of a new Flood. Somewhere in Turkey there was a shaman who lived on air. The Holy Grail. The Ark of the Covenant. And the moment of truth when the bull is killed *recibiendo* at the San Isidro festival in May. Bird thought it was in May. At any rate, he was not going to write about all the garbage that the newsdesk saw as pumping copy – no: capital – into the paper's Sunday supplements. New financial opportunities for the big shareholders who could always be relied upon to believe that superstition, gossip and garbage were of interest. He got up.

'Don't think about it,' he said. Today, he thought. Today you are not going to talk to the lions.

He spread a quilt out on the floor, dragged two cushions off the sofa, fetched his mobile phone; he was feeling better, he could tell. No withdrawal symptoms, he thought as he settled himself on the quilt in the lotus position. His sinuses gurgled. The radiator gurgled. Nothing happened. He sat quite still. A faint rumbling from his stomach. A faint flutter next to his left ear, at the hairline. He tried to picture himself as he sat on the quilt waiting for something to pass. It did not pass. He picked up his mobile and called Simen. The last of the medicine must still be floating around in my bloodstream as I make this phone call, he thought. He clicked down the speed dial list, pressed OK, and while he waited he contemplated the grey dusk settling around the blocks of flats.

It was Leon who answered. 'What do you want?' was not a good start. But Leon laughed when Bird explained that he was actually calling Simen, who was at the cottage, but had ended up with Leon in North Africa.

'Where are you? I mean, in what town?' Bird asked.

'I don't know, but I'm in a café. Some woman has ruined my shoes. She trod on them. My expensive Italian shoes. Right now I'm drinking over-sweet coffee and reading the paper. I'm eating a peach. I've just peeled off the thin skin.'

'Wasn't that yesterday?' Bird said.

'Wasn't what yesterday?'

'That that woman trod on your shoe.'

'How do you know that?'

'Simen called,' said Bird.

Leon laughed. 'Not bad,' he chuckled. 'That's right, it *was* yesterday. You know I was in a square. You also know that the square was filled with the scent of dates. Sun-warmed dates that smelled of mucus. A woman from another millennium trod on my shoe. My secret G-spot, if you must know.'

Bird belched.

'Bird,' said Leon. 'What's up? I can tell from your voice that you're not feeling too great. Where are you?'

'At home,' Bird said. 'I'm sitting on a quilt with some cushions at my back, waiting for it to pass.'

'When did you get home?' Leon asked.

'Half an hour ago,' Bird said.

'Your speech is slow. Far too slow. I would hardly know it was you.'

Bird did not reply.

'You're still chock-full of drugs. They're roiling around the half of your brain over which you have little control. Don't think you're going to be right as rain in a matter of days. You'll have to take it easy.'

'How do you know all this?'

'These things don't vacate your body in an afternoon. There's so little I can do from this end.' Suddenly Leon whispered: 'You've picked a bad moment,' he ventured. 'Can't it wait? You're forcing me to call Simen.' Bird was sure that Leon had retreated into the shade of the awnings. He actually would not have minded being with him down there in North Africa. It was all he could do to hear Leon through the chatter from the other tables and since he had never been to Africa he listened more to these sounds than to Leon's hoarse voice.

'Who came to see you at the hospital?'

'The lions,' said Bird.

'The lions?'

'That's right,' said Bird.

He felt the muscles at the back of his neck withering. And as he tried to raise his head he told Leon that the doctor's name was Gerda Hansen. 'She's from Denmark and she plays handball. She's beautiful, a professional. Skinny. She's a failure. She's good. Are you listening?'

Leon had hung up. 'Typical Leon,' muttered Bird. He wasn't happy about me calling. But I got the message. I shouldn't have chucked those pills down the rubbish chute. Maybe it is too risky. The heart, the pills. Patients who suddenly stop taking their medication. He had read about this, of course. Was it normal for the hairline to flutter?

He went through to the kitchen. He opened the fridge: butter, cheese, sardines and a bag of broccoli in the freezer. Nothing else.

According to Sofia

I can afford to buy a whole cold cabinet full of food, but my own fridge is empty. He pulled off his pullover, stared in surprise at the sweat stains on his shirt and listened to his heart, which was beating as steadily as when he jog-trotted. 'You'd better sit on the quilt,' he cautioned.

It was so quiet in the flat that he stifled the sound when he coughed. Bird liked the quietness of the block of flats. 'It makes me feel good to have all these anonymous people round about me,' he heard himself say. What sort of things do the families in a block of flats do? he wondered. All sit in front of the television? The aroma of fried fish drifted through the open window from the flat below. He did not know what to do; he thought of Hansen the waiter who always walked two hundred metres on his toes on his way home from the restaurant. 'It builds up the calf muscles,' he asserted when Bird looked doubtful. The waiter was the only person in the block whom Bird really knew and he was back on the quilt in the lotus position, a little sleepy, but he tried unsuccessfully to lower his shoulders.

'Easy now,' he said again. 'The only thing that can happen is that you'll pass out.' He was getting ready to roll over on to a stable side position when the phone rang.

'Are you awake?' Leon said.

Bird raised his head. 'Is that you?' he said.

'Is everything all right?'

Bird shifted into a crouch. He knew that when Leon called to ask if he was awake he ought to be so. 'There's very little that's all right,' he said.

'You must be okay then,' Leon said. 'As always. You're making the right sort of complaining noises. That's reassuring.'

'Why are you calling?'

'You mustn't go to sleep,' Leon said. 'You have to stay awake for a few hours. Are you playing 'La Bohème'? You usually pull out Maria Callas when you're in this mood.'

'What kind of mood am I in?' Bird asked.

Instead of answering Leon said: 'Are you still there, Bird? I can't stop thinking about those pills you didn't take. I wish you'd talk to me? I take it you are still listening. Are you there, Bird? You were talking about your friend Maria Callas. She was beautiful. More than beautiful. I admit it. A haughty yet sensitive face. She was of the people, liked men with power and died young. She sang beautifully too, although not as beautifully as the obituaries would have it. Artists don't get better by dying. Just less difficult. I was reminded of this in the Basque country. The editors there tend mainly to write European obituaries. They have them on file, just waiting to be printed. Exactly the same as in Northern Ireland. Wasn't it Polynices who attacked the city and forbade Creon from burying his body? Or was it the other way round? Bird, are you there? In any case, he was a traitor and should be left to lie on the street for the dogs to eat. Creon's word is law. He is the State. Your friends, Brecht, Espriu, Anouilh and Gide have all written about it. A racy little piece of a score or so pages, written five hundred years BC. It's not that long ago. It just seems that way. In any case, that's not bad going, Bird. Ahead of their time, those Greeks. Are you still there? Why don't you answer me? You have to stay awake. You mustn't go to sleep now. Why don't you treat me to a fresh observation on some painting by Monet. That, too, is a bad habit. You, who could never get past Antigone. She, who represents the law of nature and religion. She insisted that man should have his last resting place on earth. Creon with his vetoes and death sentences. It's all coming back to me,' Leon said. 'Antigone, who wanted to try to forget. Both are caught, and both are heading for the abyss. Can't we talk about how all this is connected? Later,' he added. 'When you're feeling better. Isn't this what you talk about when you've had enough of Maria Callas? Bird, you mustn't fall asleep.'

'Nice try, Leon,' said Bird. 'Very nice. I'm still awake. I am a little – not much, but a little – impressed.'

'Then you are awake.'

'You've got your times and events a bit mixed up. But you've got the main drift of it I can tell.'

According to Sofia

'The main drift of it,' Leon said. 'That doesn't sound very reassuring. That's not an expression you would normally use. Couldn't you get just a little bit mad. Is it at all possible to offend you?'

'You're a real pal,' Bird said.

'Should I take that as an insult?'

'I rarely, if ever, feel insulted.'

'Do I detect a touch of temper?'

'No,' said Bird.

'Not true,' Leon replied.

Bird heard the whine of the lift. 'It is true,' he said. 'I'm feeling a little light-headed. I've got this fluttering sensation around my ear and hairline.'

He heard footsteps in the corridor. 'Thanks, Leon. I won't go to sleep for some hours yet. You can rest easy down there among the men who smoke hookahs.'

'There aren't any hookahs here,' Leon said.

Bird laughed. 'Nice try with *Antigone*,' he repeated.

'Do you have some pills?'

'No, I chucked the tub down the rubbish chute.'

'That doesn't surprise me,' said Leon.

Bird heard noises outside the door again. A sort of rustling, or like fingers scrabbling at the doorbell. 'There's someone at the door. Can you hang on a moment?'

'I think I know who it is,' said Leon. 'I called the hospital, and they got in touch with Gerda Hansen. She was on her way over.'

Bird opened the door. Dr Gerda Hansen stumbled in. She made a beeline for the fawn-coloured quilt and just made it as far as the cushions.

She fell very neatly, made the most elegant of nosedives. She looked like a country doctor after three extra shifts, falling apart; she floundered about, lost a shoe, then picked it up and stared at it in amazement.

Then she looked at Bird, a long look, made an attempt,

attempted to speak, gave up, placed her hand under her cheek and dropped off to sleep on the red cushion. Bird smiled. She really was beautiful, even if she was too thin. Her face was peaceful. Her car key nestled in her curled palm. She had the appearance of a woman who had run too far and too fast, and just at that moment, with her lips drawn tight, she looked as if she was taking a break.

'Has she arrived?' Leon asked.

'Yes,' Bird said. 'She's here.'

'Can I rest reasonably easy?'

'Indeed you can,' said Bird.

Bird got a surprise when he looked at her hand under the pink cheek. He had no idea what to do and he was glad that she was asleep. He switched off his mobile, went through to the kitchen to see to the coffee machine, stood on tiptoe, but kept an eye on her lying in there on the quilt. He looked at her and knew that nothing would be the way he had thought it would be, and because she was sleeping deeply with her mouth half-open he refrained from looking at her.

Not very romantic, he conceded. A hushed kitchen in a quiet block of flats. He opened a tin of sardines, sat down at the table, stared out at the fir trees, the path running up to the floodlit forest track, all the joggers aiming at eternal life, and as he munched sardines the woman on the quilt gave a moan. Through the window he watched the old die-hards, a bunch of sprightly pensioners, and he could tell which of them would stop at the gate to pummel aching muscles. Suddenly it all seemed such a bore. Almost everything, he thought. But the sounds coming from the doctor in the living-room were encouragement of a sort. He burped up wholemeal bread, sardines, light beer and filter coffee. All at once he thought of Maria Callas and *La Bohème*, the first tentative notes, like an experiment on Puccini's part, a void being filled, and the way that sentimental chaos was turned into everyday Italian truths. Highly unreliable truths, that is. 'Bird,' he said to himself. 'Go for it. You've nothing to lose.' He found his deluxe Walkman, slipped in the cassette, studied Callas's profile,

According to Sofia

gave a little smile, adjusted the volume and rested his elbows on the table between the sardine tin and his coffee cup. The fluttering at his hairline was still there. It was neither better nor worse. Was he relaxing? Was he calmer? A little calmer? Did he feel the tension in his shoulders at all? He fell asleep in the middle of a tragic aria; somebody had died; Maria Callas handled it with style, stillness and reconcilement. He slept long, way too long, because he was woken by Gerda.

'You look like a way-worn pilot,' she said, easing the headphones off his head. 'Are you okay?' she said patting the sides of his mouth with her hands. 'Wake up now.'

Bird, remembering something he found embarrassing, stood up, took hold of her and buried his face in her short mop. She smelled of cigarette smoke, stale liquor and sleep, but he held her close and knew that he would not regret it.

'She's skinny. Really thin,' he told Sofia two months later. 'You know what I'm like. I found it a bit embarrassing, standing there beside the kitchen table, holding on to her. I didn't seem to want to let go of her. It was a little unusual. She is my doctor, after all.'

'You're shy, that's all,' Sofia said. 'You always have been, and you should think yourself lucky.'

'Why?'

'I think it's good to be thin,' Sofia continued. 'I'm a lot thinner myself now. I weighed ten kilos more three months ago.'

'Are you ill?' Bird asked.

'No,' said Sofia.

25

The hangover from the injections lasted for most of the next day; periodic bouts of dizziness left Bird hunkered down while Gerda sat quietly on the sofa, contemplating the blue wallpaper. She crept around the flat as if searching for something that was gone forever.

Bird, who wandered fitfully and gingerly from room to room and still thought he could smell the hospital, had his own worries, but he smiled at Gerda on the sofa. She looked all in, as if she had just been playing in a handball tournament, he thought, and the sour-sweet tang from the health-drink bottle didn't help any. She did not eat, hardly spoke, simply waited. And when Gerda did speak she explained in lowered tones that it came in bouts, two bouts a year, occasionally three, never more.

She eyed Bird warily.

His general light-headedness meant that he had to tread carefully, so when Bird left his nice, safe seat in the armchair by the fire and padded around the flat he felt his way along reassuring bookcases, sofa and doors. He was scared. He had never really been scared before, and of that he was glad. Work was going to come to a halt for both of them. 'Five days,' Gerda said. 'Maybe a week.' She admitted that this was the way of it. When Bird thought of the office, the light falling through the yellow Venetian

According to Sofia

blinds and the smell of coffee from the machine before the canteen opened, the newspaper building seemed so far away that the thought of it struck him as faintly absurd. First Dr Vige rang, then a consultant surgeon with a commanding voice called three times to speak to Dr Gerda Hansen, his voice quivering with controlled panic. Bird heard the duty roster being mentioned as he fumbled with the bag of coffee. He gathered that two of the hospital's surgeons were weather-bound at an airport in Germany. The consultant had no one to assist him but two housemen whose palms grew clammy whenever he walked into the room. Gerda was trembling slightly. By twelve o'clock she had smoked ten cigarettes and Bird coughed demonstratively, asthmatically, almost fervently as he opened the veranda door, causing them both to feel cold.

It was a chill, clear winter day with a yellow sun and long shadows. Frost scrunched under the shoes of housewives and joggers. Gerda lit a fresh cigarette from the previous one. 'Does it bother you?'

'Yes,' said Bird.

She carried on smoking, gazed at the wallpaper, her fingers shaking when she flicked her lighter, and Bird eyed her steadily. She succumbed two, or was it three, times a year. It started with red wine. 'Spanish red wine. It tastes like reddish-brown earth. It's a disease, of course,' she said. 'I don't want to destroy anything. I have no conscious desire to destroy myself. It's so simple and it happens so fast. Do I need to say it's awful? I see it in my patients and I detect it in myself. Are you scared, Bird?' she asked, stubbing out her cigarette in the ashtray.

Bird made no reply. He tossed the half-smoked cigarettes into the fire, vaguely aware that he was starting to feel hungry. 'It's getting better,' he said. 'I think I may be over the worst.'

He knew that Gerda still had some hours to go before her hangover eased off. He sat down in the armchair, stretched his legs out under the table and thought of nothing. The situation was not a complete mess, but it was demoralising. He glanced at the computer. He was nine clicks away from being able to send a finished article to the newsdesk, but the thought of having any sort of opinion seemed so repellent that he opened his mouth. He tried to breathe slowly, then he read an American magazine in which it was admitted that bears could change sex: it was simply a matter of genetics and all it took was a heap of dollars, patience and a little luck. Not only that but genetically modified bears would become a stock market commodity. Nordic sperm, Aryan sperm, would be an attractive proposition on the stock exchange. Women would pay a fortune for a drop of Aryan seed in which links with Odin and Tor were preserved. Hitler's dream of refining Nordic arrogance would finally be bourse-listed. Skilled doctors would freeze every form of Aryan madness in small sterilised tubes. Neuroses would be modified and manipulated. No mention was made of why bears should change their sex. This soothed Bird's nerves. He looked out windbreakers for them both, wrapped Gerda in a scarf and woolly hat. He kissed her on the forehead. She was trembling slightly. She smelled of deodorant and soap. They locked the door of the flat and made their way to the lift, looking like a tolerably happy married couple. Both were feeling a little rough, but they were going to take a walk around the big lake and drink in the first breath of winter air. It took time. Everything took time. Not that each step was an effort, but it did require a certain amount of forethought. Bird smiled. Gerda had two spots of hectic red on her cheeks. She pressed her lips together. She looked determined. Not the slightest bit peeved. Right now, he told himself . . . He had to do it right now. He would have to ask her to marry him or to move in with him. He stopped there and was not surprised. He was forced to rethink slightly when he saw that she was about to throw up. He did not back down, though, was working his way round to it, but before he could say a word she told him that if she was ever to hear good news it had to be here. 'It has to be here. Right here.'

According to Sofia

They were down by the beach, today with a thin crust of ice surrounding the frozen water lilies, and the good news was to come from a man who always wore Harris tweed jackets. She pointed to the logo on his windbreaker and wiped her nose with a tissue. Bird felt better with the chill wind in his face. He liked the sound of the ice crackling as they crossed the puddles and he thought: Come on. Don't take so long over it. There's no need for that. And in order to gain some control over himself, as he stood there in the mellow winter light, he talked about what he knew best. He launched into an account of the catastrophic war in which Tiglath-Pileser played a leading role after ascending the throne in 745 BC; a conflict which ended with Nebuchadnezzar's famed victory over Necho at Karkemish in 605 BC.

Dr Hansen took it well, stared at him in amazement as he described how Assyria had destroyed entire capital cities and taken the inhabitants into captivity: Damascus in 732, Samaria in 722, Musasir in 714, Babylon in 689, Zion in 677, Memphis in 671, Thebes in 663 and Susa in 639. Although Bird was not so sure about the last one.

'Of all the capitals within reach of the Assyrians only Tyre and Jerusalem survived.' Bird coughed, cleared his throat, tried to look at her, but abandoned the attempt. 'Some did survive,' he elaborated as he watched the ducks struggling to gain a footing on the ice. 'Nineveh was plundered in 612 BC. Death and destruction all around. Assyria was a disaster. Sometimes it seems as if everything is a disaster. The victims of Assyrian forces fought their way back to life and, in most cases, glorious futures. Nineveh was the only city which fell, never to rise again. There are always some who don't survive,' he said, observing one duck which was having trouble hauling itself up on to the ice. 'I wonder which of us it will be?'

'Of us two?' said Gerda.

Bird shook his head. 'No, not us,' he laughed.

'Are you really into all that?'

'All what?' said Bird.

'Nineveh. Ancient times. That whole long, banal train of events staged by historians?'

'Yes,' he said.

Bird looked at her standing there with the light behind her. She was looking better. She had faced up to the winter. The sunlight lent her skin a golden cast; starkly, pitilessly it revealed that she had been on a bender, and he could tell that the lines around her mouth were there to stay. Not only that but she had spots, little pimples which she had forgotten to cover up. 'You're so young that you actually have spots,' he said. 'It still surprises me you're being so young.'

She did not bother to answer. 'I'm fifteen years older than you,' made no impression. She pointed to the duck which had now heaved itself up on to the ice. It waddled towards the shore, shaking its tail. Then it joined the flock and was lost among all the rest.

'Fifteen years,' said Bird.

For the first time that day she laughed. 'Fourteen,' she said.

'Do you think it's dangerous?' Bird asked.

'Is what dangerous?'

'Drinking.'

'Of course it's dangerous. You know it's dangerous. But it's necessary.'

'Necessary?'

'Well, what else?' She took three steps along the path, removed her hand from her pocket, held it out to him and smiled. 'Come on,' she said.

'That blue down jacket suits you,' said Bird. 'I was quite convinced that it would never be worn. It's been hanging in the wardrobe for at least three years.'

'I can smell that.'

'Am I talking too much?'

'No,' she said.

They walked on along the path. The water was pale-blue. Bird saw a cloud reflected in the water and pointed to it. She nodded,

According to Sofia

let go of his hand and stepped aside for a jogger then laced her fingers through his again, squeezed his hand lightly, just a little squeeze, he barely felt it and Bird breathed in the cold air, glanced at her, surveyed the ice, the pine trees: silent, patient, a little sombre, expectant even. 'I feel as though I could drink air,' he said. 'Mouthfuls of ozone.'

'Do you want to talk about the ozone?' she said.

Bird did not reply.

'Do you want to talk about drinking?'

'Definitely not,' she said.

They walked across a pontoon bridge. It rocked under their feet. She bent down and broke off a piece of ice the size of a hand. She nibbled the ice, crunched it, held it out to him. 'D'you want some?'

Bird shook his head.

'It's really good.'

She dried her fingers on the down jacket, settled the scarf closer around her neck, took his hand in hers and slid both into her pocket. They crossed the pontoon bridge, passed the big rock, and he pointed to a crevice in the cliff face, dark, green moss, a slither of scree ending in a heap of stones. 'I almost fell down there,' Bird said. 'One day early in the summer, in June, I almost took a header on to that pile of stones. It's the first time I've ever been truly scared. I come up here sometimes to remind myself of it. It almost went badly wrong,' he said. 'For the first time it almost went seriously wrong.'

'Do we have any time to lose?' she said.

'Not really, no,' said Bird.

Two joggers ran past. He caught the scent of sweat mingled with cold air and felt the urge to run.

'Feeling better?' Bird asked.

She shrugged.

'Are you cold?'

'A bit, yes.'

She walked a little faster. She had lowered her shoulders. Bird noticed that suddenly she was stepping out like a sprinter who, to everyone's amazement, has won on the line. He regarded her neck and shoulders. Looked mainly at her shoulders.

She stopped beside the red bathing hut. 'It's nice here,' she said. 'This is where I'm going to swim in the summer.'

'It's dangerous.'

'You already said that.'

'I'm a little unsure.'

'No,' she said. '*That* you certainly are not.'

'How would you know?'

'Have I destroyed something?'

'You mean someone,' said Bird.

She worked her hand free of his and pulled the scarf tight around her neck. He could tell from her eyes that she was actually smiling.

'Who?'

'I've no idea,' said Bird. 'How would I know?' he added. 'I've only known you a few days.'

'It doesn't feel like that.'

Bird buried his chin in his scarf and smiled. It was funny. He was funny, without meaning to be and he liked that.

'Don't try to teach me anything about Nineveh.'

'I promise,' he said.

She slid her hand into her pocket. 'Bird,' she said. 'Can I move in with you? Right away, if possible. Today. Or tomorrow. It seems so right. I think it might work. For years. Maybe for ever. I think we deserve it.'

Bird looked at her. 'Of course,' he said.

26

Antonio Nerida had just rolled over on to his back. He wiped his brow with the back of his hand. 'There's nothing wrong with my heart,' he said. 'I'm a Basque. I'm hardened,' he said with a grin. 'I'll throw every cliché in the book at you.' He grinned again. 'This is mine. All mine.' He pointed at his chest, in the region of his heart. 'The Basques have never been conquered. We've thwarted every attempt. Even the Moors had a go at us. A bunch of jumped-up Berbers if you ask me.'

He dug his elbows into the bed, cleared his throat and swallowed the last drops of water, peering at Sofia over the rim of the glass.

He was rather surprised. 'I've thought of you. Often,' he added. 'For years.' He rolled on to his stomach. 'I've thought of you for fifteen years. Almost every day. You don't have to believe me.'

He looked at the empty water bottle on the bedside table. Shook it suspiciously, muttered, threw back the bedcover in order to get up, changed his mind and put his head back on the pillow.

He considered Sofia's left breast, seriously and at length.

'He was actually serious. Can you imagine Antonio Nerida being serious? You've no idea how sweet he was, though,' Sofia confided to Linda Olsen when they were chatting on the phone.

'He studied both my breasts,' she went on. 'For ages, felt them with his hands, lifted them and rested them in his palms, went all soft-eyed and ran a hand over his brow. He was restless. He was gearing up for another round.'

'Not right now,' Sofia said.

He shook his head.

You're not a very nice man, she thought. You're in good shape, but I don't like you. You eat too much, you work and smoke and do all the things you're not supposed to do. It's annoying. I'm a plain, ordinary Norwegian puritan and I envy you. There's not a thing wrong with you. You've never jogged more than a hundred metres. You've never had a molar removed. You've never been diagnosed as having a fatal disease. You've never screamed in agony. I just know you haven't. You've never been in hospital. You're small, but brimming with energy. And you make no apologies for anything whatsoever. It's something of a relief. I admit it.

Antonio Nerida thought of his new sound system. He plumped up his pillow and smiled when he remembered the loudspeakers which he had hidden under a rug.

They were bound to be discovered, but not today.

Everything would be discovered. But not right at this moment. He knew it would come to light that he was sleeping with Sofia. When he returned home and lied about a job in some village in the mountains one look from his wife would be enough. She would eye him up and down and greet him with a peremptory toss of the head. The nape of her neck. He thought of the nape of her neck. That all-knowing nape. Followed by a snort. Then she would turn away. Turn her back on him. She would march out of the room and slam the door behind her. He almost dreaded it. But that would come later. Right now he was lying in bed, gazing at Sofia's left breast. Gazing at it for a little too long. He knew that. She didn't like it. He knew that too. The air in the room smelled sweet, a little too sweet. She had spent most of the evening and the night before in a bar, drinking Fanta, eating tissue-thin slices of Basque ham and listening to Nerida discoursing on the Basque talent for survival.

She had been so bored.

'Do you see me as a patriot?'

She still did not bother to answer.

'A nationalist?'

She observed him.

'Or neither?' Nerida asked.

'Something like that,' said Sofia.

Nerida laughed. He ran his fingers through his thick locks, breathed deeply, left hand at the back of his neck, and to Sofia's surprise he suddenly seemed so relaxed. 'No clichés,' she warned, sitting up in bed. She drew the sheet up to her chin, ruffled her hair and went on: 'I don't want to hear another word about all things coming to he who waits. I mean it,' she smiled.

Nerida looked at his fingers. Two gold rings glittered. The larger was inset with a flat, black stone which he studied, rubbed against his cheek and regarded again. It was a beautiful ring, old, worn, with scratches in the stone. It was a little tight and looked as if it had become embedded in his finger.

'Don't tell me that's your dead father's ring, the one he used to twist round and round whenever he was feeling depressed,' said Sofia.

'Yes, it's Father's,' said Nerida.

'He stole it.'

'That's right,' said Nerida.

'From the bedside table of a married woman. She was very careful and didn't want to scratch your father's back. So before they went to bed she took off all her jewellery, including that ring,' Sofia said.

'No,' said Nerida.

'But he did steal it?'

'At a market. He stole it at a market in a village not far from here. From a locksmith.' Nerida picked up his tobacco pouch, rolled another cigarette, lit it, drew the smoke deep down into his lungs and smiled contentedly. 'Now don't go telling me that as a surgeon you've seen the lungs of people who smoke as much as I do.'

'I promise I won't,' said Sofia.

'He was an anarcho-syndicalist as it happens. The locksmith,' he added. 'He was a patriot. That too is a disease. He was a nationalist and a patriot. He was a nationalist who believed in Lenin and Durutti. He sometimes maintained that the revolt of the tobacco workers in Barcelona was the high point of his life. He believed in Lenin, Mao and Pol Pot. That is more dangerous than smoking.'

'Do you smoke hash?' Sofia asked.

'Not here,' he said. 'I smoke it at home. At the weekend,' he added. 'When I'm listening to music. LaFaro,' he murmured. 'The great LaFaro. There aren't too many things I wish were different. But I would love to have had Scott LaFaro's ear. He's dead. I know. It doesn't seem right. I think it happened in a car. A crash. The best people die in such stupid ways. In cars. Driving through red lights. How stupid can you get? Gaudi was mown down by a tram. He had a roll of drawings under his arm. I'm superstitious. We Basques often are.'

'*Du er et nek*,' Sofia told him in Norwegian.

'What did you say?'

'That you're a *nek*.'

'And what does that mean?'

Sofia told him: 'It means you're a twerp.'

'True,' Antonio Nerida said. 'But I've never given in. I've never had the chance. The hardest path is often the simplest. One feels duty-bound. I come from a sensitive family,' he said and smiled. 'We do not give up. We are intemperate, homeless and nationalistic. We've no idea who we really are and would rather not know. That's the stupidest part. We claim that our long dialogue with the Spaniards is at an end. We are stubborn, reactionary, opinionated, intriguing. We weep when we read our epics

According to Sofia

about the horses' hooves pounding across the plains. We abhor facts. Ours is not a family one marries into without good reason. We fight. I laugh it off. But I don't give in. No bloody way,' he smiled.

'You're a child,' said Sofia.

He tapped the ash off his cigarette.

'This is the strongest tobacco in the world. Every single draw on one of these cigarettes is packed with all that is bad. Nicotine. Cancer. Tar. Gall. Hate. Anger. Curses. And, not least, opinionatedness.'

'What else?' asked Sofia.

'Isn't that enough?'

'You're a proper charmer,' she continued. 'It's always been charming to act like a child until one is forty. I don't know why that should be. After that it's banal. So in your case it's been banal for some years. Wouldn't you agree?'

'Yes,' he said.

'Do you intend to do anything about it?'

'No,' he said.

'What do you want of me?' asked Sofia.

'Nothing,' he said.

'Do you know what I want of you?' said Sofia.

'Of course. You're using me,' said Antonio Nerida. 'You're using me as you use most people. You don't mean any harm by it, but you exploit me more ruthlessly than I do you. You're in big trouble. And it shows. Only you know what the problem is. Maybe you don't even know. Yet,' he added. 'You have some notion of what might be wrong. Seriously wrong. With you personally,' he added. 'You won't say, though. Not yet. Not to a soul. Not to Leon. Not to me. And definitely not to Simen. But you need a man. A man whom you know. It should be someone who knew you years ago. And he should be here right now. I don't know why. I just know that's how it is. Am I right?'

'Yes,' said Sofia.

Nerida got out of bed and went to the bathroom. Sofia

observed the way he squeezed the toothpaste out of the tube, smeared it on to his index finger, gave his teeth a good scrub, gargled, scrubbed again, washed his face, his compact neck, his armpits. He was naked. A handsome naked man who had not been lying in the sun. He had spent years sitting in a blue office chair, but still he looked like a hurdler. 'You look like Bird,' she said, following him with her eyes. 'I don't like Bird,' Nerida replied. 'There are very few men whom I like less than I like Bird. I've never liked him. He's a sportsman. A jogger. Just about everything has been handed to him on a plate. Such things do not go unpunished. Not ever. He's in hospital,' Nerida said. 'He was admitted yesterday. Perhaps the day before yesterday.'

Sofia swung her legs over the edge of the bed. 'In hospital? Why didn't you tell me?'

Nerida stood in the doorway. There was a fleck of foam from the toothpaste in the left-hand corner of his mouth, and he had never concealed himself from anyone when naked. Neither man nor woman. 'There's nothing wrong with him. He was out running and he collapsed. I've spoken to a doctor. A woman. Dr Gerda Hansen. Do you know her?'

'No,' said Sofia.

'You were in a state,' Nerida said. 'You had actually been arrested. But I got them to put you up in this suite. You didn't need to be told before. He's perfectly all right. You're all right. It's just nerves.'

'Just nerves?' Sofia repeated.

He screwed the top on to the toothpaste tube.

'I had been thinking of making love to you again. I suppose that's out of the question now?'

Sofia got out of bed. 'Out,' she said. 'I've got to shower. I need to call Simen. Do you know where he is?'

Nerida looked at the toothpaste tube.

'No, you don't,' Sofia said.

She stepped into the tiled bathroom. The bidet smelled new and exclusive. 'Bird,' she whispered. 'No funny business now. No

According to Sofia

fancy notions. No excuses. I need you. I'm going to need you like never before. I don't know why, but I need you near me right now. You and Simen. And Leon. That much is clear, although I don't know why. I'm a bit touchy at the moment. I'm scared. You understand that, don't you? I've been flattening waiters with ashtrays. Which is not exactly normal. I usually have some sort of control. I don't know what's happening to me.'

She showered, washed her hair, rested the back of her neck on the bidet and noticed a little cut on her shin. She smiled. 'Simen. You really ought to be here now,' she said, while Antonio Nerida lay in bed thinking about Bill Evans. His touch, he thought. He has a touch so exquisite that it makes most other pianists seem like amateurs. I've never heard anyone but Bill Evans play with such intimacy. What couplings of brain and fingers could give rise to a touch like that? Can it be learned? I have heard it copied almost perfectly by Leon. And by Therese Somoza.

He jumped up from the bed and smiled. 'Easy now,' he said slowly. 'That blasted Somoza family. There seems to be no end to it. They know everything, but say nothing. They turn taciturnity into an art form. They keep their mouths shut. About everything. They are capable of suppressing absolutely everything. After ten years most of it is only a distant memory. Antonio, why don't you stay away from them? You really ought to.' He was talking louder than he liked.

'What did you say?' said Sofia.

'Nothing,' he replied. Then he rolled another cigarette and lit it. He thought of Therese's profile when she bent her head over the keys. Then Sofia's profile on the pillow. She slept as if there was no such thing as evil. He thought of how she seemed calm and how she had laughed at the police officers, the law and him.

'I have to go shortly,' he said.

'Why do you have to go?'

Again he thought of Therese's profile. Nerida heard sounds from the shower. Sofia's humming, he thought. I've been thinking of her for twenty years and all I really want is to go home to my new loudspeakers. It's stupid. And vaguely comical. He considered leaving while she was in the shower, but instead he retreated to the warmth of the bed, the smell of her, still strong, aromatic, heavy, the rather pungent perfume which she had not bought in the Basque country.

'I'll have to feel my way,' he whispered. 'It's going to take some time. Everything takes too long. I always have to bide my time. Lawyers are always so suspicious. It's an occupational disease. I hope she'll stay in there under the shower for a while.'

To pass the time, he thought again about Leon, Therese and a touch on the piano which was unmistakable. He had come across it before, often, most often from guitarists who made the guitar look as though it sprang from some secret spot in their chests. He felt happy because he had thought of the chest, not the heart. A Spaniard would have said the heart. 'They're so boring,' he said, swearing under his breath.

'Antonio, you mustn't swear. There will be no cheese and ham for supper if you swear,' he heard his mother say. That voice was grumbling away at the back of his mind as usual.

'It's so complicated,' he went on. 'Or maybe it's more of a bore. I'd better pay a visit to Pater Rafael, to find out for sure.'

Not many people knew that pious Pater Rafael slept with his young colleague in Santander, he thought to himself.

Only the female clerk with power of attorney knew how Antonio Nerida persuaded Pater Rafael to open his books. Knew of insights into cupboards in which knowledge and facts, confidences and gossip were stowed away in files. Nerida sat down abruptly on the edge of the bed. 'Does he know who Therese Somoza's mother is?' he asked himself.

'Who do you mean?'

Sofia stood in the doorway. She looked demure, damp, untouchable in one of the hotel's towels. She seemed so relaxed that he regretted having said anything at all.

'Do you mean Simen?'

He made no reply.

According to Sofia

'Of course he knows,' she said.

Still Antonio made no reply.

'Why do you keep going on about Therese?' Sofia said.

She wrapped the towel round her head like a turban.

'Do I?'

She smiled at the mention of Therese's name.

'Are you bored?' Sofia asked.

'No,' he said.

'Never?'

'Never is a Nordic word. It's the most Nordic word I know. You lot are so hopelessly resigned to the idea that most things will never happen. No disasters. No political assassinations. And if any such thing should occur it comes as a shock and gives rise to national neuroses. No civil wars. No dangerous differences of opinion. And you assume that this is how it will always be. But you're in for a disappointment. You're doomed to disappointment. I'm guessing that it always happens. Maybe not today, but some time soon, I'm sure. It's bound to happen.'

'Really?' said Sofia.

His eyes went to the thick black hair on his arms. Rested for far too long on the long black hairs on his white arms, and it looked as though for the first time he did not like what he saw.

'I think what you need is a case,' Sofia said. 'A big case, one that has nothing to do with money.'

Nerida sprayed his reading glasses. He plucked a tissue from the pink box on Sofia's bedside table, gave the lenses a good long rub without looking at them. 'I'm sure that the one thing I do not need is a big case,' he said, holding the glasses up to the light. 'I have far too many big cases running in this city as it is.'

He put on the glasses.

'Are you going to warn her?'

'Who?' said Sofia.

He peered at her over his half-moon spectacles. 'You're here to talk to her. To explain how it happened.'

'Must I?' said Sofia.

'Can't you see that you must? Is it really so hard for you to understand something so simple?'

'Yes,' said Sofia.

'Then it's worse than I thought,' said Antonio Nerida.

27

Simen ran hot water into an old shaving bowl. It had been bought at an auction in a hamlet in the back of beyond which he did not care to think about. That was a long time ago, in his great-grandfather's day – the founder of the family, the timber merchant with the big ears.

'He was stubborn, a bit mad,' his grandmother had whispered when the housemaid had been to the chemist and measured eight viscous drops of Hoffman's Anodyne into her Chinese tea-cup. 'He had a bastard child,' she continued once the housemaid had closed the door.

She sipped from her cup, patted Simen's head, flicked her hair forward on to her cheeks to hide her ears, sighed, drank the bitter brew from the tea-cup and sang a song about far Andalusia. 'It's a bawdy ballad, you know. Your great-grandfather was fond of it. Only drunken peasants, aristocrats and wealthy timber merchants have a true appreciation of bawdy ballads. We've been rich a long time, but we have a lot in common with the country folk. We owe our livelihood to the forest owners. We despise the greedy, grasping barrow-boys in the towns. Remember that. We're the raw material. Amsterdam was built with our timber. The docks in Bilbao are constructed out of oak timbers. Solid Norwegian timber. Carried over the North Sea by us. In our ships. Don't yawn when I'm talking about our ships. Your forefathers swindled just about everybody. And they took pleasure in swindling. Swindling is an art. But they've never fooled the peasants. Understand?'

Simen did not understand one word of what his grandmother was whispering to him, but he liked sitting with her when she drank tea. She was a superstitious woman. 'When you grow up, you're to pour the hot water for your shave into that old bowl. You have to do that as often as possible. Every day if possible. All will be well with the men of this family as long as you use that old bowl for your shaving water. Your grandfather was a modern man who set no store by common sense. He read books, went to the barber on the corner and died young. He didn't smoke, didn't drink and had no bastard offspring. Illegitimate children are not always a bad thing, you know. They're often the best. He loved only me. He was never unfaithful to me. He was a fine man. A boring individual who exported timber, eels, acorns and berries and never set foot on a ship. He was a sore trial,' his grandmother said. 'Imagine a man who had never been to sea. Imagine a man who had never thrown up all the way across the Skaggerrak. Simen, don't you forget to use that old bowl when you shave. The past is always there, and yet it's never there. Don't pretend you don't understand what I'm saying.'

Simen had woken early. The cottage was warm, dampish and smelled of winter. He made coffee, wiped the condensation off the window-pane with a towel, sat in the chair by the window, sat there a long time. He could not see a single ripple round the beaver's lodge on the point and he sat in silence, a little tense, but he forced himself to lower his shoulders while he waited for the coffee. He wandered through to the bathroom: it smelled of pine panelling and synthetic varnish, a modern bathroom with jacuzzi and sauna, built with his own hands. He picked up the old bowl, a little piece had rusted and fallen off; he contemplated setting it on his head, then thought better of it. He wouldn't have minded sitting on the back of an old farm horse, singing that bawdy Andalusian ballad as he rode past the police speed trap in the lay-by. He smiled, set the bowl at an angle in the pale-green sink, ran a little hot water into it and lathered his face. The face he saw in the mirror was grey, woefully grey, rather weather-beaten, a Spanish face Sofia would have said consolingly.

But Sofia was in the Basque country and he forced himself not to think about her.

He was at the cottage. He was shaving with Great-Grandad's bowl for reasons he did not care to think about. It had been bought in an out-of-the-way corner of the country in a village he was trying to forget. Was that where his great-grandfather had been born? Had he been born into poverty and kept alive with the aid of two cows and four sheep? He hadn't ridden into town on a horse. Nor had he marched into town with a hayfork for a lance. That much Simen knew. Instead, he had come to town on a raft which carried him and two cows to the upper ferry landing. There he dragged the cattle ashore, drove them up to pasture, sold them, borrowed money and built a notorious hotel. He gave houseroom to drunken peasants, whores, money-grubbers and seamen lugging duffle bags or sea-chests. He got rich. He got rich far too quickly. 'Which is not a good thing, you know.' And when his grandmother reached this part of the story, she would sigh again, settle back in the armchair with her head resting on the starched lace antimacassar and give a little sniff before falling asleep; her breathing became slow and steady and smelled bitter. 'You have to leave this earth once you've done all you can do,' she whispered. 'Not before. And not too long afterwards.'

Simen's father's preferred game was five-card draw. He did not enjoy playing poker, but at the poker table he won more than he lost and sometimes he won a lot. One ice-cold day in December 1932, two days after Christmas and long before Simen was born, he won a house in the centre of town. It was here that Simen grew up, though he had no idea that it had been won at the poker table until he read his father's will. He could not believe it, read the deeds, felt first mortified, then indignant and sold the house at a knock-down price.

'You're impossible,' Sofia said when they moved to the expensive flat by the sea. 'We sell a house for next to nothing and move to a flat so pricey that we'll have to scrimp and save for years. Who was he? Your father,' she added, with a smile that moved Simen to lower his eyes.

He told her again that his father had been married to a woman who looked like an English lady. She was rosy-cheeked, cool, calm and collected, liked Great-Grandad, the sea, boats, well water, ice, oak timbers and cod-liver oil. Gossip had it that she had had a child by a newsagent. That didn't bother her. Gossip had it that she had a fortune in English pounds. 'Apparently I have two illegitimate children. Three,' she laughed and looked at Simen. '*And* English pounds in a bank in London. Don't you worry about what people say. It'll only wear you down. We're the sort of people folk like to gossip about.'

She was not afraid of living. One day at spring tide, she dived off a cliff nine metres high, and Simen remembered how she laughed when she surfaced with seaweed in her hands.

'I just want to sleep,' she explained when she stopped having breakfast. 'I'm not well,' she said when she did not eat dinner. 'Now it's getting serious,' she said three months later when she did not have the strength to climb the stairs to the first floor. After the first twelve stairs she had to rest and wait until she was breathing normally again. 'Simen, I don't want to be put into hospital. Promise me. I won't let them operate on me, but Dr Steffensen can give me pills. For the pain,' she added. 'Only for the pain.'

She wanted to die alone at the cottage.

'I want to die in this mausoleum.' She sat in the chair by the window, smoked, read Horace and ate herring and beetroot. She told Simen what it was like to die. 'What it's like to die young,' she enlarged. 'I'm far too young. There's so much I haven't done,

According to Sofia

and so much I haven't managed to ruin. It's gone so fast, but I don't feel cheated.'

She believed she was at last going to meet Great-Grandad, the timber merchant, and have the chance to chat about oak timbers and Rotterdam, about the docks in Bilbao, about opium, and Simen only realised what pain she was in when she spoke Dutch. She died young. She died of cancer. She passed away. 'I'm going to sit out on a point,' she said. 'Not the point where the beavers have their lodge and where they slap the water with their tails in the morning. But a sunlit point. I want to die early in the morning when there's a nip in the air, with only a pack of cigarettes for company. A pack of Golden West. Simen, you're to stay away. Well away. I mean it. I want to die in silence, alone, and I don't want you to remember me that way, in that silence.'

While she waited she knitted wrist warmers, polished copper, made jam and played patience. She removed all mirrors from the cottage.

'I'm nothing but skin and bone. I'm vain, and I don't want to be reminded of the fact that I look like a bag of bones. This disease sucks the juices out of everyone it touches. The willpower. Me. Changes me. Degrades me. My strength is gone. All desire. I've lost all pleasure. That too is gone. Why don't you go back to town, Simen? I won't weep and wail. You won't hear me do that. I want to be alone. When the end is near I want to be totally alone. Promise me that, Simen. My wrists are cold. And my back. My face is cold. And between my thighs. My hair. My feet. It's silly. Very silly. But I'm cold between my thighs. I'm like ice. I feel like a glacier. And that I certainly did not deserve.'

Simen forgot her.

He had to forget her. Even when he remembered her. When he put his mind to it, which was not often, he remembered her. Then he would sit in the chair by the window and gaze out at the spit of land across from the beavers' dam. He had shaved, showered, eaten. 'You're to have breakfast every day. Eggs, bacon, wholemeal bread and coffee. A lot of coffee.' He had drunk four cups of coffee. He had eaten bacon. What he remembered best was her laugh. He remembered her laugh in the mornings when she brushed her auburn hair and gathered it at the nape of her neck with a brown clasp, her conversations on the phone before she had breakfast, the scent of tobacco and perfume, and the way she baked, roasted, preserved, laughed, beat rugs, threw out rubbish and sniffed when a game of patience did not work out. She laid out hands of patience at the breakfast table to divine what the day ahead might hold. 'You see, Simen, the cards only act as a guide. They don't reveal what's going to happen, but what I can prevent from happening.'

The only thing which could really throw her was one of her husband's fits of rapture. Every year, in the bright light of spring, he would take to singing an aria. 'Your father, Simen, thinks he is a singer. That he is actually a great performer. Every spring when he gets drunk, really drunk, he gets it into his head that he is a famous Italian tenor. It's harmless, but tiresome. Luckily he rarely gets drunk, but it does happen.' Simen searched for the usual laughter lines on his mother's face when she spoke of the singer, but she never laughed about it, nor did she smile, instead she laid her hands in her lap in a way which said that this was one battle she had lost.

Simen's father had a mellow tenor voice with a solid vibrato which sliced through the night as he stumbled homewards. On such nights, on unsteady legs, he would feel his way along the cemetery wall, stopping when he reached the chapel. There he would catch his breath. Rest. Clear his throat. And then he would fill his lungs with air. 'He sings to the dead. I swear he does it for his kinfolk. He sings to his genes. He's a timid man who kicks over the traces a couple of times a year. There's nothing wrong with that.' The chapel was a plain white building sheltering under the maple trees. With his hands against the whitewashed chapel wall to steady him he would take a deep breath, lift up his head and sing '*O mio bambino caro*'. Always the same aria, sung over

According to Sofia

and over again, till the lights went on in the living-rooms round about. It was actually quite beautiful, to hear him singing in the warm spring night. He conjured up a memory of what would have to be described as love. There was something slightly unreal about this unassuming man, who usually never talked about anything but timber, herring, syrup and eels, singing so tenderly of emotions of which he had, in fact, no memory. He struggled to stay on his feet, and he succeeded. He was a stubborn man. He ate bread and syrup every morning, and also after he had sung his aria outside the white chapel donated to the town by his father, or was it his grandfather? Maybe that was why the cemetery's neighbours let him be. He would sing for at least an hour before they called the police, who brought him home, not in a police car, but a taxi, almost always with the same driver, Skogen, behind the wheel. The latter would escort him slowly but relentlessly up the steep steps to Simen's mother who nursed him back to his senses with lager and some kindly sex. She did not laugh at him. Because he was afraid. Very afraid.

'What's happening to me?' he would ask in the morning when he looked in the mirror. He shaved with hands that trembled and combed his few strands of hair across his scalp. 'It drives me crazy when I think of what I might have done. I don't dare think about it.'

He was comforted.

'So you sing an aria outside that dreary old chapel. So what? It happens twice, maybe three times a year. Skogen gives you a lift home. I take good care of you when you get here. Why mope about, thinking that all is lost?' He tried to explain that it was his nerves. The family nerves. 'It was my forefathers' nerves and foresight that gave rise to shops, ships and timber yard, and told us when to buy and sell. Those uncanny nerves which get out of hand in the spring. I'm a sensitive and not particularly brave man,' he said, biting into white toast with syrup. 'Why won't it stop?' he wailed. And while Simen's mother brushed her auburn hair she reminded him that it was bound to stop. 'So you will just have to laugh it off. It doesn't matter. Certainly not if you can bring yourself to remember that the chapel, the chandelier in the cathedral and the bishop's palace were all donated by your grandfather,' she said. 'You're complaining because you love opera. Isn't that rather stupid? You rule over office hacks, labourers, sailors and farmers. They depend on you. I'm thinking particularly of all the seamen getting on with their work from Stettin to Cuba.' And when she said this, Simen, who caught the sigh breathed over the syrup, realised that she was angry. Not because he sang. But because spring was such a trying time. 'I saw the first glimmer of green on the birch trees today,' was the first sign from his father. And everyone knew the Italian tenor was on the way. 'I'm wasting my breath, I know,' his mother said. 'But can't you see that it's a finer thing to be a timber merchant than an artist? Is that so hard to understand? I know that every spring you feel a need to talk about your grandfather poling himself down the river on a raft with two cows. He was out to conquer a town. The world, as he thought. And that was exactly what he did. But won't you stop it now? It's so depressing and we've heard it so many times,' she said, considering the skin at his hairline.

'That was my great-grandfather, not my grandfather,' he replied and stroked his chin. 'He had three cows with him, and a horse. He built a hotel for farmers. A cheap, solid hotel for country folk bringing their beasts to town. He liked their steady hands and the fact that they always paid up front in cash or cattle. He recorded the sums paid in a leather-bound book. When he slept, the book lay on the bedside table between the candlestick and his Meerschaum pipe. He loved the town, never left the riverbank, the ferry landing, the loading berths, the timber and the shop. I don't know how he managed it. He lived till he was ninety. And he was never ill.'

After three weeks they both laughed. The return of spring was a tough, lengthy, expensive, wet, and ruinous business, but it was a passing phase. After two, sometimes three, weeks the worst

According to Sofia

would be over. For months they would see neither hide nor hair of Skogen the taxi driver.

Simen, who tended to suppress just about everything, sat in the brown chair by the window and gazed out at the beavers' point. 'This place really is a mausoleum,' he muttered and thought of the new extension he was going to build in the summer. He glanced at his mobile and knew that at the touch of a few buttons he could throw light on Leon's situation down there in North Africa, Bird's last night with the lions, Ted's frustration, Sofia's orgasms and Linda's latest conversation with the butcher. He could be in touch with the stock market, the reporters, the newsdesk, the switchboard or old Iversen. All within a matter of minutes. All of them, all of it, Simen corrected, simply by pressing a few buttons on an instrument which he hated. It was so embarrassing. Everything happened at once. 'This mobile phone can make me believe anything,' he muttered as the waterfall down by the beavers' point rumbled. 'Or so it seems to an editor who has to form an opinion each and every day on a world which is, in fact, a complete mystery to him.' He closed his eyes and pictured the family relics hung on the walls and buried in cupboards and boxes. The family's fear preserved here in this costly mausoleum. We can retreat to this when everything falls apart. He heard the way the chair creaked when he moved. Almost two hundred years of success. Almost as long a period of asceticism. He was still bending over the old shaving bowl in the morning. He would go on doing that. If he forgot to shave at the cottage it made him uneasy.

'Don't worry about that,' he admonished himself. 'You don't have to do anything. You're going to sit here for three days. Drink Clausthaler and eat steak. You're going to sleep and read. That's all. It takes time. But it will pass. It always passes if we sit here in silence for a few days. It's simply a matter of waiting.'

28

Had he fooled them all? Had he remembered everything? Was it really that simple? Bird bent forward to peer out of the window of the little city hopper which was to take him to Bilbao. The propellers dragged the reluctant plane towards take-off and as he slid his feet forward he was ticked off by a stewardess who pointed at his seat-belt. Bird had had three days of being poked and prodded by Dr Vige, the registrar and the nurses, so he immediately felt nettled. No, furious. The nurses would have pumped him full of tranquilisers, in pill and injection form.

He had been thinking about dope when he watched the 100 metres final in Sidney. What a field. Had the world ever seen so much talent assembled on the white starting line? He thought of the sprinters' reflexes, the quiescent weight of the muscle mass, the eyes. What had they crammed down their throats? What manner of drugs? How many kilos? he had wondered.

The rain was laced with snow. Huge flakes. He gazed glumly at the slush and thought of Simen. Bird knew that he was up at the cottage all alone, conversing with his forefathers.

And as the aircraft was buffeted by gusts of wind, he peered out at the snow-ploughs on the runway. Amid the whining of the propellers he tried not to think. Instead he watched efficient men in orange overalls waving their arms and motioning to the city hopper pitching in the squall. Somewhere, something snapped. Was it the wheels? The elevator? The engine mount? Might it be the wings? Just for a second he hoped it might be the wings. A woman opened her handbag, fiddled with a pack of Valium and swallowed one dry.

The pilot – calm but alert, with a voice made for sitting in a queue of planes – informed them of sleet at below-zero temperatures and Bird, still a little woozy after his visits to the lions on the synthetic savannah, raised his head and thought: We're going to crash.

'We're not going to crash,' he said to the woman, who stuffed the strip of Valium into her calfskin bag without a smile. At last Bird was alone. Alone in a stubby little plane. He was protected by titanium. He got it into his head that he was protected by titanium, it had to be: titanium and thick steel plating, he hazarded, in a stubby little, no – a slobbish little plane, he thought. Who designs planes anyway? Because they're not pretty. Sitting at a standstill on the runway like officious geese. They looked ridiculous. Expectant. Mean. Sitting there like that, waiting, they looked as though they were keeping an eye on one another. And almost as if they were hoping for plenty of air pockets. Great plunges into nothingness. Towards Mother Earth. A huge bang. Was he actually hoping for a disaster? Earthquakes? Landslides? Avalanches? For earth? An emergency landing on some sturdy farmer's fields? A great blaze. Bird, who had not the slightest fear of flying, not at this point anyway, thought of Bilbao, coffee, chocolate and a newspaper in a foreign language. He hoped for *Le Monde*, which was such a wholehearted advocate of the modern world while still sticking to a lay-out more readily associated with typesetters who smelled of lead. Newspaper offices were Bird's only strongholds. And as always, it struck him that there was something ominously superficial about newspapers. Everything. Absolutely every piece was considered, laughed at, discussed and written within the space of four hours. He opened his mouth. He yawned. A clear sign that it was time for the stewardess to get her act together and bring on her trolley.

He came down in favour of perhaps. He had perhaps fooled everyone. That ambiguous word 'perhaps' was the closest he could get. There was actually a chance that all of those who expected something of him had been fooled. That was some comfort. The whine of the propellers rose to a screech. The drifting snow settled in a white band behind the plane. He had, of course, done his research, planned it all down to the last detail. His run that day, Dr Vige and the lions, his heart and the pills had simply delayed things. He was on his way. He slipped off his shoes and turned to the stewardess in the seat next to him, to be met by a reassuring smile and demure knees as the aircraft's titanium housing rocked and rolled. She smiled at him. That smile, thought Bird. He raised his hand, placed it over his mouth and eyed the stewardess's calves and professional shoulders, steady shoulders which played it cool as the plane bounced along. The woman who had swallowed two Valium, kneaded her throat with her fingertips. It looked as though her throat was protesting against this flight. The aircraft juddered, the noise of the engines increased and Bird found it funny when someone screamed. They were screaming before take-off. They were screaming while they were still on solid ground. They were truly terrified. Had he remembered everything? He meant everything. For the trials ahead. Guiltily he shut his eyes. The trials ahead, he thought.

He thought of Linda. She had not lost her grip. That she would never do. The little city hopper heeled over, lifted its nose into the gusting wind, the captain was quiet, far too quiet and the stewardess made no move to get out of her seat. The plane wobbled and wavered, rain pelted across the windows. They needed to climb higher, into more amenable air streams. Below them stretched the mighty North Sea. Bird had spewed his load so many times going over the Skagerrak that he, for one, had no wish to be down there in one of those boats laid to in the storm.

According to Sofia

He remembered the smells of rust, seawater, salt and herring in barrels. He remembered the squalling wind, the smacking of the tarpaulin over the hatches and he felt the stewardess's eyes on him, as if she were expecting him to sneak open a plastic bottle and take a slug. A hearty slug of Rémy Martin. Bought in the duty-free shop and paid for with plastic. But Bird was having too much fun to drink. He did not want anything at all. And certainly not alcohol. The plane wobbled again. Tilted to one side. Was someone actually screaming now? Or hooting? He hoped they were hooting. And while he was wondering why he should hope this he was not thinking about Therese Somoza, Linda, Nerida, Leon and Ted Fichter's son He could not remember his name. Bird closed his eyes; for a moment the plane was pointing straight down; the silence, the total silence signified that in just a few seconds the first proper screams would rip through the cabin. He stared down at the fishing boats rolling in the swell. It was blowing a gale. They really had their work cut out for them down there. He was thoroughly enjoying himself. It was a long time since he had had so much fun. The overhead lockers sprang open and coats and handbags spilled down into the laps of passengers who made no move to get up. Bird scratched the back of his neck. There were signs of panic in the seats. A suggestion of genuine terror. More juddering. No soothing captain's voice could quell the disquiet. This he knew, and wisely held his peace. The little city hopper resolved the matter, however, by battling its way skywards, to eventually come out above the clouds and level off, droning contentedly, reassuringly, confidently: we're not going to die today. Silence reigned in the cabin, to be broken by the clinking of the trolley. Bird smiled. He glanced up at the stewardess's blue cap, slightly askew after all the commotion, and he lifted his hands and clasped them behind his head.

'All that worry for nothing. A complete waste,' he told Linda in the restaurant at the airport outside Bilbao. She was sitting on the restaurant balcony eating a prawn sandwich.

Bird had slept on the plane and did not wake until the captain brought the aircraft down on to the tarmac with a bump. He yawned again. A sure sign that he was actually feeling pretty good. He smiled at Linda's open mouth, at her teeth, her palate, the prawns disappearing along with the dill and garnish of green stuff. It gratified him to behold such an appetite. Linda had put on ten kilos since he had last seen her. Valiantly she went on eating. 'I love prawns. They're good for the kidneys,' went unheard. 'I'm going to Algiers,' was dismissed by Bird. 'That's as may be,' he said. 'But first we have to stay on here in Bilbao. A couple of days,' he added. 'You have to help me find Sofia, she listens to you. Then you can go wherever you want.'

Behind Linda, on the marble from La Mancha, a graffiti artist had scrawled 'Euskara' in white paint.

'I know,' Bird said. 'Bilbao is a shitty little town with a fantastic museum.' The Guggenheim, in the Basque country, its walls hung with the works of all those once-exiled artists, he thought. Picasso had been brought home. They had nailed him to the wall. It was he who declared that once art is properly understood we will be able to paint pictures to cure toothache. Any common or garden witch-doctor would agree with that. And the Sami shamans. What was the story with Guggenheim? Was he a financial witch-doctor? Of course he was. At any rate, that grey picture from Guernica was there on the wall, disguised as a national treasure, the war about the war, about yet another war, about a new civil war: money, nationalism and politics locked in blissful embrace once more. Politicians parading geniuses they once kicked out of the country.

'It makes you weep,' he said.

Linda stopped chewing.

'We're meeting some people here,' he continued. 'I don't know how many are coming. But this is where we've arranged to meet.'

Linda shook her head: 'What's wrong with you?' was checked by Bird with a nod towards the stairs in the departure lounge.

According to Sofia

There was Nerida.

He was standing next to a pillar, staring down at his tickets. Dressed for the occasion in a yellow coat and black scarf, with steel-grey hair curling round his ears. He looked good. Bird had to admit it. Linda laid her fork on her plate and regarded Nerida. A stewardess could not help smiling at him as she strode past. But Linda was not impressed. 'Harrison Ford,' she said. 'He's copying him. In that coat and with that hat it's too obvious. He's unsure of himself. I don't know how he can be bothered. It's laughable, really.' She ate some vegetables from a small plate which Bird had not noticed, stuffed them in, munched, tore the cellophane off a pack of duty-free cigarettes. 'Was that good?' Bird asked. She sent him that look which said that she had never liked him. 'Are you still running?' sounded like a reproach. 'Is it still the sports pages of the newspapers that interest you most? Whenever I think of you, I see you on your way to the shop to buy running shoes. Set any new personal records lately?'

'I was hoping to be met by a dwarf,' Bird retorted. 'I had been hoping he was here in town.'

Linda was no longer munching. She swallowed. 'A dwarf?' she said. She tapped the plate with her fork. The look in her eyes said he had fallen foul of her and was being shown the yellow card after only three minutes of play. He had fouled up in the compassion stakes, deliberately and with malice aforethought. Linda's trembling fingers told him that he was a bastard.

And he returned the compliment with: 'What are you looking so guilty about. It doesn't suit you at all.'

'You never know where Leon is,' she replied. Did Bird detect the ghost of a smile on her lips? Had she realised right away that he was goading her by bringing up the one subject that could upset her? 'He could be anywhere,' she went on. 'He is bound to feel at home anywhere. He has no choice. Dwarfs are the bravest people in the world. They get on with their lives. They stick at it. They make money, they work, they like girls, big girls, preferably fat girls. They don't cause any bother. They're always busy. They don't have time for fooling about,' Linda said.

Bird did not answer.

'Are you afraid of him? Is it because your sister went off without telling you?'

Still Bird did not answer.

'Why don't you like him?'

He sighed heavily, but smiled anyway.

'According to Sofia – Sofia the compassionate – compassion can often be mistaken for love. And the first person you have to learn to love is yourself. Do you love yourself?'

'No,' he said at length.

Linda turned almost triumphantly to the lady behind the counter and pointed to her empty plate. She looked at Bird. 'Well?' she said. 'What do you take Leon for?' And when he again refrained from answering she explained that she always took a table near the counter. 'You can see why. You know why, in fact. I'm lazy. I admit it. Things improved greatly once I got round to admitting it. It took me half a lifetime to admit it. That's why I sit close to the sandwich counter. Which also means that I don't have to get up. If I am nice and smile at them the waiters bring my sandwiches to me. Ever tried that? Smiling at them?' she repeated.

Linda lit a cigarette.

'Have you been ill?' she asked out of the blue.

Bird shrugged.

'Was it serious?'

Bird shook his head.

'For long?'

'No,' said Bird.

'Ought I to sympathise? Were you ill enough for me to act all soft-hearted and sorry for you?'

'No,' said Bird.

Linda was surprised, slightly embarrassed, but more taken aback to hear Bird actually admitting this. 'You don't usually talk to me about this sort of thing.'

'Maybe not.'

According to Sofia

'Are you better now?'

Bird did not answer.

'Where's Leon?' Linda said.

'Isn't he in Algiers? You said you were going to Algiers. Or at least, that's what you said a moment ago.'

Linda looked at Nerida. 'He's boring a hole in that ticket with his eyes. Isn't he ever going to stop looking at it?'

*

Bird took a deep breath, drummed his fingers on the plastic table-top, which was gleaming after being wiped by hard-working Basque hands. Everything was so neat and tidy. Everything was so European, new, the product of a EU directive, solid, scrubbed, polished, washed and tended as if this were a nation of skinflints. All of a sudden he wasn't sure he liked what he saw. 'This place smells of milk,' he said suddenly to Linda. 'Last time I was here it smelled of wine. Red wine. Heavy red wine. Now it smells of butter and cheese.' Linda stared at him in astonishment. 'Were you scared?' she said. 'I mean . . .' She looked at Bird, paused before continuing. 'I'm not talking about some hair-raising plane journey. Were you scared?'

Bird, sulking now, tried his luck with: 'Today. Today of all days I wish everything was the way it used to be. That something was the way it used to be. I wish Bilbao smelled of rotten vegetables, rust, oil and the welding torches at the shipyards. I miss the reek of fish, salt and diesel from the boats. I wouldn't mind eating in a restaurant that smells of leftovers and *vin ordinaire*. Wine that's been doctored slightly: a dash of alcohol to tone down the taste of resin. A sprinkling of cloves giving the scent of summer. A little bit of jiggery-pokery. These days I'm willing to accept that. I can't abide the thought of the truth. What good is that to me? I mean: today is not a day for truth. I wouldn't mind the stench of tainted meat, mouldy-rinded cheese, ham and herring.'

He peered out at the freshly-washed splendour of Bilbao. The whole thing was as inanely neat and tidy as it was buffed and polished and primped, the menus were in English, French and Swedish. No one bothered you and the sandwiches were packed with calories and health. Not a single harmless bacterium could thrive under those plastic lids. 'May I,' he said to Linda, picking a greenish-yellow lettuce leaf off her plate. 'Do you mind?' was answered with: 'Do you never feel hungry? Really hungry?'

Bird gave her a quizzical look.

'What's wrong with that guy? Nerida's not reading, he's only pretending to. He looks as though someone parked him there.'

Linda nodded towards Nerida.

'He's resting,' said Bird. 'He's standing there so all the women passing by can get a good look at him.'

'No,' said Linda.

Bird picked another leaf off her plate.

'He's just standing there,' said Linda. 'He looks as though he's feeling the first symptoms of an attack.'

'What sort of attack?' Bird asked. 'You know what,' he said. 'This is the best lettuce leaf I've ever eaten.'

'How should I know?'

'Know what?'

'Nerida has an attack coming on. He won't admit it. Not yet. But he will.'

'Who's paying?' Bird broke in.

'For what?'

'For you to sit here. For you imagining, until a few minutes ago, that you were going to Algiers.'

'Who do you think?' Linda said.

'Ted Fichter?'

Linda smiled.

'What about that guy down there? His eyes haven't moved for a good few minutes. Not even when the stewardesses turn and stare at him. There must be something wrong with him.'

'He's reading,' said Bird.

'For a quarter of an hour. 'Reading the same ticket. He hasn't budged. Couldn't you go down and speak to him?'

'Why should I?' said Bird.

'Because he's making me nervous.'

'Nervous? You?'

Linda snorted.

29

The first suspicion was aroused when Sofia thought she was in London. Antonio Nerida had tried to dismiss it with a smile, but he felt miserable and his head suddenly started to ache. He hardly ever had a headache, it was a problem he only suffered from when there was something which he refused to admit. What was it he knew? What was it he had seen? Did Spain not agree with her? Sofia was not the first person whose blood had congealed after a couple of weeks in the stark, white Spanish sunlight. It threw everything into relief and it did not agree with everyone. But Sofia was used to the wrought-iron gates; she liked the women's silent disdain, the death in the arena, the smells, the sounds and the stupefying vapours of the African heat. It began as they were driving past a park containing palms and pine trees and a huge sign advertising Sobrano brandy. Sofia spoke English in the hotel reception and said that they were going to the Savoy Grill. It was nothing really. She had walked out of the hotel, hailed a cab, climbed in and spoken English to the driver.

Nerida took charge, explained in Spanish that they were going to a restaurant, but Sofia carried on speaking in English.

He was somewhat alarmed when she again referred to the restaurant as the Savoy Grill, and when she ordered lunch and

According to Sofia

meant dinner. It surprised Nerida to hear her chattering away. She never did that. She spoke English to the head waiter until it eventually dawned on her that she ought to be speaking Spanish.

Not the least bit put out, she lifted up her hair, slowly, and informed the elegant head waiter that she had lived in Alicante. Nerida tried to comfort himself with the fact that Spanish is an intricate language in which idiomatic subtleties can give rise to misunderstandings. Normally – this he admitted – she ought to know that she was in Vitoria and not in London. Sofia was too much of an old hand to forget the Spanish word for waiter. She ought to know that Rioja was produced in the vineyards around the city. But that she had suddenly forgotten. She ought to know that Vitoria was in Spain. During the meal she had difficulty in placing Malaga, Lisbon and Oslo. This he remarked on when Sofia was talking to the head waiter about swordfish. She adored Andalusian swordfish. She remembered one dinner in Ronda. 'That was the best. A long time ago, but far and away the best I've ever eaten. Quite delicious.' She had stayed at a hotel right opposite a park. Suicidal people climbed over the fence and leapt into the gorge. 'It's a popular park for suicides.'

The head waiter was completely won over. He had a brother who worked in the Hotel España in Ronda. 'A noble hotel,' he said. During the season he worked double shifts and earned a quarter of a year's salary in tips. He had bought a Seat Cordoba and was engaged to the daughter of the town archivist. The head waiter was interested in the Roman occupation of Andalusia and each summer in August, when the weather was at its hottest, he would sit in a cool basement at the archivist's offices, reading documents. Sofia suddenly revealed that she was confusing Ronda with Cadiz. It was not too embarrassing, because she laughed and shook the waiter's hand.

Antonio Nerida acted as if nothing were amiss, but when Sofia started cleaning her sunglasses with skin lotion he ordered a double Larios and tonic. She sprayed a good layer of skin lotion on to both lenses. It might have been an accident, but she smeared the cosmetic gunge over the glass, rubbing briskly, almost gaily. He stirred his drink suspiciously as Sofia daubed her napkin with skin lotion. Then she gazed at her hands as if they belonged to a stranger: 'I feel my hands look so old,' she said. 'Don't you think so? They don't seem to be much good for anything.' He shook his head, and did not find it reassuring when she started fiddling with her sunglasses and tucked her napkin under the tablecloth. All of a sudden she called to the waiter, fumbled with the menu and asked him to fetch Mr Leman the head waiter, who worked, Nerida knew, at the Savoy Grill in London. He drank water, nodded pleasantly to diners at neighbouring tables who had noticed the napkin tucked under the tablecloth, and in the silence which ensued he asked the waiter for a towel. The latter bowed. 'It will be an honour. Nothing is too much trouble for a guest with whom one can discuss Andalusian swordfish. We are delighted to have you here. Tomorrow you shall have the table by the window.'

Antonio Nerida felt uneasy. Sofia spoke Spanish almost without an accent and he said nothing when she asked the taxi driver to take her home. She gave the driver an address in London. 'It's a small hotel, but it's where I always stay,' she explained to the driver. 'I have such a terrible headache. On the left side. Around my ear. It's worse than usual. I'm sorry I didn't recognise you, Antonio. I got you mixed up with that dean with the chronically sweaty upper-lip. What was it with him? Did he ever amount to anything? He was sweet. He was keen. He was wild and wanton and never gave up. Didn't he move to a town by the sea? Of course he did. Did he write poetry? Did he leave Salamanca? Surely not. How old was I when I met the dean? Did he become foreign minister? The dean, I mean. He was pushy. Persevering is possibly a better word. He was so young. Nervous. He followed me to Hamburg when I left home. I was sure he would do all right for himself. Did he move to England? Or do I misremember?'

According to Sofia

Antonio Nerida had tried not to think about it until suddenly at the airport in Bilbao his suspicions would no longer be denied. He put down his leather suitcase. He knew that something was seriously wrong. He was quite sure of it. And all he wanted to do was to stand next to the grey marbled pillar and stare at his tickets.

He stood quite still and waited for Bird.

Nerida regarded his general feeling of nausea as understandable, but a nuisance, it persisted, came in waves, little burps, harmless, but unpleasant. His experience as a lawyer told him what he ought to do. He tried to ignore it, to no avail. If he had not felt so alone he would have divulged what was going to happen to Sofia, but it would have been taken the wrong way. It was always taken the wrong way. And anyway, what would he say? That sometimes she didn't know where she was? That she was liable to switch, without any warning, from Spanish to English? That she plastered her sunglasses with skin lotion? That suddenly she would not recognise him? He had consulted his medical encyclopaedia without any idea of what he was looking for. He had called the doctor who assisted him with difficult cases. The doctor was in a bar, eating shellfish, and what he told Nerida was not encouraging. And again: Nerida felt the diagnosis like a weight on his shoulders, he felt trapped by his profession. From it he had learned never to speak too soon. Occasionally, when he was in the possession of all the facts and could have revealed what was likely to happen, even his best friends got mad at him. They would grow tight-lipped, distant, traitorous even. And far too often, when a complex case had finally been won – this too he tried not to think about – his fellow lawyers would be all over him. They made it sound as though he did not predict the future, but presented it to them.

Antonio Nerida knew why this was.

'Sometimes you have to wait with telling what you know. Keep it to yourself. And you should never mention yourself by name,' his father had whispered to him. 'Especially not to people you know. People you think you know. Remember that. You were born to be friendless, almost everyone will be infuriated by you.'

That was the only piece of advice he remembered. His father had never in fact done anything but tramp about the hills, visit the village markets and roll around in the beds of married women. He described himself as a happy man. When Antonio Nerida shaved, the mirror showed him what his father had been talking about. He was almost all the things his father was not. He was handsome. He was successful. He was a parvenu. Idiosyncratic. Charming. A star lawyer, so the papers said. He won most of his cases by dint of charm, bold moves and grim facts, backed up by the tactical manoeuvring of the young whippersnappers in his office. Young lawyers were queuing up to become his dogsbodies. He was notorious, but he was also brilliant, a combination which appealed to him, and he was duly bad-mouthed in the city bars after he had gone home to his loudspeakers and Miles Davis.

'If he had only got roaring drunk instead. Once in a while, at least,' his wife complained.

She never became privy to the fact that he celebrated his victories, described in terms of fees, in intimate tête-à-têtes with Keith Jarrett.

He sat quite motionless for ten minutes the first time he heard Jarrett's new interpretation of 'I loves you Porgy'. There was something unreal about it. Too much feeling. It was a little too raw. The jump from this to his colleagues joining in the sing-song in the back-rooms of bars was a little too pronounced. He was not one of them. Nor could he ever be like them. They roared out Basque hymns to the thousand hoofbeats on the plains, to conquest, to the fire of nationalism, suicidal gall and the wild and joyous rovings of their genes. They sang of women swollen by men's orgasms while the other conquerors waited their turn, their trousers around their ankles. In other words: of the rapes committed by their fathers, and the ancestral codes implanted in the women with the aid of horses and lances or Russian Kalashnikovs. The women had shrieked in conquered bedrooms and dark barns while deep-red wine, lust, tactics and pride swilled about in the men's stomachs. They sang till the sun rose in the east. They sang until they had no voice left. And somehow it wasn't quite the same when Nerida confessed that he could not sleep for thinking of the saxophonist Zoot Sims. His wife, Pilar Nerida, as virtuous as she was beautiful, admitted it, reluctantly but pitilessly, as she lay in bed masturbating, eating chocolates and reading magazines. She didn't give a damn for LaFaro's intricate chords when what she longed for was orgasms, and when she lay still the sound of the bass reached her from the basement and she got upset. It did not help that Antonio Nerida had been working flat out for three months and felt exhausted at the very sight of her. Nothing was said about the fact that he had worked fourteen nights in a row along with two worn-out female clerks who staggered home every morning at the crack of dawn. No mention was made of his having to be in court by ten a.m. In just three months he could wear out two members of staff. He was a bastard, no question about it. He would never be any different. Such was the verdict in the bars. The men who liked him least were married to women who would willingly have followed Antonio Nerida anywhere.

'Not to mention anytime,' whispered the sober bartenders, who heard everything and remembered it too. 'It's a bit scary. And all he can think about is some woman from Norway who's supposed to be a surgeon. Who'd want to sleep with a woman surgeon?' the taciturn waiters asked as they washed glasses, placed them carefully on the shelves, totted up drinks bills on a slate underneath the bar and swept the tips into the cardboard box. The bartenders knew just about everything, said nothing, but were happy to relay the gossip to Nerida. He drank Fanta, tipped lavishly, spoke refined Spanish with a touch of the Salamancan dialect: intelligently, softly and somewhat wistfully. This last he had learned at the university from an enthusiastic professor who thought he would end up stranded in an office in Brussels.

'You mustn't give up. The future lies there,' was a prediction on which the young Antonio did not act. And this he had never regretted.

Needless to say it was a demoralising business. It took it out of him, having to explain every evening to Sofia that they were not in London, but in Vitoria. He wanted to move to a hotel in Bilbao, but she would not hear of it. He wished that she was drunk, but Sofia drank only iced water, tea, coffee and Fanta. She bought rain gear and went for walks in the hills and when she got back she ruffled her hair and looked at her hands. They were covered in dirt and grit and grass stains, and she said: 'I keep falling down. I don't understand it. But suddenly I'll just collapse on to a path. I never used to do that.'

In the morning when he arrived at the office, heavy-hearted and still with snatches of Zoot Sims at the back of his mind, to be met by a scene of overwhelming chaos, he was still asking himself why. Although he did not really like to admit it, he was sick of the whole thing. It was such a mess and he hated mess. He was sick of Sofia unexpectedly breaking into Norwegian. Of her calling him at the office and speaking English. It was too much for him. The doctor's diagnosis, which was not particularly accurate. But frightening. Almost unreal. Because Sofia was not so different from before. And sometimes, as now, next to the stairs leading up to the restaurant in Bilbao, he felt a little twinge in his chest, on the right side fortunately; a twinge, distinct, but innocuous. This last the doctor had told him. Nerves, that's all it was: nerves. Nerve endings in conflict. Things weren't connecting in the brain the way they should. 'When you're stressed.' And, as always, it was accompanied by stiffness, first in his knees, then in his feet and he felt nauseous, but not anxious. He stood next to the pillar, pulled the tickets out of his pocket, stared at them, thought of Sofia, all too often he thought of Sofia. He thought of her hair and her eyes.

According to Sofia

He had heard her say saddle and mean bed. It was easy to deceive oneself. 'Forget it,' he breathed.

He had spotted Bird and Linda up on the restaurant balcony and he turned his back on them. He knew that Linda regarded him as a pedantic little lawyer. Not that she didn't admire him, but compared to Leon he was of no consequence. And he wasn't nearly bright enough for Sofia, but he was acquainted with members of the shadow cabinet in Vitoria, men of power great and small; he was also power-mad, ambitious and wrapped in Italian suits. He was a sophisticated high-flier, but he trod Basque soil in hand-sewn Italian shoes. He couldn't resist it and he was made to suffer for it.

He didn't feel like talking about Sofia.

He guessed that Linda must have given the word for him to be approached. He had, after all, been standing stock-still for half an hour, gazing at the tickets. Bird, who was making his way down the stairs, unhurriedly, almost carelessly, was just about the last person Antonio Nerida wished to speak to.

He had a sudden urge to walk away. To move. He told himself that he ought to get out of there. Or even better, become invisible. But Bird: at that very moment – Nerida closed his eyes – Bird smiled that little smile which said that he had the upper hand.

30

In Dr Vige's Audi, Gerda Hansen described what she had done with the day. Dr Vige sat straight-backed behind the wheel, listened, remarked on her voice – a little too animated, a little too articulate – and he realised that she was worried.

She was talking about a patient, a super-fit diver, a product employed by the oil industry at great depths, a silent, sun-tanned man with a medallion around his powerful neck; a little husky-voiced, but with a physique that drew appreciative nods from the doctors. His marks in every exam from secondary school to the last little test at Statoil were not just good, they were sensational. He was wealthy, mild-mannered and worked only eight months out of twelve. He had been pictured in Statoil's monthly magazine: open shirt, medallion, muscles, blue eyes and a beach with palms and parasols as a decorative backdrop. He had been on a visit to his other home on Lanzarote.

'A Greek parody,' Gerda Hansen had whispered. It was uttered so spontaneously that the consultant, Dr Hanich – arrogant, but brilliant – removed his glasses. 'Do you know him?' he asked.

'No, I'm glad to say,' she replied.

There was silence round the table.

'It's just a routine check-up,' Dr Hanich continued. 'The usual

According to Sofia

thing. He wasn't recommended for the *Kursk* job. He was pretty upset. Because he wasn't picked,' he added. 'A parody, you say?'

He glanced up from the green documents which sanctioned diving to great depths. He set his pen down gently on top of the papers, drummed his fingers, looked at her, then at the other doctors, who made no comment on her remark. Dr Hanich did not attempt to conceal the fact that he liked the Danish psychiatrist who spoke so impulsively about parodies. In the previous millennium, which he was glad to see the back of, no one had ever disputed his professional opinion. It would have been unthinkable for it to be described as a parody. He had two years to go until he retired, so he had little to lose and his curiosity was piqued. He put his index finger to his nose, and paused a little too long as he peered at Gerda over his half-moon glasses.

'What do you think?'

'Know,' Gerda corrected.

'Okay, know,' he laughed, setting his glasses down on the pile of paper. It was so quiet in the room that they could hear every sound from the corridor.

'He chews khat,' she said.

The consultant surgeon screwed the top on to his fountain pen. 'Chews?'

'Khat,' Gerda repeated.

It was still very quiet around the table, but two of the doctors put their hands to their mouths.

'Are you absolutely certain?' The consultant tapped the pile of paper on his desk with his glasses. 'I mean. . .' he began.

'You need to know for sure?' Gerda said. 'Well, naturally you need to be quite sure.'

'Indeed,' said Dr Hanich.

'Note the teeth,' she said. 'It's a dead giveaway. I've seen that colour before. Yes, I'm certain. If you tell him he needs to see a dentist he'll start to worry. He's smart, he'll know right away that he's been found out. He'll find some excuse to resign.'

'You mean he'll do a runner?' the consultant said.

'I think so,' said Gerda.

Dr Vige, who never touched coffee, tobacco, alcohol or meat, had been there at the table when Gerda had this conversation with the consultant. He jogged along floodlit forest tracks in the evenings, listened to Mozart, read biographies, journals and medical literature. No mention was ever made of the fact that the other doctors at the hospital assigned him the simplest cases. He had been married and still wore a wedding ring. This was noticed but never spoken of. He was dependable, but anonymous. What he liked best was to listen, and what he heard was that Gerda was worried.

'What's up?' he asked, changing down a gear on the steep uphill slope. He drove carefully and as if he were constantly listening to the engine.

'It's bad,' Gerda said.

'What is. . .?'

'Bloody awful,' Gerda finished.

He pulled up, astonished, at the lights before the tunnel, turned down the volume on the Mozart emanating from the Audi's four loudspeakers, sat watchfully behind the wheel, tapped the gearstick with his wedding ring, glanced at her, waited, noted that she was breathing steadily and said again: 'What's up?'

'He's one of them,' she said. 'One of many. One of a growing number. He sits alone in his luxury flat and chews khat. He chews and chews. It's a real grind, I tell you. Just imagine the number of hours they spend chewing. Most of them drink, some chew khat, others drink, chew khat and sniff cocaine. Don't think it's confined to divers, either. They can be brokers, divers, doctors, drivers or psychiatrists. It's a disease. Everybody knows about it. Nobody talks about it.' She looked out of the window, at the sunshine. 'Fine flying weather,' she said suddenly. 'It worries me because there's nothing I can do. He already knows all the tricks. The only thing he can't hide is that his teeth are rotting away and that his gums bleed. When he gets home at night he slumps in front of the television. He's single, childless and in very deep

According to Sofia

water. He wonders what he should do while he's sniffing cocaine instead of chewing khat,' she said.

'This really upsets you,' Dr Vige said.

'No, worries me,' she replied.

'Why?'

'Khat isn't particularly dangerous, but it's not entirely harmless either. And did you notice his nose? The hairs in his nose? Within the past couple of months, the last six months maybe, he's moved on to the harder stuff. That's the rule. The law,' she added.

'Why aren't you moving?' Gerda nodded at the lights.

'Can I drive you to the airport?'

She stared at him in surprise. 'Why would you do that?'

Dr Vige changed gear so smoothly that Gerda could tell he took pleasure in it. He fingered the walnut of the dashboard as lightly as he would have tinkled the keys on a Steinway grand. She heard not a sound from the engine and she could not recall ever having sat in a better car seat.

'Do I look as if I could do with it?' she asked.

'Yes,' he said.

A new, four-lane motorway to the airport had just been opened, he indicated to switch lane, did not look round, glanced in the mirror as the turbo kicked in, upping the revs. 'Nice car,' she said.

Dr Vige made no reply.

'Do I look that bad?' Gerda asked.

He was on the new motorway now, Gerda caught the faint hiss of the wind rushing by, and the doctor, who had smoothly eased his way into the line of traffic, turned his head a fraction and regarded her eyes, ears and chin as he steered the car into the left-hand lane. 'No,' he said.

'No what?' she said.

'You don't look bad at all.'

Gerda suddenly opened her bag, closed it, smiled at the doctor and laid her hands in her lap.

'You can smoke if you like,' he said.

She looked at him, did not answer, then she fixed her eyes on her hand and fingers. Silence reigned in the car.

'How did you know?'

He did not feel like replying, simply drove on quietly and it struck Gerda, who had been dreading the bus journey to the airport, that she had never come to feel at home in a car so quickly before. She considered the doctor's profile, a little hazy in the light off the sea behind it, and she felt as if she had known him a long time. He said no more than was necessary, drove fast, a little too fast, and he took pleasure in it. 'Do you think that diver is seriously at risk?' drew no response from Gerda. Her eyes followed his hand as it shifted back and forth between steering-wheel and gear stick, confident movements; he's an almost phlegmatic driver, she decided, feeling drowsy and relaxed because she was being chauffeured right to the Departures entrance.

'When do you get back?'

This took her by surprise.

'Monday?' he asked.

He showed no sign of embarrassment or awkwardness in asking this. He pulled on the hand-brake and waited.

'Yes,' she said.

'Alone?'

'I expect so.'

He waited.

'Here?' he asked. 'To this airport? Give me a call and I'll come and pick you up.'

She opened the pack of cigarettes, but did not flick her lighter.

'Is there anything I can do?'

'No,' she said. 'Like what, for instance?'

'Whatever,' he said.

'I don't think so.'

It seemed perfectly natural for him to kiss her on the cheek, on both cheeks, lingeringly, she thought in the plane, as she fastened her seat-belt. Before she fell asleep she heard the voice over the loudspeaker telling her where she could find the emergency exits.

According to Sofia

She was still awake when the captain informed them of their cruising altitude and she thought to herself that there were no emergency exits, and then again maybe there were.

She woke up in Bilbao.

She had not been to Bilbao since she had played handball for Denmark – as a reserve, it's true, probably because she had slept with one of the assistant trainers, she told Bird five hours later, when she met him at the hotel, where he had cake and drank Turkish coffee. 'This tastes quite disgusting. Kind of sweet and kind of bitter,' he said and stared at Gerda. He jutted his chin upwards, as if his ear was blocked.

She had slept for three hours at the hotel by the beach, gazed at the harbour across the water while she ate, waited for Bird, thought of Dr Vige, the diver, and all at once she felt like listening to opera. '*La Bohème*,' she said, trying to explain to Bird. 'I don't know why, but I feel like listening to opera. I'd like to spend an evening at the opera. Do you understand?'

Bird looked at her and blinked, several times, swallowed, swallowed again, straightened his back, his arms dangled down by his thighs, his head was tilted, his mouth hung half-open as he stiffened his shoulders, his neck, his back, then he blinked again. A thin film of sweat covered his brow. He jutted his chin, pressed a hand to his ear, patted his cheek gently with two fingers, cleared his throat again and again and laid his head on the table.

It was so sudden.

'Come on,' she said. 'We're going home. We'll take a taxi.'

'Why?' Bird said.

She paid in dollars.

'Why?' Bird said again.

The man behind the counter – adorned with fake tattoos, rings in his lips and nose, in his tongue, his ear – was sharp, experienced and did not hesitate when Gerda waved away his offer of change. She took command; she did not ask if she could make the call; she ordered the immediate dispatch of one of the taxis used in emergencies. She did not have to tell the young waiter that they needed to get Bird out of there within five minutes. 'We'll just make it,' she told Bird, who was hiccuping and did not really know what was happening.

'Where are we going?' he asked.

'Home,' she said.

'Where's home?'

'Relax, now,' Gerda said. 'We'll just make it,' she repeated. 'As long as you don't cause any trouble, everything will be fine. Nothing will happen if you do as I say.'

'To the hospital,' she told the driver.

He eyed Bird, who was gently tipping towards the front seat. 'Which hospital,' he asked, handing Gerda a plastic bag.

'You must know that, surely,' she replied.

'Wasn't it here? I mean in Bilbao, that you played handball for Denmark?' Bird said. 'You mentioned something about a trainer. Am I right? It was a long time ago, I know. But I'm pretty certain it was Bilbao.'

He spoke slowly and distinctly.

'Yes, that's right,' said Gerda.

'What now?'

'Take it easy,' Gerda replied. 'From now on it's purely routine.'

During the interval Dr Gerda Hansen called the hospital and was advised that Bird was doing fine. After an hour with Puccini in the beautiful, albeit somewhat run-down opera house, an experienced doctor gave Gerda to understand that Bird was weak, but on the mend. The down-to-earth woman doctor informed her briskly that he was sleeping. He would sleep until the morning.

'How could he be so stupid, with *his* history! Do you know him? Couldn't you tell him it's dangerous?' Gerda was happy to listen to a cool, detached voice reeling off factual information. Professional data. Logical expectations. Bird had got off lightly, with no haemorrhaging.

According to Sofia

Gerda was not entirely reassured by Puccini, but the music, the red lamps in the foyer, the carved wood panelling, the soft, burgundy carpets and the paintings on the stairways allowed her to distance herself slightly. From what? She was not sure. The ironic paintings lining the stairs, painted by unknown masters, testified to Spain's colonial history. Less than honourable, but studiously shaped by artists who committed to canvas exactly what they saw. What one discovered, she realised, standing there on the mosaiced slate floor, looking up at all those faces, was that after the generals it was always the civil servants who conquered the world, and lost it. The colonies which were won, then plundered, tormented and lost. The wordless faces on the wall revealed not only why, but also how. And prior to the silent conquistadors: Roman busts, warriors fulfilling the usual objectives: conquering, changing, then putting the end result into the hands of the civil servants. She spent a long time looking at those Spanish copies of Roman masters. The silent disdain of the bureaucrats, their faces sombre, but patient. They prompted her to retreat, reluctantly, slowly, to Puccini, who promised her not a moment's peace.

She took her time. It *took* time to walk up the stairs and it took time to find her way back to the soft, red-plush seat.

She was thinking, of course, about Bird.

He was now lying on a white hospital sheet, burping, feeling a little shaken, but really quite content. While Puccini endeavoured to make her believe in timeless love, she went on thinking about Bird, then about a handball trainer and, a little later, about Dr Vige, and the drama unfolding on the stage failed to grab her.

Before going to the opera she had walked down a street full of souvenir shops. A mixture of the usual crap and sham ornaments, but with the odd genuine piece here and there. She did not yield to temptation. Bought nothing. She did, however, spend plenty of time at the museum. She doubted whether Picasso would have applauded being identified with those asymmetric curves. They, too, were a sham. The engineers had had their off days. And

Gerda, who was on the look-out for something beautiful, for beauty, she made so bold as to whisper to herself, was not disappointed, but felt a little cheated. She had been looking forward to seeing the museum. Soundless boats full of tourists taking photographs slipped past the docks. It was cold out on the water; chilled Japanese swathed in voluminous scarves of French design stood ranged on blue sightseeing boats. With hats pulled low down on their foreheads they snapped memories of a sensible city with old warehouses sitting right on the seafront. Norwegian timber, Gerda thought. Danish connections. Dutch design. It was raining. Heavy rain. She pulled on the sou'wester she had brought with her, slipped two bocadillos into her bag, bought from a stall on the corner next to the hotel. She would eat when she got back from the opera, with the voice of the Italian tenor still ringing in her ears. She knew that both Linda and Antonio Nerida were in town.

She tried to forget this.

She had not met them before, but she had a note of their mobile numbers and her apprehension grew even as Puccini did his best to take the edge off things. While the mock opera was not a disappointment, it was not exactly what she had been hoping for. It could have been so cleverly done, but right at this moment, she thought, in a city full of Spanish barrow-boys, she wanted to go home.

The barrow-boys were nowhere near as relentless as Puccini. So there was some comfort to be drawn from the tenor's sedate vibrato and she had no doubt that she ought to be getting home as soon as possible.

But here she was in Bilbao, and she had shaken her head as she looked at the ticket while changing her dress and getting ready for the opera. Why was she here? Why did she feel so sexless? Why couldn't she be like Sofia? She could never be friends with a man.

When Sofia met a man there was never any doubt, that much she had grasped.

According to Sofia

Gerda outlined her lips with a deep-red lipstick. She was attractive. That she knew. In the mirror she saw a face she liked. No more than that. She liked what she saw and was content with that. All this, including the visit to the opera, to shield herself from that little word 'cancelled'. She tried replacing it with the word 'postponed', but knew that this was small comfort. A meeting in Bilbao to resolve a certain matter had had to be cancelled when Bird was rushed to hospital. Did he always fall ill when there was something to be resolved? Was it that simple? What exactly was it that was destroyed every time he fell ill? Had he fooled everybody? This was the thought which crossed her mind as she stood in the bathroom, naked, after her shower. Comfort, however small, was not the worst thing she could think of right now. The consumptive beauty on the stage sang staunchly of love, and on this evening Gerda allowed the magic of Puccini to enfold her.

But still she felt edgy.

She felt so uneasy that she got up from the soft plush seat. In the forenoon, when purchasing her ticket, she had wangled herself an end seat. 'I suffer from bouts of claustrophobia,' she had lied to the woman at the box office. So did just about everybody, the latter had declared.

'Have you tried carob beans?' received no response from Gerda.

Ten minutes later she left her seat. She went out to the cloakroom, asked for her coat, took her mobile from the pocket and keyed in Simen's number. 'Could you set up a three-way conference call? For you, Bird and me? He's in hospital, I suppose you know that. Do you have the number?' And because she was feeling so efficient, so desperately efficient, she burst out laughing. The neat little cloakroom lady stopped knitting. The clatter of knitting needles ceased. Utter silence.

'It became so bloody quiet, you see. And all of a sudden I was so scared,' she told Bird three days later.

Simen organised the conference call. He sat in his office at the newspaper building, staring out of the window at a snowdrift. A bit of an exaggeration, admittedly, but the caretaker had shovelled the snow up against the garages. Simen had got someone to help him set up a three-way link and when it actually worked he was so happy that of course he blurted out the one thing he definitely did not mean to say.

'Bird, now you're exaggerating. There's no need for that. We know it's embarrassing. But it's not as if it's the first time you've had to bring your sister home? Why don't you just take it easy for a couple of weeks? What are they doing to you in that hospital? Is it one of those typical EU palaces? Are they stuffing you full of pills? I hope it's a decent hospital. I insist on it. Gerda, you know a good hospital when you see one. I really hadn't expected this, Bird. Did you really have to fall on your face? Right now. Couldn't you have waited?' he asked. 'At least until you got home.'

Gerda, who was sitting on a chair in the foyer, feeling a little dazed – this was not exactly how she had expected her trip to Bilbao to turn out – was more than somewhat distracted by the tenors, those irritating high Cs, and the smells of gin, white wine and tapas from the bar. She heard at least four languages being spoken by the crowd of young people with new money. They were so beautiful, so many and they laughed so loudly and so senselessly. The cloakroom attendant ate on the sly while she knitted. Doggedly, determinedly she knitted enormous white mittens. Or was it a balaclava? In which case, who was going to wear those mittens or that balaclava. For what purpose? Gerda closed her eyes. She heard Bird hoisting himself up in the bed. He lowered his voice, it was a little hoarse; had he really got the nurses to smuggle his phone into the secure unit? Or was it intensive care? Was he really as calm as he seemed? This conversation? Gerda dropped her shoulders. Was it a conversation or actually an

According to Sofia

exchange of suspicions. Did they know, or did they merely suspect what was coming?

They acted as if nothing was amiss. Three comments from Bird and then they were gabbling on as usual, although possibly a little disconcerted by the fact that a couple of them were in Bilbao. And Gerda got drawn into it too.

'I was stupid,' Bird said. 'I was wrong. I shouldn't have made the trip, that's obvious. It was at least a week too soon. I was far too weak to leave the flat. I should never have left the airport. I can't believe I did that. Not at this time. Later, maybe.'

Bird was certain of it. He had not been prepared. He had not eaten. For two days he had not eaten a thing. He did not count the lettuce leaves he had picked off Linda's plate. Where was she anyway? She ought to be informed. She and Ted Fichter. Of what? They were involved. In what way were they involved? Once a week they doped each other up.

'Was it on Thursday?' Bird said. 'Catfish and *crème caramel*, that's pretty good dope. *Crème caramel* baked in the oven. Particularly when washed down by Rioja. I'm trying to make light of it, you see. It's odd, but I feel perfectly fit. My gall bladder hurts a bit. Or is it my lungs? You sound so worried. Wasn't that what you said, Gerda? That I seemed so uneasy. That's not a bad way to describe the situation. Right now, I mean. Simen, are you there?'

Yes, he was there. Simen was there. Solid and dependable, he was there. On the desk in front of him were soda water, lemon wedges and ice cubes. He was not writing the leader. Not today. Iversen was seeing to that. Yes, he had been to the cottage. Two days. Or was it three? No, two days. He had not been too bored. A bit. Especially to begin with. 'Stop it, Bird!' Again a remark which made them aware of the silence.

'Listen, since we're all in this together, why don't we just head for home? It would be so much simpler. All things considered. Gerda's sitting in the foyer of the opera house. Bird is being fed from a bottle on a stand. I've eaten three bananas. There doesn't seem to be any reason to proceed until something conclusive happens. There has to be some conclusive development before I can proceed. Do you understand that, Bird?'

Yes, Bird understood that.

'Don't you have anything to say, Gerda?'

'Not really, no.'

'What about you, Bird?'

Bird did not answer.

'What's that supposed to mean?' Simen said.

'That? Not a lot,' said Bird.

Gerda sighed so loudly and clearly that Bird and Simen could not help but hear.

'I've been looking at myself,' Bird said. 'I've been taking a long, hard look at myself. You have no choice, really, when you're lying in a hospital bed hooked up to a drip on a stand. I've been looking at myself,' he repeated. 'Long and hard.'

'What did you see?' asked Gerda.

'Do I have to say?'

Simen was silent. They knew he was sitting at his desk in the newspaper building. He did not want to say anything, and it sounded as though he had parked his voice up there in the satellite.

'I run,' Bird said. 'I gamble with my life. Work when I have to, worry too much, have no expectations whatsoever, and have forgotten what it was that used to make me happy. That's the worst of it, that I've forgotten that. It seems to have disappeared. Lying here, I feel as though someone has stolen it.'

'Bird,' said Simen. 'Why don't you come home? And why don't you bring your sister with you? You're in a bed in a hospital in Bilbao, for heaven's sake. Wouldn't it be better for you to come home? You're a bit weak, but no worse than that – you'll be up and about in a week. Things have got a bit mixed up,' he said guardedly. 'But no worse than usual. You can always go back. For good, if you like.'

'I'm on my way,' said Bird.

Also in translation available from WWW.MAIAPRESS.COM

Merete Morken Andersen AGNES & MOLLY
£9.99   ISBN 978 1 904559 28 3

Agnes and Molly are childhood friends. At nineteen their paths in life diverge widely – Molly sets out into the world to study, travel and eventually become a talented and acclaimed set designer, while Agnes has just been diagnosed with multiple sclerosis, and her world and possibilities are rapidly narrowing. Aksel is the man they both desire. When his ex-wife is taken ill, he asks a favour of Molly: would she take care of his two children in her summer house? Agnes is jealous of Molly's relationships with Aksel and the children and, when she comes to the summer house to help, the real struggle for power begins, with the women battling for the affections of the children. This is a richly atmospheric novel about friendship, jealousy and love.

Translated from Norwegian by Barbara J. Haveland

'Her best, most complex and most inspiring novel' *Hamar Arbeiderblad*

Merete Morken Andersen OCEANS OF TIME
£8.99   ISBN 978 1 904559 11 5

It is midsummer in Norway. A long-divorced couple meet in the wake of a family tragedy. Finally they are forced to confront what went wrong in their relationship and the effect it has had on those around them. In the psychological drama that follows, they plumb the very depths of sorrow and despair, before emerging with a new understanding. This profound novel, which draws on the myth of Persephone and on Mozart's *The Magic Flute*, not only deals with loss and grief, but also – transformingly – with hope, recovery, and love.

Translated from Norwegian by Barbara J. Haveland

'Beautiful' *Jostein Gaarder*   **'Bravely clear-eyed'** *The Times*
'Remarkable' *Guardian*   **'Intensely moving'** *Independent*
NOMINATED FOR THE IMPAC AWARD
SHORTLISTED FOR THE OXFORD WEIDENFELD PRIZE
LONGLISTED FOR THE INDEPENDENT FOREIGN FICTION PRIZE

Also in translation available from WWW.MAIAPRESS.COM

Maria Peura AT THE EDGE OF LIGHT
£8.99   ISBN 978 1 904559 24 5

Growing up in a village in the far north of Finland, Kristina falls for Kari; together, they are desperate to escape the restricted life of an extraordinary and remote community. Peura evokes the passion and curiosity which they struggle to conceal and which is in danger of destroying them. Her book brims over with the haunting light of the arctic north and the presence of deep natural forces.

Maria Peura's first novel was shortlisted for the Finlandia Literature Prize in 2001, and received three other awards. This is her second novel.

Translated from Finnish by David Hackston

'Haunting and inspiring' *Independent on Sunday*

VOICES FROM THE NORTH: NEW WRITING FROM NORWAY
Edited by Vigdis Ofte & Steinar Sivertsen

£9.99   ISBN 978 1 904559 29 0

Seven prize-winning writers showcase their work, both prose fiction and poetry, in this celebratory anthology. Exciting and innovative, these young writers use images of life and death, the past and the future, of Norway and abroad, of the poetic and the everyday, to illuminate our current lives and issue warnings about the future. They challenge tradition and reveal a distinct take on modern life. An introduction by Steinar Sivertsen and a piece about Stavanger's history by Kjartan Fløgstad, one of Norway's leading writers (author of *Dollar Road* and *Grand Manila*), complete this imaginative and vibrant anthology. Contributors include Johan Harstad, Tore Renberg, Sigmund Jensen, Einar O. Risa, Øyvind Rimbereid and Torild Wardenær.

Stavanger, together with Liverpool, was European Capital of Culture in 2008
Published in association with Stavanger2008, with the support of NORLA